BY MARIA KUZNETSOVA

Oksana, Behave!

Something Unbelievable

SOMETHING
UNBELIEVABLE

SOMETHING
UNBELIEVABLE

A NOVEL

Maria Kuznetsova

RANDOM HOUSE

NEW YORK

Published in the United States by Random House, an imprint and division of Penguin Random House LLC, New York.

RANDOM HOUSE and the HOUSE colophon are registered trademarks of Penguin Random House LLC.

LIBRARY OF CONGRESS CATALOGING-IN-PUBLICATION DATA
Names: Kuznetsova, Maria, author.
Title: Something unbelievable: a novel / Maria Kuznetsova.
Description: First edition. | New York: Random House, [2021]
Identifiers: LCCN 2020014097 (print) | LCCN 2020014098 (ebook) |
ISBN 9780525511908 (hardcover: acid-free paper) |
ISBN 9780525511915 (ebook)
Subjects: LCSH: Domestic fiction.
Classification: LCC PS3611.U985 S66 2021 (print) |
LCC PS3611.U985 (ebook) | DDC 813/.6—dc23
LC record available at https://lccn.loc.gov/2020014097
LC ebook record available at https://lccn.loc.gov/202001

Printed in Canada on acid-free paper

randomhousebooks.com

2 4 6 8 9 7 5 3 1

FIRST EDITION

Title-page and part-title art: © iStockphoto.com

Book design by Dana Leigh Blanchette

To all of my grandparents—the ones I knew,
the ones I didn't, and the ones
I wished I knew better.

For some a prologue—for others an epilogue.

—MIKHAIL BULGAKOV,
The Days of the Turbins

LIST OF CHARACTERS

PRINCIPAL CHARACTERS

Antonina, called Tonya

Arkady, Tonya's first husband

Alexandra, called Shura, daughter of Antonina and Arkady

Pavel, called Pasha, son of Antonina and Arkady

Fyodor, called Fedya, son of Antonina and Arkady

Dimitrev Senior, Tonya's second husband

Dimitrev Junior, Shura's husband

Natalia, called Talia, wife of Fyodor

Larissa, daughter of Fyodor and Talia

Polina, called Polya, daughter of Fyodor and Talia

Anatoly, called Tolik, son of Larissa

Valentina, Anatoly's wife

Natasha, daughter of Anatoly and Valentina

Licky, a cat

THE ORLOV FAMILY

Konstantin, closest friend of Fyodor

Tamara, Konstantin's wife

Misha, son of Konstantin and Tamara

Bogdan, son of Konstantin and Tamara

THE SHULMAN FAMILY

Yuri, Natasha's husband

Natalia, called Talia, their daughter

Sharik, a cat

PART I

As Easy as Being
a Woman

Larissa

My granddaughter, Natasha, has a long history of caring for unfortunate creatures. When she was a little girl, a recent transplant to America, she and her father would rescue endless varieties of pathetic fauna from the woods behind their dilapidated New Jerseyan duplex—broken-winged birds and feeble rabbits and one-eyed kittens that they would fail to nurse back to health until their dim flames were nearly extinguished. Whenever I visited from Kiev, I would try to put a stop to this nonsense, of course. Natasha's mother and I would take the pitiful creatures to the backyard and put them out of their misery with a frying pan under cover of night. Oh, her mother, Valentina, was a force, a stunning, steely woman with a vicious gleam in her eye as she wiped the bloody pan on the grass, wanting to harden her daughter against the cold world. But what can you do, she died of breast cancer when Natasha was seventeen, leaving her alone with my hapless son, so the girl has remained as soft as a whore's bottom.

When my son was felled by a heart attack five years ago and handsome Yuri, his former student, began courting Natasha, I thought finally, finally, she will settle down, stop caring for useless men, and have someone care for her. And last year, when she told me she and Yuri were expecting a child, I thought, Well, yes, she will have to make some compromises with her acting career, but she will be a natural! I recalled her rapturous, Madonna-like gaze when she beheld her ailing creatures, and later, the slew of stinky pets she took into her various cramped New York apartments, and I thought, She has my simpleton sister's animal-caretaking genes; she'll also love holding a crying nothing to her breast, much more than I did anyway. But when she first materialized on my computer screen with the rat-faced girl in her arms, she looked weary and ruined and sweat-covered, shaking my faith in her abilities. She has spent most of the three months since her daughter's birth chained to her infant and lately, also caring for Stas, Yuri's overly young, greasy-haired deadbeat of a friend who fled the Boston suburb where they were raised under murky circumstances, whom she was kind enough to take in.

When I see her this evening, her pale skin emerging in the morning light of her living room, her dark eyes swollen and sleepless, she brings to mind a clump of hair I yanked out of my shower drain just last week. She is holding her hideous baby girl, Talia, stroking her cheek in hopes that she will drift off.

"Now, listen, child," I say. "If you train that girl to sleep in your arms, she will become a mother-dependent namby-pamby. You should do what my parents did to me, and what I did to your father. Put her in her crib until she is filled with existential understanding. She will see that she is all alone in a cold universe and must drift off on her own. And while she's in there, you should leave the apartment and go for a stroll or see a movie."

She laughs and shakes her wilted head. "I'll consider it."

"Some would call that child abuse," says Stas from a dark corner of the apartment. Lately, his presence has been as reliable as that of Sharik, Natasha's vulgar orange cat.

"Oh please," I tell him. "Everyone did it in the Soviet Union, and we raised a generation of strong men."

"Alcoholics," he says.

"Strong alcoholics," I concede. "Don't you have somewhere to be?"

"Not at all," he says, approaching the computer to give me a slick little smile, and I shake my head at Natasha for not telling this pesky creature to leave.

She turns to the derelict boy at last. "Why don't you go take that stroll my grandmother was talking about?"

"Fine, fine," he says, lifting a grubby hand at me, and soon enough the door slams shut. Natasha watches him go and then fusses with the quilt on her worn green leather couch and then the threadbare garage sale rug on the floor with her free hand, a desperate attempt to create order. When her gaze returns to me, she looks even more out of sorts.

"Listen," she says, "there's something I wanted to ask you."

"Oh dear," I say, and I feel nervous all of a sudden, though what could she possibly want from me? Could she be asking for money at last?

"Don't freak out," she says, but she does nothing to calm me down. "But I was wondering—would you mind telling me the story of how your grandmother died during World War Two?"

I take a moment to collect myself. Why on Earth is she asking now? "Of course I can tell you," I say. "She threw herself under a train. Then the war ended."

"Right," she says. "But I was wondering if you would go a bit more in-depth? You always promised to tell me the whole story, and I thought, Tally would want to learn her history one day—"

"And soon I will evaporate and you will have no story to remember."

"That's not what I'm saying."

"You didn't have to."

I take a drag on my cigarette and consider the days ahead. I wonder if she truly wants the story, or if she is only asking because she thinks I need more help than one of her mangled rabbits, a distraction to keep the abyss at bay. I have told her bits and pieces of the story over the years, but never from start to finish, because the girl has the attention span of a ferret and because talking about the war for too long wears at my heart. But what else do I have to live for?

Old isn't gold—I am approaching my ninetieth brutal year and wouldn't mind being clubbed over the head with a frying pan myself. A season has passed since I buried my husband and the days are long. My body is betraying me and my dear Kiev is of no use to me now. Seeing it in its early summer glory without having the able body to enjoy its lush gardens and verdant parks reminds me of longing for Styopa Antonov, a graduate student and Lermontov scholar who studied under me in 1962, a charming man with the firmest buttocks whom I could not touch on account of my marriage—well, now that I think of it, we did carry on after a while, but you get the point. So! I used to hold literary salons in my elegant home filled with obscenely youthful, lust-crazed students arguing about whether or not Yesenin truly committed suicide and sneaking off to neck on the balcony. Now my main source of entertainment is packing up the few things I'd like to take from my apartment down to my cottage on the Black Sea, and letting my husband's men sell the rest. Chatting with Natasha could only ease my suffering.

"Fine, fine," I tell her. "Why not?"

"Really?" she says, her bloodshot eyes lighting up in genuine surprise. "I thought it would take a bit more convincing."

"Let's get on with it."

She is startled once more, caressing the limp strands on her daughter's head. "Right now?"

"I don't have forever."

"All right then," she says.

She puts a finger to her lips and tells me to wait a second, she has to figure out how to record the call, if that's all right with me. Then she pats her girl's butt, and the helpless thing shuts her unknowable eyes, a creature as alien to me as a space monkey, as far away from my Kiev kitchen as a distant planet, an American-born girl whose parents left their homeland as schoolchildren and will hardly be able to pass their Soviet legacy down to her, though they did surprise me by naming her Natalia after my mother, and now Natasha seems to think the girl will one day feel tied to her mother's Motherland from hearing my sad story. Currently, the only Soviet thing about the child is that with the cosmically disappointed look on her face, she brings to mind Gorbachev during his resignation announcement. Well, what else is there for me to do? I wait for my pathetic little great-granddaughter to settle, and then I begin.

My grandmother Tonya was a weak, spoiled woman, though I must admit she had a rather difficult life. She came of age at the turn of the century, in a palatial apartment in the center of Kiev, a buxom and brainless banker's daughter, wasting her youth flitting about endless soirees draped in the season's finest gowns, smoking long cigarettes and flirting with any man with two eyes like the frivolous woman that she was. She married a banker, a colleague of her father's, and gave him three children: first horse-faced Aunt Shura, then my dear father, and finally my sweet Uncle Pasha.

But when my father turned twelve, the Revolution blazed through Ukraine like a flame through a silk handkerchief. The Bolsheviks seized my grandparents' fine apartment overlooking the Khreschatyk, inheriting all the velvet curtains and blinding chandeliers my grandmother spoke of until her dying day. They left her family with two trunks of finery they dragged to their tem-

porary home at the residence of the Dimitrev brothers, friends of
the family whose ties to Lenin made them immune to the upheaval,
whose apartment overlooked Postal Square and had four floors
and gilded windows and a separate entrance just for carriages. My
grandparents decided to flee Ukraine before they suffered the
worst of it—I am not certain where to, perhaps London, or Milan,
or even Paris. They planned to take a train to Odessa and transfer
to a more enlightened capital from there.

But as they plotted their escape, my grandfather died of typhus,
you know how these things go. And so, the day before my grandmother and her three children were to leave, stern typhus husband
still tepid in the ground, the older Dimitrev brother pulled her
aside with a double marriage proposal: she could marry him, and
her daughter, Shura, could marry his younger brother. What did
she think? She was not a product of the first freshness, but she still
had her youth about her, she was not yet forty, and her daughter
was a spirited sixteen, and they could have a good life together, and
furthermore, it was unpatriotic to leave the Motherland when it
needed you most. Could she really see herself raising her children
in some dainty land like France, or among the blanched Brits, with
their tasteless food and inferior literature?

But after some hesitation, Baba Tonya turned down Dimitrev
senior, got her children and suitcases ready, and had her hosts' carriage drop them off at the train station. Can you imagine it? Utter
chaos. Blood running through the streets. People swarming around
like flies on a heap of manure, trying to keep their wits about them
as they prepared to face the great unknown. My grandmother hovering over her children like a hapless mother duckling, wondering
if her destination would prove more bountiful than her Motherland, home of her ancestors, the Kiev Rus, land of Gogol, cradle of
Russian civilization. Or would it be even worse—was she walking
her diminished self and her three children into more dire circum-

stances, which she would have to navigate without a man by her side?

My grandmother was no heroine. She was no Catherine the Great, riding her horses and taking her lovers and corresponding with Voltaire and changing the world with the force of her fist and tremendous cleavage. The thought of emptying her own chamber pot brought her to tears. She had a large, substantial frame, but she was as wobbly as a holodets. She liked her dances, powder on her face, Champagne at her bedside, a maid to clean up after her thoughtless messes. She heard the train moan like a whale in heat and turned her children around and jumped into the nearest carriage she could find. And so she fell into the arms of Dimitrev senior and accepted the brothers' dual marriage proposal. Who could blame her?

Of course, if she could look back on her choice from the vantage point of history, she would see she made an awful mistake, but there was no way to know that at the time. And with senior and junior Dimitrev, Babushka Tonya was able to maintain her lavish lifestyle—to a point. Shortly after the rushed nuptials, the upstairs of the brothers' apartment was seized and divided up for the so-called proletariat, and suddenly, there was no more room for my twelve-year-old father or his nine-year-old brother, or so the story goes. Dimitrev senior decided to shuttle the boys off to an orphanage all the way out in Kharkov, can you believe it? And my grandmother did nothing to stop him.

The way my dear father told it, the establishment was quite dignified, for an orphanage. He and his brother shared a bunk bed with warm blankets and had enough porridge to eat. The place was run by a distant Dimitrev cousin, so the boys were given special privileges, and my father became an aide to the teachers, helping care for the younger children, never shedding a tear, reading every book on the institution's modest shelves until he ruined his eyesight and was forced to wear bottle-cap glasses. He even maintained his composure on the rare days when his mother would summon him and his brother to Kiev for a visit. They had shined their boots so hard in preparation for their first reunion that Uncle Pasha immediately slipped on the parquet floor at the entrance to the apartment, breaking his nose and dripping blood all over the place, and though a doctor was sent, his nose was never the same afterward. Perhaps that was why his grudge toward his mother was more severe than my father's.

When my father turned sixteen, he returned to Kiev to attend the Polytechnic Institute, while his brother chose to stay behind at the orphanage instead of joining him in the ancestral city. My father had left the orphanage in what, 1922, 1923? The Bolsheviks had run everything to the ground, but my father had managed to stay out of trouble. Meanwhile, on the other side of the city, my dear mother, who had been truly orphaned due to a parental cocktail of typhus-cancer at the age of seven, had been slaving away at the restaurant of two mean old aunts ever since, spending her days washing dishes and occasionally wringing the necks of the chickens they kept in the backyard for stew, learning everything from the books she snuck into the closet where she slept. She taught herself to read and write by closet candlelight, well enough to finish school and eventually become a secretary at the Polytechnic Institute, and that was where she met my father.

They married in 1924 and in 1927 I was born. A year later came Polya, my smelly, spoiled, and achingly gorgeous sister. Papa had done quite well as an engineer at that point, having dug himself out from the horse-stink of the orphanage to the upper echelon of the Industrial Engineering Institute, even becoming the closest friend and confidant of Konstantin Orlov himself, Institute founder and leading expert of Soviet welding, the sneaky fire-breathing business of fusing metal without the pesky need for nuts and bolts. He was a stony man whose only redeeming quality was his handsome son, Misha. My father, however, maintained his humility in spite of his lofty connections. Though Uncle Konstantin offered our family a private apartment in the blocks designated for Institute employees, Papa chose to live among the masses, and my equally austere mother supported him wholeheartedly. He recalled how helpless his mother had been because of all her maids and bedrooms and parquet floors and did not want his daughters to be similarly weak, so he condemned my dear family, the Volkov clan, to a one-room communalka on Vladimirskaya, only a few blocks from his workplace, while Baba Tonya and Aunt Shura continued to enjoy their finery near the bank of the Dnieper.

Uncle Pasha, now a crooked-nosed bachelor, completed his studies in Kharkov and worked for the Engineering Institute there, showing no interest in returning to live in Kiev, so he was rarely subjected to seeing his mother and sister, though he did love horsing around with me and Polya during his visits to our home. My family also tried to avoid my grandmother, but on special occasions my sister and I were shoehorned into our only starched dresses and shuttled to the Dimitrev half-home, which was twenty times the size of our communalka, plush with velvet divans and gold-tasseled curtains and vodka gleaming in crystal tumblers and excessive Frenchy foods I pretended not to prefer over the kasha and herring of home. My parents weathered these events with resignation, like patients enduring a rectal exam, and I followed suit. Of all of us, Papa suffered the most. He tolerated his mother, sister, and sister's husband well enough, but he could hardly stand to look at his stepfather, Dimitrev senior, the man who had sent him away to the orphanage. He never forgave him for a second.

Dimitrev senior was a tall, red-faced man who had gray hair and a silver mustache though he was not very old, perhaps not yet forty, a decade younger than my grandmother, at least. He would twist the handles of his mustache around his index finger, and the more he twisted them, the longer they grew. He had a menacing twinkle in his eye that suggested he was always internally laughing at a private joke told to him by the vodka tumbler in his hand. Talk about a strong alcoholic—perhaps his proclivity was the very reason Papa and his brother were never aficionados for drink like most of their compatriots. After several generous sips of this elixir, he would pinch my father by the ear, and poor Papa would bear it, but other than that, he left him alone. He was too busy fussing over my grandmother. How he loved to tease the old woman! She spent most of our visits splayed out on the divan with the back of her hand to her forehead like some long-suffering beauty—and she might have been a beauty once, but the dead husband and endless soufflés had made her into a stout, large-nosed, dark-haired matron.

"I am exhausted!" she would declare, sighing loudly.

"My darling," her husband would say, indicating the cooks and maids milling about. "How could you possibly be exhausted? I cannot remember the last time you lifted a finger."

"Exactly!" she'd fire back. "Do you know how tiring it is, giving commands all day?"

My parents and I tried not to laugh at this ridiculous woman. Giving commands! What I would have given to, just once, have someone iron a shirt or do a dish or brush a hair on my head for me, instead of having to be tough like my father wanted me and my sister to be. But anyone could see that his communalka convictions had no effect on my sister. Dear spoiled Polya found nothing humorous in the exchange about our grandmother and her supposed exhaustion. In fact, she took the woman quite seriously. My sister lived for these visits to my grandmother's home.

Darling Polya possessed the vapid beauty of a lobotomized swan. Her wild red hair coiffed about her head like the petals of a delicate flower. Her blue eyes, two shining jewels set in the center of her round, startled face, as pale as a porcelain toilet! Her lips, as lush as the banks of the Dnieper in spring. And her figure, as developed and buxom as a sixteen-year-old woman's by her eleventh birthday. How I loathed her. Well! Like attracts like, so Babushka Tonya and Aunt Shura lavished their love on my sister, donning her with delicate garments and ivory hair clips and powdering her face until she resembled a china doll, and even, on occasion, taking her shopping.

Dimitrev senior loved flirting with my baby sister, twirling her around and inviting her to sit on his lap, though she was far too old for it. The only time I saw my parents hold hands was when Dimitrev senior planted Polya on his lap and laughed, vodka sloshing in his mustache, because Mama was telling Papa to steel himself, that making the man back off would create more trouble than it was worth. Thankfully I was spared any affection from this mustachioed man. Men had a long history of preferring my sister over me. Was I jealous at eight, nine, ten years old, angry that I was a stern, reptilian version of my sister? No, no, not at all—my stark appearance forced me to have my wits about me. Why do you think I outlived my sister by more than half a century—and counting? But I am getting ahead of myself.

During our visits, my grandmother and aunt even allowed my sister to wear a ruby necklace that belonged to my grandmother's own grandmother, supposedly given to her by the Empress Maria herself. The rubies were shaped like enormous teardrops and were punctuated by diamonds. The necklace was such a beautiful thing that even I was not immune to it, though my pride kept me from wearing it the one time my grandmother offered it to me, which was perhaps when the gulf between her and me widened and was never again bridged.

But I could not stop staring at the beguiling and borsch-colored string of rubies around my sister's long neck, over the years. Just once, I touched the necklace, and my grandmother slapped my hand away.

"Why, Larissa," she said. "I did not think you cared for nice things."

"I don't," I said.

"Whatever you say, dear sister," Polina said with a sly smile that made me want to throttle her. I watched my smirking sister fluttering around with the necklace on and vowed to avenge this injustice one day. I can still feel my hand smarting from the assault.

Once my sister was adorned with the jewels, my grandmother would put on the gramophone and pull out her second most coveted item—a white boa long enough to wrap around a New Year's tree. She would take the feathery, wild thing and drape it around Aunt Shura and Polya and herself, and the three women would begin cavorting and writhing under the feathery monstrosity like dirty boudoir girls. The women laughed, the women shrieked, they would cry out and shimmy their fingers and kick up their feet in a primitive imitation of a can-can, it was something awful. Just once, Aunt Shura asked if Mama and I would like to join and Mama lifted her hand and shook her head. "Not for us, thank you," she said, and that was that.

During these unseemly cabarets, Dimitrev junior and my parents sullenly sipped their tea while Dimitrev senior sucked down his vodka and stared lustily at my sister and grandmother while I sat with crossed arms on the divan and counted down the minutes until the car would take us home. The worst part of it was the smug look on my sister's face, like she belonged among those rich witches because they made her dance like a monkey and bought her dresses a few times a year. Only when I saw her with them, getting ideas about herself, did I see that Papa had a point about making us suffer in the communalka, a place designed to remind you of your place in the universe.

The dreaded boudoir boa dances stopped my twelfth year. Life is strife, as they say—in the span of two years, all the inhabitants of the shiny apartment were dead except my dear grandmother. The brothers were purged, or perhaps one was purged and the other died in a sledding accident, who can remember? As for Aunt Shura, it was cancer that did her in, or perhaps it was gangrene of the foot. What difference did it make? Dead was dead, and the living were left to figure out the rest. Aunt Shura was the last to go, and my grandmother could not do so much as pour a cup of tea on her own, so my sister and Mama and I folded her clothes and stuffed what we could into three velvet suitcases that Papa hauled out of her palatial apartment. She arrived in the winter of 1940, which then seemed to be a time of extreme privation because Papa had to sneak home a bag of clementines from the Industrial Engineering Institute's New Year's party so we could have a small celebration of our own.

My grandmother drifted into our communalka with dead eyes that were not offset by the ruby necklace and boa she insisted on wearing from that moment on—needless to say, she was already a bit cuckoo at that point—and I did not know how she would survive without her former splendor. My family shared one large room of a three-family communalka; ours was the most desirable because it had a balcony. Our apartment also contained three lovely items: two ivory cabinets with engravings of dancing elephants that the Dimitrev brothers gave my parents as a wedding gift, and a pink divan of unknown origin. Mama and Papa slept on a cot they folded out at night and Polya and I rested on two tiny mattresses behind a seamstress's curtain Mama had fashioned to give us some privacy. Now Polya and I would have to share one tiny mattress and Baba would dominate the other. When Mama showed my grandmother her new sleeping arrangement, she looked like she had been backed up against a fence and shot.

However, my grandmother's arrival soon became a matter of secondary concern. By spring, I could feel the tension rising in our communalka and our streets. By eavesdropping on my parents and the occasional neighbor, I was gaining troubling intelligence: Hitler could be invading the Soviet Union, and Kiev, any day now. In June, Molotov's voice shook over the radio when he confirmed it: the Germans had bombed us, and we were going to war.

The next month, Uncle Pasha and his colleagues from the Kharkov factory evacuated to Shalya, a town to the west of the Ural Mountains, halfway to Siberia. In August, Uncle Konstantin called in the middle of the night to tell us to pack up our things to prepare to head into the vast nothingness, just as my uncle did. From now on, my father and the engineers who had erected practical structures like bridges and university buildings would have to put their minds to the nasty business of war, constructing tanks and other weapons. The next morning, the workers of the Industrial Engineering Institute and their families would evacuate to the remote town of Lower Turinsk, where we would stay until it was safe to go home.

"And so the war begins at last," says Stas from somewhere in the distance, approaching the screen, his face shiny with sweat from the outdoors. When did the homeless boy even return to the apartment? "With all due respect, Larissa Fyodorovna, I thought you'd never get there," the impudent creature adds.

"Every word I have said is necessary. And with all due respect to you, I did not invite you to listen to begin with."

"I couldn't help myself."

"Then my story must not be so dull after all."

He shrugs with a smile, tucking a greasy strand of hair behind his ear, rascal that he is. Natasha smacks the boy across the chest. "Don't be rude."

He shakes his head and picks up Sharik, and mercifully disappears from view. This impudent long-haired homosexual—if only he could go back to where he came from and leave Natasha alone.

My sun has gone down hours ago, but Natasha is a radiant wonder on the screen, having perked up from my opening salvo. Her unsightly daughter rudely slept through the entirety of my tale, and is only now waking up, grumbling and flailing her crooked limbs.

"And what happened on the train?" Natasha says. "I remember there was a little girl who died."

"This has been more than enough for one day," I say.

She nods and moves her silly tot closer to the screen, as if her blighted face would compel me to keep talking. "Isn't she a beauty?"

The nearly bald, snot-covered girl scrunches up her face, preparing to unleash a torrent of cries. I scowl at the girl, yet her mother has the nerve to ask again if she is a beauty and then shoves her nipple into the girl's mouth.

"Her nature must make up for her looks," I assure Natasha, and she shakes her head.

"She's your blood, Baba."

"Of course she is mine. You think I myself am some great beauty? Even in my heyday, I did not look much better than this rodent-child, though I made up for it in charm—and you should have seen your father. As hideous as the day was long! His rear was far superior to his face for quite a while. Until he was a university student, at least. But you, on the other hand—a beauty from the moment you were born."

How can I explain it? When I first held her tiny form, I knew Natasha was the child I was waiting for. After her father lowered her in my arms, she spit up all over my new blouse and broke into a devilish smile and I thought, Thank heavens, the girl has spirit! Her father was mild, considerate, and melancholy almost from birth—how he bored me! When Valentina forced the family to America—claiming she was discriminated against as a Jew, and perhaps she was, but was it worth the turmoil?—my heart crumpled, I couldn't bear Natasha's absence. I had to resign myself to a yearly visit to America and having the girl visit me at my seaside cottage for a few weeks every summer, I had to pour all of my happiness into those days like it was the fine Georgian wine Volodya Shoshenko, a charming Gogol scholar with a beguiling goatee, had once gently guided into my patiently waiting lips one evening on the patio of the cottage in question while Natasha was resting.

Though I look forward to returning to my seaside home for good in a few weeks, I would give anything to be walking along that shore with Natasha again, as she danced by the water and recited Shakespeare. " 'O, wonder!' " the girl had cried as we maneuvered around the sunburned seaside flesh to stake out our own sandy territory. " 'How many goodly creatures there are here! How beauteous mankind is!' " Even as she grew up, I could not help but see her as the sharp, curious creature in my arms.

"If only you could have seen yourself," I tell her. "Your eyes were as big as moons. It was something unbelievable."

"They still are," Yuri interjects, giving me a wave and a wide grin.

Had he been there the whole time too? No, no, he has just walked in the door, it seems. He is a competent, handsome man with thick hair and a solid nose, a substantial patriarch compared to his wimpy friend. I love him as my own. He was the only man able to calm down my granddaughter during her wildest, darkest years, pacifying the frenetic girl at long last, and I will always treasure him for it.

"You're looking lovely, Larissa Fyodorovna," he tells me.

"Stop it, you rogue," I say, waving him away.

"I can't help myself. How are you?"

"Awaiting the grave with open arms, my boy."

"A lucky grave it will be, to have you all to itself."

"You butter me up, silly man," I tell him, and he chuckles until Natasha pops the child off her breast and tells him to knock it off.

"How's the packing?" he asks.

"You know how it is. Either I will finish it, or it will finish me."

"Enough of that," Natasha says, burping her little nothing. "I'll call you in a few days, Baba. You must be tired."

"Remember what I said. A few hours alone in the crib will only make her stronger—and you as well," I tell her.

"How could I forget?" she says, mustering a laugh as she hangs up.

I feel uneasy after I say goodbye to the girl. Of course, delving into the war doesn't do my spirit any favors, but my main concern lies in the present: how far gone is Natasha? Is she simply feeling the eternal mother blues, or is it something more? She does not look like a complete wreck like I was when my son was born, when I was hardly capable of changing the child without weeping, though then again our worthless cloth diapers were enough to undo the strongest of women. No, no, Natasha is faring far better than I did, or at least, not worse. I prepare for sleep, telling myself I have nothing to worry about.

Natasha

"You think you can afford me, Mr. Robertson? It is impossible. You can have me, for a price, but you can never truly afford me, you understand? Natasha—she is priceless," I say in my best Russian accent. I give one little swivel of my hips and add, "Thank you."

"Thank you, Ms. Sterling," the casting director says, nodding to say there's nothing else he wants from me. He and his crew shuffle papers at their desk and whisper to one another, not giving me another look. I usually know at least someone in casting, but this time, they're all strangers, which doesn't help my case. I leave the cramped room with my back straight and head high, as if my heels aren't killing my still-swollen feet, like I have places to be and don't care if I book the fucking gig or not, as if I can't tell they were completely unimpressed.

I walk down the too-bright hallway into a too-dark room filled with other hopeful would-be prostitutes-and-secret-spies who look like me, with long wavy hair and pale skin, five foot nine and one hundred and ten pounds—or that was my pre-pregnancy fighting weight anyway. Though the character in question is supposed to be in her thirties, they all look like twentysomethings trying to look older, brushing their hair and chatting nervously in a sea of hairspray and perfume.

And these bitches have a right to be nervous, because this isn't just another audition for one of the thousands of Russian prostitute parts all over the city but one for *Pen & Sword,* a real NBC political prime-time show people like my bland mother-in-law actually watch, a role as a series regular who wins the heart of Mr. Robertson, aka Greg Spade, played by Mark Sims, my childhood TV crush, and in fact, one of the first men I ever masturbated to at the probably-too-young-and-the-cause-of-so-many-of-my-man-problems delicate age of ten.

Though I promised Yuri I'd take the summer off from auditions, when my agent said she had another top-notch prostitute audition for me, one that was even more prestigious than my respectable three-season gig as Katya Andreyeva, the telepathic crime-solving hooker on CBS's *Seeing Things,* I couldn't turn it down. When I got the text after spending the better part of the past three months getting my nipples chewed on, I thought I might blow my brains out if I couldn't get out of the house and be someone other than a mom, even if that someone was a prostitute-spy conveniently named Natasha, as they often are. But seeing these younger, skinnier, smooth-skinned, perky-breasted women who have slept more than three hours in a row in the last month, I know I've wasted my time, that I would have been better off talking to my grandmother at our appointed time instead of rescheduling for later in the day for this bullshit.

I take off my jacket and leather pants and bright-red lipstick in the bathroom, my prostitute gear which had gotten me plenty of hooker roles before I got pregnant, though now I just look like a plastic bag my cat, Sharik, ingested and threw up. My boobs are killing me so I squeeze some of my milk into the toilet and change into a T-shirt and leggings and flats, my default mom garb. But as I head for the door, I see I'm not getting off that easy. I spot Marianna, Sofia, and Vera, three girls from the Borsch Babies—or as I call them, the Borsch Bitches—who seem to haunt all the same auditions as I do and whose tiny asses and thigh gaps make it clear that they most definitely do not have babies of their own. And they've spotted me too—it's too late to sneak away.

For a while there, the Borsch Babies, a Russian-Jewish theater troupe, was basically saving my life. When I dropped out of NYU after a semester and was spending my time bartending and failing at auditions and hating my dead mother for saying I told you so, the only thing that gave my life meaning was meeting a bunch of equally dubiously employed Russian immigrants in the founder Vadim's dim little theater in Brighton and trading immigration stories and then looking further back, to our parents and even our grand- or great-grandparents, talking about the collapse and perestroika and communal life and the purges and wars and pogroms, trying to make sense of that ancient rubble, asking how it made us who we were.

None of our plays were very good, I can say that now, though we pretended otherwise, as if the people in the audience were there for art's sake, not because they were related to or had fucked or wanted to fuck one of us. But talking about the poor dead Russians who had been royally screwed by the government to bring us here to live our strange uncertain lives did something so essential for our souls that we couldn't see past it to the stiff accents and melodramatic plots we forced our audiences to endure a few times a year. Plus, we partied hard and had a good time. In fact, too good of a time, and once I got involved with Vadim while he was already involved with Sofia, and then, it turned out, also Marianna, things got too messy, culminating in an ill-advised foursome on a waterbed after too much blow that we were convinced would solve the awkwardness instead of making everything impossibly worse. After that, I left the Babies, traded my last name, Orlova, for Sterling, and then I got some money doing voiceover work for *The Americans,* basically just chitchatting in '80s-appropriate Russian as background noise for three full seasons for an impressive hourly rate, and then I got my big break in an eco-friendly tampon company commercial for a brand called Lady Planet that was big for a while, where I paused in front of the camera to tie my shoe and declared, "It's as easy as being a woman!" It didn't exactly make me Flo from Progressive or the Mentos man, but people recognized me, for a while. Then I signed with my agent and booked *Seeing Things,* and sure, it seemed like I left the Babies for bigger things, but the timing of me leaving and then getting lucky with work was a coincidence. And now my former Babies costars are winding through the crowd just to be bitches to me, I'm sure.

"Looks like Mamachka is back in the game," Vera, the queen of the troupe, says as she runs a cold hand over my head. She still weighs about ninety pounds and her long black hair is impossibly thick and shiny. "But oh, she looks so tired. Unless you've had your eyes done recently."

"Have you slept since the baby was born?" says Marianna, the prettiest and meanest of the three. "We should come over, say hello. Bring you some bouillon and rub your feet."

"At least you've put on weight. That's good. You were too skinny before. Now you look like a real woman," says Sofia, the sexy one, squeezing my side while I try not to flinch.

"Did you actually stop shaving your arms?" says Marianna, stroking my stubbly forearms.

"Always a pleasure, ladies," I say. She's right about the forearms, but fuck her. "Really. So lovely to see you."

They cackle like little witches, Shakespearean cunts without cauldrons. "Natasha thinks she can be this Natasha," Vera says. "We will see, won't we?"

"You know, the Borsch Babies are putting on a play about Chernobyl this fall. You are welcome to join us anytime," says Marianna, and I know she's keeping herself from adding, *If you don't think you're too much of a hotshot for us.*

"Thanks," I say, trying not to visibly cringe about this stupid idea. Who would actually give a shit about Chernobyl? It's not exactly a sexy topic. "I'm pretty busy with the new baby, but I'll keep it in mind," I say.

"Of course," says Marianna.

I nearly trip over her leather boot as I step away.

"Oh, Natasha?" says Marianna, and I turn back to her steely smile.

"What?"

"Congratulations."

I have no idea what she's talking about. I have the crazy thought that she's congratulating me because I somehow already booked *Pen & Sword,* but then I remember I have a newish baby at home. I mumble a thank-you and choke on hairspray all the way to the elevator.

Outside, I catch my breath. I take a selfie and post it on Instagram: *#backinthegame #auditionlife #threemonthspostpartum* and watch the likes crop up on the screen, people I never see in real life telling me what a badass I am, a warrior, even, for going out for roles. I hate doing this shit, I'd literally rather have a screwdriver shoved up my ass while getting my teeth cleaned than write these dumb posts, but everybody else does it and if I don't, then no one will remember that I exist. Anyway, it's a nice change from posting pictures of Tally, though anything I share about the little rat gets more love than my posts about my career, such as it is.

I'm never out in the wild anymore, so I don't even mind the mean June heat or the garbage-sewer summer smell of the city. I strut to the subway because I'm in full makeup and feel human and smile at everyone I pass, hoping someone cries, "It's as easy as being a woman!" at me or at least tells me I have a nice ass. As I round the corner, a guy in a suit leers at my tits, but as he gets closer I see he's not turned on but horrified, and then he points at my chest. I look down and realize he's trying to be a good citizen, telling me my boobs are leaking. But I just give him the finger and cry, "Fetishist!" and stride past the poor man. My face burns as I throw my prostitute jacket back on and skulk into the subway.

Stas puts away the little black notebook he's always scribbling his poetry in as soon as I walk in the door. Old Sharik is sitting on his lap and Tally must be sleeping in her crib, a small miracle. I peek in the bedroom to see the rise and fall of her chest. When Stas rolled in a few weeks ago, with his compact little body and pony-tailed blond hair, wearing a tattered button-down shirt and black jeans though it was a hundred degrees out and the middle of May, reeking of cigarettes, flies practically swarming around him, I wasn't exactly thrilled. I hadn't seen the guy since our wedding, when he got blacked out and boned sexy Babies Sofia in a broom closet, and he's been a waiter-slash-poet-slash-heartbreaker ever since, according to Yuri. But then he held my girl and I had a hard time reconciling this fake bohemian guy who called himself a poet with the sweet man holding my daughter, and I hated him a little less.

He has experience with babies because he practically had to raise his kid sister on his own. His dad left his family to start a new one right after his sister was born when Stas was a teenager, and his mom was so depressed that Stas had to do most of the work when he wasn't in school, or when Yuri's parents, friends of his family from Minsk who lived in the same Boston suburb, couldn't help out. Though Yuri was in college when this was going on, he came home on the weekends to check in on Stas, take him out for a burger and cheer him up, treating him like his baby brother. Now Stas's baby sister is a teenager herself, and he's obsessed with her, always facetiming her on our balcony. It's a lifesaver that he's showing some of that love for Tally.

"You have the magic touch," I say, nodding toward the bedroom.

He smiles broadly. "She's easy. How did it go?"

"Complete waste of time," I say, kicking my shoes off. "I don't know why I bothered."

"You underestimate yourself."

"I think I have a pretty realistic view of things."

"If you don't get this prostitute role, then you'll get the next one. With that orange turd in office, there's no shortage of them, I'm sure."

"That may be true," I offer, because I can't deny that there have been more roles as Russian prostitutes and spies since Trump got elected last fall, since everyone loves having Russians be the villains again like it's the fucking Cold War. "But it doesn't matter if there are a million parts like that right now. I've been out of the game too long and I look like ass on a stick. I don't even think I'm good enough for the Borsch Bitches anymore."

"You don't really miss them anyway, do you?"

"I'd rather die than crawl back to them. But I'd also rather die than—not work," I say. He looks like he wants to further pursue the topic of my train wreck of a career, but I am way too tired for that. I say, "Really, thank you so much. You're saving my life."

"Likewise," he says. "The pleasure is all mine."

I consider asking: *What am I saving you from, exactly?* But I don't want to make it weird. All I know is that he told Yuri that he got into a "messy situation" with a girl back in Boston, which was so bad that he placed a desperate call to Yuri asking if he could crash with us, insisting that sleeping on a couch in a one-bedroom with a newborn in it was preferable to his current situation, and of course Yuri didn't bother asking whether this was preferable for me. Yuri, Yuri, always eager to please everybody because he was the only child of parents who were impossible to please—quiet, distant people who drove down from Boston to take one look at Tally and told us they would return after the summer, when there would be more they could do—even if it was at my expense. Once I clean up a bit in the kitchen, the man himself is back, opening the door loudly enough to wake Tally up. He doesn't wait, doesn't give her a minute to settle, he just runs into the bedroom and picks her up from her crib and raises her in the air, the sunlight flooding her few feathery strands of hair.

"There's my baby girl," he declares. "Let's have a look at her." He kisses her forehead, her cheeks, her little nose, and she gives him a smile, which obviously has melted his fucking simpleton parent heart, just as those early smiles are supposed to do. "Yep, everything is in working order," he says, kissing me on the forehead like he's a priest offering his blessing to a dying child. "We won't have to take her back to the store for repairs."

"I did my best," Stas says, saluting him.

"You always do," Yuri says. Once Stas steps out on the balcony to smoke, my husband turns to me and says, "How did it go?"

He's just come back from class so he's in his adorable professor gear, with his khakis hiked too high over his button-down shirt and his plaid loafers that could have belonged to my dad.

"It was fine," I tell him. I don't know why I don't admit how awful it was.

"That's great," he says, failing to read my level of enthusiasm, turning back to Tally.

I could go on, but he won't hear me. He doesn't care about me at the moment. Talia is the apple of his eye and I'm old news. He cradles her and strokes her cheeks. "Little butterball," he says, kissing her nose again. Right then, I could tell him my vagina split in half on the subway and he would just nod and smile.

I stop and fix my hair in the mirror that hangs above the one photo I have of my great-great-grandmother Antonina, who looks so stylish in her long black coat and famous white boa, the only picture Baba had of her, maybe the only one ever taken, not long before her world was thrown into chaos. And sure, she was batty, but she's also the last woman in my family who was glam in any way—not my practical-minded great-grandmother, or my tough grandmother and her plain matching cardigan and pants and simple pearls, and not my own mother, who never wore makeup and kept her legs hidden under ugly work suits, though there was no hiding her beauty, a woman whose gorgeous hair I saw down exactly once. None of the other women, as far as I know, ever wore a lick of makeup, while Antonina was inches deep in rouge and powder, Revolution or not, and bless her for it. I tell myself that the women in my family had made it through the Revolution, and the Great War, and that surely I can make it through the early days of parenting, which reminds me I have to call Baba in an hour. I turn back to my nearly bald, big-eared little girl who has the face of the man I love, the man who is now staring at me.

"What?"

"Nothing," he says, and then he kisses me on the lips, a big improvement over the lame forehead kiss from a moment ago. "You look pretty, that's all."

"Pretty?" What am I, a high school girl? I consider pointing out my leaking boobs, but no, this is sweet of him, he's making an effort. It's nice to know he can still see me that way. "Thanks," I say, and I run a hand down his slightly stubbly cheek. "You're not so bad yourself, Shulman." He laughs before turning back to our girl.

The kiss lingers, though, reminding me that there had been a point when we kissed all the time, when we couldn't keep our hands off each other, which kind of diminished when I felt too gross to hook up during my pregnancy and had totally gone away once Talia was born because I felt even more gross then. But I'm hoping things will change, even if it's hard to imagine a sexy opportunity presenting itself anytime soon, what with Talia waking up every hour and Stas puttering about, though maybe we could exploit Stas for a night out when we're feeling up to it, or when I am anyway.

Yuri sits down with the girl in his arms and she is fast asleep again, like magic; well of course she sleeps in his arms, there's no scent of milk to put her on high alert. I sit next to him and watch her resting there, as still as a pile of stones by a riverbed.

But when Stas returns, she whimpers and opens her eyes, giving me her signature cranky face, like she smells something foul and is certain I'm the one responsible. Those are basically her two states for me, either annoyed or asleep. She saves all her heart-melting smiles for her papa.

"Sorry," Stas says.

"No worries," I say. "Girl's gotta eat anyway."

I take her in my arms and am about to whip out my tit when I see Yuri's eyes get huge and I realize that this is because while I've been nursing Talia in front of Stas when Yuri's at work, I've never actually whipped it out in front of the two of them. Maybe it's weird to just have my tits on display for a guy I'm not married to. Or maybe this is deeply anti-feminist, maybe I have a right to do whatever I want with my fucking blown-out body, and actually I have, I've done it at every park all over town. But now I look at Stas and Yuri again, and both of them are noncommittally looking around like something weird isn't happening and then I say, "Excuse me," and take Talia into the bedroom and whip out my boob just for her. I'm kind of pissed Yuri acted all weird, but on the other hand, I see his point—his wife showing more of her body than he has seen in a while in front of some dude she's not married to, fine, fine, fine. I'm just surprised he still sees me as a human woman at this point; after all, you wouldn't tell a bag of Doritos or a porcupine or a shopping cart to cover up.

Tally clamps down on me, hard, and I wince, but then I feel a sweet relief, my engorged, leaking boobs finally releasing some of their weight. It still takes me a moment to understand this is my life now, that this is as normal for me as it used to be to put on my heels and walk five blocks to the Lair, the bar where I worked for years, where I would do a shot of Tito's before starting my shift like clockwork. Who could have imagined it, even a few years ago? Me—somebody's fucking *mom*. One of the reasons I never wanted a kid, beyond my general too-fucked-up-to-have-one state, my lack of higher degree or money or maternal feelings toward anybody except Sharik and all my beloved long-gone former pets, was that I wondered, by the drawn-out end of my poor bitchy mother's life, whether she was glad she even had me at all.

What was the point? You spend all this time trying to get pregnant, and if you're "lucky," then actually getting pregnant. Then you feel like ass in a glass for nine months if you're "lucky" enough to carry the baby to term, and then you push the little shit into the world, you give all your blood and sweat to the helpless thing and it saps your strength and resents you, makes you its enemy, doesn't remember the nights you spent rocking it or holding it to your breast or changing its poopy diapers. Then you spend the next decade fighting, and if you're "lucky," you come out the other end with an understanding—but that's like twenty years of work for a best-case scenario that doesn't feel all that worth it to me. And in my mom's case, she never got to the other end of it, because she fucking died, because the breasts that gave me life turned against her in the end, just like I did.

After Mama died and I dropped out of NYU, I lived with another actor for a while, kind of more of a mime-actor, then a not-funny comedian, then a guitarist, then a muralist who only painted bare feet, and then another actor-bartender who was really just a bartender. I gave these men everything, sometimes getting it back but most of the time not, spending hours fighting with them in the middle of the night, breaking mirrors and bottles and once, even a window. Then I'd flee their places to live with friends or my poor dad in Jersey City, but I'd always end up returning to them, drinking too much, having wild, sweaty sex in poorly air-conditioned studios as we'd take back everything we said and affirm how much we loved each other. Sometimes we'd even scrape together whatever money we had to take desperate vacations upstate to try to get away from it all when we were just trying to get away from each other. But then we'd come back defeated, starting the cycle all over again. On top of that, I kept bartending and auditioning and occasionally even acting, and when I thought about that lost decade after it was over, I wondered if those late-night glass-breaking sessions would have been better spent getting a bit of sleep, or even nursing a cute little baby. That was what I wanted when Yuri and I got together after my father died, well, maybe not the baby part, but just a bit of rest, and if the baby was a necessary component of that necessary peace, then so be it, I guess.

There was just one problem.

I never thought Talia's arrival would solve my issues, but I thought at least there would be some indescribable bond the second she emerged, something wild and instinctive I couldn't explain, not even to my husband. But she arrived after a disappointingly short natural birth and, well, when I held her in my arms, she was a pink, hairless, rat-faced little gremlin with enormous ears that made her look like a lost little space alien, her face angry right away, as if asking me, *Why did you push me out—into* this? Who could blame her for feeling that way? And who was I, her orphan mom, to give her an answer? The weeks wore on and moony-eyed Yuri and my too-old-to-really-help-out in-laws from Boston and various theater and bartending friends came over to coo at her, while all I could feel was exhausted from round-the-clock waking and holding the girl to my cracked and bloody nipples. I kept waiting for it, that feeling I had heard about, a crazy exhausted ecstasy that when described by other moms sounded like a good night onstage, when nothing else mattered, when I might as well have melted into the stage lights and exploded like a star.

But even now, three months after her arrival, after the so-called fourth trimester has passed, when I hold Tally to my breast, I only feel like Momland, population two, is the loneliest place in the world. Like Yuri and our friends and everyone who reacts to my desperate Facebook and Instagram posts about how full my heart is are the normal ones and I'm the fucking space alien. Yuri just thinks I'm tired. He doesn't know I'm waiting for my soul to be filled.

When I return with Tally, the boys are doing their thing, Stas telling Yuri that Tally was a babe magnet when he took her to the park.

Yuri: "Pick any of the ladies up?"

Stas: "Of course. I invited my top three prospects up for dinner, I hope you don't mind."

Yuri: "How will you choose between them?"

Stas: "Who says I have to choose?"

"You never learn, do you?" Yuri says. He only speaks this way to Stas, while being so proper with me and the rest of the world. I wish he knew I actually wanted him to let loose a little more with me too. But we hardly have time to joke around anymore because we're too busy tracking the last time Tally was changed or napped or spit up everywhere. Now he cleans the litterbox and gets the trash together and he and Stas grab the trash and take off to get groceries and run a bunch of other errands.

I'm alone with a whimpering Tally in my arms, and I try to rock her with one hand while checking my Insta with my other and I see I've gotten a few dozen more likes on my audition post, even from the Borsch Babies, and feel a little better about showing up there at all. After I prop Tally up on my lap and sing "Itsy Bitsy Spider" to her and shake a rattle around for a while, feeling my remaining brain cells ooze out my ears, the sweet girl looks sleepy, so I take her to her crib and lower her down and by a miracle she actually settles down after a little while, just like Baba said she would. I curl up on the couch next to Sharik, resting my head near his haunches, and try to do the same, but I can't, all I can do is wonder what Mama would think of me now, if she would judge me or praise me for auditioning when I'm at the end of my rope.

A few months after Mama began chemo, I woke up in the middle of the night to this beautiful singing. I thought I was still dreaming, or that Papa was listening to Pugacheva or something, but it was four in the morning, so I went downstairs to investigate. We lived in a cramped condo but it had this big wooden patio that faced the woods where Mama liked to sit with her morning coffee. And that was where I found her, bald as a gosling in her bathrobe, with the sliding glass door open. It was a fall night, and pretty cold, and I wanted to throw a blanket over her like she always did to me, to tell her she would catch cold, or to beg her to go back to sleep—the chemo had exhausted her—but for some reason, I just stood there. She was singing a song I had heard before, one of the

Soviet ballads Papa would play on his record player during their occasional date nights, filled with longing and darkness, a song by Lev Mishkin from his album *Heartsongs for the Drowned,* a song I had seen her rocking her head to but never, ever singing. But there it was:

> My heart bleeds for you, darling
> Rivers of the blackest blood
> It bleeds so sweetly, my darling
> The world is a wild, mad flood
>
> My heart is torn open for you, darling
> My flesh has been chewed right through
> My body has been ravaged for you, darling
> My soul is mangled, ancient, and blue
>
> But I don't care because I want you, you, you
> The only thing I want is you
> You, you, you, darling
> The only thing I need is you.

I knew it was something I wasn't supposed to see, like the time I walked into my parents' room when I was in elementary school and understood that they were having sex, that the strange grunting and sweating shadowy shapes belonged, crazily, to my parents, so there I was, unable to turn around, but knowing I couldn't announce myself, until I slowly backed away. My relationship with my mother hadn't exactly been healed by all the chemo and in fact had gotten steadily worse since earlier in the fall, when I sat my parents down and explained that I would not be applying to colleges, that I would move to the city to be an actress after my senior year was over. Papa was upset but not surprised and didn't put up much of a fight, but Mama had been livid. "Are you trying to kill me even faster?" she had said. "You're not thinking clearly. Life is long, child, or at least it should be, for most. You can go to school and try this actress business on the side, but do not bank your life on it." "But I know what I want," I said to her. "I don't want to spend all day in pointless classes." She didn't speak to me for a week after that.

So there I was, listening to my mother sing in this gorgeous voice filled with dark passion and love. I had never heard my mom sing a single note before. Even on lame family vacations when I was a kid, sometimes Papa and I would sing to the Beatles or whatever he put on, and Papa was terrible and knew it, and I was just slightly above average, but Mama would sit in the passenger seat with this pained little smile on her face, which I thought was just because we were not very good at singing, but then I saw it might have been more complicated.

I moved forward, toward my mother, without even realizing it was happening. It was breezy out and Mama's robe and the trees in front of us were rustling. If she still had her long flowing hair, it would have danced in the wind. Mama turned around, looking absolutely horrified, far worse than I imagine she would have looked if she knew I caught her and my dad fucking when I was a kid. Her eyes were wild and she looked absolutely mad but also beautiful in her white robe, her head completely bare and her eyes black and slick and her collarbone sticking out in a not-unstunning way, my mother even when she was dying.

"What are you doing?" she said.

"I didn't know you could sing."

"Go to sleep, darling. You were just dreaming."

"I heard you—"

"You are mistaken. Go back to your room. You have school tomorrow."

"But it sounded beautiful," I said. "I didn't know—"

She grabbed my wrist, hard, and looked like I had let her down worse than I ever had with all the boys or the drinking and skipping school or even the whole no-college thing, all of it, as if it had somehow snowballed into this one moment on the patio, when I was pretty sure that I hadn't done anything wrong, for once. If anything, I was trying to be nice and get to know my mother before it was too late.

"You didn't hear a thing. Now, leave me alone. I just need a bit of peace."

I didn't fight her, for once. I went back inside and grabbed a blanket, but Mama looked so fragile and ghostlike on the patio that no blanket could warm her up, that it would only make her more angry and would invade her privacy even further. I had already stopped her from her beautiful singing, which seemed like the worst crime of all, and I knew then, standing by the sliding door with a scratchy old blanket my grandmother had brought from Kiev, that Mama was not long for this world, that she had one foot out of it already.

I was right. Though I thought maybe if I could bargain with God, not that I believed in that kind of thing, if I promised to be a good girl and stopped driving down the Shore with older boys in the middle of the night, if I stopped popping the Xanax I got under the bleachers after school in exchange for blow jobs, if I ate my dinner and didn't skip class and even got B-pluses in English and history classes and even Spanish, and forced myself to apply to college and tough it out for four fucking years, then maybe God would let Mama live. Of course the big joke was that, for once, I was acting like the good daughter Mama had always wanted, but it was too late.

She hardly noticed that I went to school and stopped talking to boys and wearing the short shorts and tanks with exposed bra straps that had gotten me sent to the nurse to change into my gym clothes on a weekly basis. She barely cared that I even filled out applications to Rutgers and NYU and Marymount though I made a point of doing them at the kitchen table, but none of it did any good. Mama quit chemo after Thanksgiving and died, fittingly, just before the New Year, which had been her favorite holiday, the only time she got dressed up and festive and hung out with the other Russians, sometimes even hosted them, and stayed up drinking and laughing until the sun came up, but no, not that year, which me and my poor father had to face on our own.

The hopeful trill of Skype from my laptop wakes me from the thin sleep I managed to get after I stopped thinking about Mama. I check the clock and see I'm half an hour late for our meeting and Baba has grown impatient. I run a hand through my hair before I answer, trying to look marginally presentable, to brush away any lingering thoughts of my mother for the moment.

It's already evening in Kiev, and the kitchen lamp shines over my grandmother's long silver braid. As long as I have known her, she has kept her face plain and put on the same pearl earrings, but I have always found her long braid extravagant. Though my grandfather was one of the most well-known and wealthy men in Ukraine, she doesn't act like it: she insists on public transportation, refuses help around the house, and wears the plainest clothes. And she wants me to be the same way, which is why she doesn't spoil me and hasn't even floated the idea of giving me a cent of the profits she'll get from selling her furniture, though she's been this way for so long that I'm not mad about it, most of the time anyway. I'm just happy for her company.

"You look exhausted," she says, peering at me.

"That's because I am."

"Naturally."

"Where's the girl?" she asks triumphantly.

"Sleeping in her crib, as a matter of fact."

"Your grandmother knows best, doesn't she?"

"On occasion," I say, and I even have it in me to laugh a little.

I miss her so fucking much, right then. Her firm hugs, her un-shakable confidence. How she always made me feel like every-thing was going to be just fine, that I was getting all worked up over nothing. I haven't seen her in real life since last summer, when I visited her and Grandpa in Kiev just before I got pregnant. When Grandpa died, I was too far along to visit and help out. Which was devastating, because he had been so good to me, in his way. Since I was Antigone in seventh grade, a pretty morbid role for a kid, Papa made a habit of filming me performing and sending the tape to my grandparents. My grandmother would tell me I was stun-ning, but Grandpa would give constructive feedback in the short letters he sent me: *You overdid the theatrics at the beginning. But it was the opposite problem later on, child, I hardly felt your love for your dead brother, you were like a cold fish*, he wrote. This progressed all the way to the last thing I did, my three seasons on *Seeing Things*. *You didn't pause for long enough when you discovered that the coroner was the murderer. You needed to let it sink in. And later, you lingered too long when you were making a joke. It's all in the timing, dear*, he had written. "Thank you for the advice," I would tell him over the phone. "I'll think about it next time." "What else is a grandfather for?" he would say with a chuckle. I was not offended; Papa said I was perfect and so did Baba, and Yuri didn't really have a critical eye, and I appreciated it. He was passionless when he said it, like he was just examining a model of a bridge for defectiveness, and I could see why he was so good at his job. And the thing was, he was usually right. He could see things clearly. Which made me won-der, sometimes, if he knew about how much I drank or the losers I

dated, or how hard I fought with Mama, or even about my grandmother's seaside flings; how could he not?

My poor grandfather. He was stern but innocent, and I loved
him like crazy, though I know Baba did, too, in her own way. It
killed me that I couldn't help Baba bury him, that though she had
a bunch of Institute lackeys arrange the whole thing, I could not be
there to comfort her.

And now I'm the one who needs comforting. Though she keeps
telling me she's too old to travel, I think I can wear her down. "If
you visit us, you can see Talia firsthand," I try.

My grandmother snorts. "And do what with her, discuss eco-
nomic affairs?"

"Don't you want to see your family?"

"Foolish girl," she says. "I'm seeing you right now."

"It's not the same and you know it," I say, my voice cracking.

"You poor thing," my grandmother says, and this makes me
choke up, because there's nothing I hate more than pity, and because she's the one who is all alone, not me, though anytime I ask
her how she's doing she just says, fine, fine. She moves closer to
the screen, like she's inspecting my pores.

"Do you remember that rickety old wooden bridge in Mariinsky Park, the one overlooking the ravine?"

"Of course," I say, unsure of where this is going.

"When your father was a baby, I would take him for a stroll
there almost every morning. I would look down and oh! It was
such a welcoming abyss. I wanted to throw myself off every time
for the first two years at least."

"Why didn't you?"

"One of those mornings, as I was standing on that damn bridge,
we got caught in a thunderstorm and I had to push the stroller
home like a maniac. And I thought, Well, the gods should take me
now. I am ready to go—I can't go on anyway. But I saw your fa-

ther and his needy, shriveled-up face in the stroller, and I thought, No, no, they can't have me, this boy would be lost without me, I guess I'd better just go on and live."

"Did Grandpa know you felt that way?"

"Every woman feels that way!"

"I think some feel better than others," I say, though I don't feel better than that, not at all. But I don't have a large sample size or know a ton of moms except my friend Stephanie, who seems to be doing just fine, though she's rich now and that can't hurt, though she's always been the kind of person who doesn't get wet when it rains, nothing can bring the girl down. But I don't want to dwell on this shit any longer. I want to hear my grandmother's story, even if I'm not sure why I'm so desperate for it right now, why I finally got tired of doing my hair next to my ancient photograph of my great-great-grandmother without really knowing why she ended her own life.

"Anyway—" I say.

"Of course. Where were we?"

I smile. My grandmother is just faking it. She knows exactly where she left off, but she wants to build up the drama.

"You were leaving Kiev at last," I tell her anyway.

"Indeed," she says, but she seems distracted, giving me this odd little smile.

"What's wrong?" I say.

"Nothing," she says. "Nothing at all. For a moment there—it was the strangest thing. You looked exactly like my sister."

PART II

SINISTER SISTER

Larissa

My family stood in our courtyard in the early morning with our suitcases, waiting for the Orlovs' car to take us to the station while my sister scurried around like a maniac, trying to summon her beloved stray cat, Timofey. The night before, she cried madly when parting with the three vapid indistinguishable brunette friends I called "the three Annas," had a prolonged goodbye with Stella and Ella, the mother and daughter who lived in the room to our left and put makeup on her face when Mama wasn't looking, wept when saying farewell to our groundskeeper, Maxim, and she even shed a tear when Aunt Mila and Uncle Igor Chernak, the cranky retired engineers in the room to our right, gave us marmalades as a parting gift. Minutes earlier, my sister put a hand to her heart when the Kostelbaums, the Jewish family with six children who only communicated with us by pounding on the ceiling with a broom when we were too loud, pounded on it one last time as we left, this time in valediction. But these goodbyes were not enough for Polina. She would not feel complete if she did not see her mangy black cat, a foul creature who regularly stalked our balcony in hopes of her lavishing him with love and milk. Like many of the world's common fools, Polya had a soft spot for animals, though she could hardly be bothered to be polite to her own sister.

"Where did you go, my sweetness?" my sister cried into the void, madly waving an old bread crust as bait. Just a hint of pink and purple bled through the dark sky.

The Orlovs' car had arrived at last, followed by a car containing the Orlov family. I did not realize a Black Maria would be coming. This made our journey feel even more official and solemn. Still, my heart fluttered at the notion that Misha Orlov, the older son, was right there, waiting in the shadows.

I heard the pitter-patter of my sister's faithful cat just as the cars' headlights flooded our courtyard. Polina lurched toward her creature while Mama grabbed her by the scruff of her neck like she herself was a wayward kitten.

"Hurry up, silly girl! If we miss this train, there will be no other," she said, but Polya gave Papa her irresistible look and he nodded and lifted a hand. My sister smiled weakly and crouched down toward the vile, stinky thing.

"Good boy," Polya said, letting him lap the bread crust out of her hand as she stroked his fur. "You'll always be my good boy, won't you?"

"Unbelievable," muttered Baba Tonya as she adjusted her boa. She was Polya's ally about all things except Timofey—she, like me, did not care for animals. It might have been the only thing we agreed on.

"Really, Fedya," Mama said, shaking her head at my father, but she did not chastise my sister again.

"You'll have to be good without me now. Can you do that?" my sister told the creature.

"He can't talk," I snapped, but she ignored me. The engines of the Black Marias hummed loudly. Uncle Konstantin stepped out of the passenger seat and lifted a hand in our direction. Even his silhouette was formidable.

Papa opened his mouth to tell Polya it was time to go, but she got up on her own, turned around, and put on her best version of a brave face, like she was some big hero for leaving a stray behind. I could have put up an equal fuss over the shelf of books I was forced to leave, but did I let my lip tremble like a baby's due to our family's unknowable circumstances? Of course not, because I was grown.

We gave our bags to a stone-faced driver, and the women crammed in the back while Papa sat in the front. The Orlov car pulled away and ours followed suit. I could just make out the cat's yellow eyes against the last vestiges of darkness and my sister put her hand to the other window. I could hardly breathe in the stuffy car, but I tried to carve out a sanctified space from which to gaze out and say goodbye to my beloved city. As the car pulled away, I looked up at our balcony one last time, a place where Papa and I would chat in the evenings, where I would read on warm summer days. It was impossible to believe that the one-room apartment attached to it would no longer be witness to our footsteps, complaints, and laughter.

There was no time for a proper farewell. Our car would not drive languidly along the banks of the Dnieper, passing the gold-domed Lavra and the beaches of my youth, the endless parks, chestnut trees, and green hills. We lived just two kilometers from the station. In fact, our apartment was only a few blocks from the tracks that ran up and down our city, and every hour we would hear the screech of the train and feel our apartment tremble as it roared by. The noise was a comfort, in a way. We drove through Zhilyansky Street, past rows of tan apartment buildings nearly identical to our own. Normally the street was not particularly crowded, but that morning it was packed, and we moved slowly.

"Don't worry, dears," said Mama. "The Institute will put us in a decent home and keep us fed. And you girls will still go to school," she reminded us. This last part was a relief to me but made Polya choke a little bit.

"We shouldn't be gone too long," Papa added from the front seat. He did not turn around to look us in the eye to emphasize his point.

"We will return before you know it," Mama said, but I knew she was bluffing. The night before, I saw her sneak our winter clothes into her suitcase and understood it would not be a quick jaunt.

"It will be far safer out there than here," Mama said. "It is the best way. It is a privilege, to be able to leave."

"It is our patriotic duty," Papa added, but this didn't take.

"But what about my friends?" Polya cried. "What will happen to my friends?"

"Your friends will forget all about you in no time," I offered, which was my best effort to distract her.

"Easy for you to say—you don't have any!" she said. I yanked her hair and watched her bottom lip tremble again. It was true. I had no friends to my name, but I had my books, my city, and my beloved literature teacher, Marina Igorevna, who was always sneaking me books the way Polina snuck scraps of food to old Timofey. While my sister loved caring for Timofey, she also thrived on the attention she received from her friends and the endless stream of slightly older boys who walked her to school, though Mama made sure they did nothing more.

My grandmother, who had withered considerably since moving in with us, was swaying back and forth, as if in a trance, hypnotized by Rasputin himself. "It's just like the start of the Revolution," she whispered. "Nobody knows what will happen next."

Mama jolted upright, her hat hitting the roof of the car. She was morally opposed to chaos.

"Antonina Nikolaevna," she said. "If I were you, I would put the boa and rubies away. We don't know who will be at the station or—out there, and it is best to be careful." Mama chose to berate her over something else entirely to avoid discussion of the unknown.

My grandmother snorted. "I can take care of myself," she said, which was complete hogwash.

"Just be careful, Mama," said Papa, and my grandmother sighed and looked out at the traffic congesting toward the station, as well as more and more families approaching on foot, weighed down by suitcases. A buzzing reached my ears as I saw the chaos up ahead. Papa had already warned us: the ride would be two weeks long, and it would not be pleasant. Our train was meant for cargo, nothing like the comfortable wagons we had taken to Yalta in the summers. We should be grateful to be allowed to leave at all, and so on. But as we arrived at the station, I was scared and angry, not grateful. What did we do to deserve this madness?

The Orlovs' Black Maria stopped in front of ours and the members of its clan emerged with their luggage. Uncle Konstantin Orlov was a tall and competent man of few words who hardly seemed ruffled by the day's, or the year's, events. He wore a tan hat and light coat and was more imposing than Papa but not as handsome. He was one of the only grown men I knew who did not need glasses, yet another sign that he was above the drudgery of humanity. His wife, Aunt Tamara, walked beside him in a black frock and purple beret. She was a brittle, snobbish, and unattractive woman who ignored me and Polya whenever our families spent time together.

Their sons helped the fathers retrieve the luggage from the trunk. Even in the midst of this maddening scene, the world slowed down when I saw striking, dashing Misha, a handsome and square-jawed boy with neatly trimmed dark hair who was just one year my senior. He had consumed me ever since a family gathering where I saw him standing at his balcony window, hand pressed against the glass as he watched the snow falling outside for a full hour without moving, and decided I would give anything for the secret to his stillness. We did not speak much, and when we did, we discussed our studies in an exceedingly polite manner that Polya teased me for, but I believed there was an understanding between us, placid but knowing, like the underbelly of a lake.

Misha's only flaw was being related to Bogdan, his smug and excitable younger brother, who even in this solemn situation was jerking his messy-haired head this way and that like a demented prairie dog, in search of any distraction from his family. He was nearly fourteen like yours truly but behaved like a schoolchild, wandering off and getting into trouble with the neighborhood boys when our families convened. The only thing I could say in his favor was that he bestowed his smug charm on me and Polina in equal measure, without preferring her for her beauty. He was not like our groundskeeper, Maxim, who once looked me and my sister over and told my mother, "Polina could be a film star!" while I waited for him to declare what I should be before I saw the conversation was over.

We carried our luggage toward the train, approaching the fray. As the sun crept above the horizon, hinting at the sweltering day to come, the station swarmed with engineers and their frantic families trying to shove onto the cars, and workers who shoved metal equipment into the cars in the back of the train. Police officers attempted to keep people in line with their batons, shouting into the void. Our greetings with the Orlovs were brief and businesslike, though when Misha nodded and said, "Larissa," I felt a bit faint. "Mikhail," I answered stupidly.

"Ladies," said Bogdan, tipping his head toward me and my sister, and we dully repeated his name.

Mama and Papa and even Baba were stony, while Polya was on the brink of tears, and I mimicked the adults instead of my weak baby sister.

Uncle Konstantin arranged for us to have the first car, closest to the conductor, which was a privilege, though it meant dragging our things through the hordes all the way to the other side of the station. Mama and Papa followed him and his wife inside the car. My parents had much in common, but physically they made an odd couple. Mama was a tall, handsome, plump, and broad-shouldered woman with thick brows, and my father was a thin-haired man of average build who was quite good-looking in spite of the thick frames covering his sparkling green eyes.

Our families were joined by the Garanins, the other family that would be sharing the car with us, which consisted of Uncle Nikita, Uncle Konstantin's third in command, his pretty wife, Aunt Yulia, and their sweet four-year-old blond, pigtailed daughter, Yaroslava. I did not much care for children, but this girl was an exception. She was exceedingly sweet and curious, gazing about her like she was on a carnival ride instead of fleeing a war. "So many people!" she kept saying, hopefully, like it was a blessing.

I only encountered the girl and her parents during Institute celebrations, and my parents were always friendly to them, though once, I heard them whisper that they found them dull, and I had to wonder if Mama's true aversion to Aunt Yulia came from the fact that, though the woman dressed modestly and kept her hair pinned back, she was a dark, Mongolian beauty. Mama distrusted any woman with good looks, though this did not mean she was any kinder to me or any more cruel to Polya as a result.

The parents moved ahead of the children, while Baba Tonya stayed by Polya's side, muttering that her dress was getting trampled. My sister managed to attract attention even under duress; a man in front of us turned back to admire her until his wife yanked him ahead. The crowd swelled as we lurched forward and I grabbed my sister's delicate hand and squeezed hard.

"You're hurting me," she said.

"Good," I said, moving away from her, reminding myself what happened whenever I tried to be nice to the girl. Why bother?

"It is important to remain calm," shouted Uncle Konstantin as we followed him through the chaos.

"I'm about as calm as a rabbit on fire," said his wife, shaking her head, and for once, I agreed with her.

"I am exhausted," muttered my grandmother, to no one.

The car where our three families attempted to settle was meant for cargo, all right. Slabs of wood that would serve as bunk beds jutted out of the walls, and there were only two small windows in the entire car; I knew I would go mad without a view and jumped on the bottom bunk near the window, which left Polya to take the top. Everyone else coupled off, and Baba splayed out on her very own bed, her boa feathers fluttering on either side of her like defeated wings. The brothers chose the bed next to ours, and I was not disappointed. Misha was on the bottom bunk just as I was, so he and I would be sleeping only centimeters apart; perhaps, late into the night, if we were turned toward each other, I would feel his hot breath on my face, a more welcome intrusion than the stinky sister breath I was accustomed to. Bogdan had collapsed on the bed on top of his with a smug little grin, arms crossed behind his head like we were taking a trip to the country and this was all a grand adventure.

Mama snuck me and Polya some bread and honey she had packed up from the apartment, and it tasted heavenly. After I ate, I glued myself to the window as the train chugged away from the station, watching my city recede. I caught one last glimpse of the Dnieper. In the morning light, the river where I learned to swim and picnicked with my family looked majestic and whole. I wished I could run to it one last time, to bathe in its loving waters. The maple trees lining the embankment were in full glory, and I would not see them shedding their leaves. I loved walking by them after school in the fall, watching their propellers spin to the ground. Would there be maple trees in Lower Turinsk? Would there be trees at all? I had never been so far east. From my books, I imagined it to be a beautiful, terrifying, barren place. I wondered if I would die in it.

After a so-called lunch consisting of black bread and black tea was served and the train made its first stop, Mama and Papa left us to see if they could be of use. Papa found a cloth to bundle a baby and some valerian root for a hysterical woman and Mama found work in the kitchen, which meant she would prepare food and frantically serve it whenever the train stopped. Papa also rushed around, helping out factory workers, many of them complete strangers to him, his old orphanage-help-others-at-all-costs instincts kicking right in.

Just once, in the evening, Papa found time for us. He crouched down and kissed Polina and me on our foreheads. It had been a draining day, the air in the car as thick as butter, melting all of us.

"My strong young women," he said, stroking our hair like we were children. "How proud you make me."

"If we make you so proud, Papa, then why don't you stay with us?" said my sister.

"Because there are many people here who need more help than you. There's a newborn who is so scared she refuses to eat," he told her, but she was not convinced. He tousled her hair again and left to speak solemnly with Uncle Konstantin, plotting his next move the next time the train stopped. When I felt a hand on my shoulder a little while later, I hoped it was Papa returning, but I was not disappointed to find Misha hovering above us.

"Do you girls need anything?" he asked. His hair was slick and resolute, like the rest of him.

I looked around the compartment, with everyone rustling about and trying to unpack and create some order to face this unknowable day and the ones that would come after it. We were as beaten down and sunless as mushrooms stocked away deep in a forest.

"What more could we need?" I said, and this got him to smile.

"Of course," he said, giving me a nod as he walked toward his father and Uncle Nikita. "Well, you know where to find me."

The boy was more handsome than his father, but he had the same imposing nose and broad shoulders; I could see him one day manning a factory, a tank, a platoon. Our situation had hardened his jaw and he was even more appealing under duress. And now he was hoping the men would let him into the adult sphere as they conferenced about the bombs falling on Leningrad, speculating that the worst would come for the city once winter set in because the Germans had surrounded it; even if its people didn't run out of food, they could freeze to death.

When he was just out of earshot, my sister batted her eyes at me and lowered her voice. "*Do you need anything?*" she said, imitating Misha in a husky voice and giggling at herself. She had teased me about Misha before, but I did not mind it until that moment. Normally, I enjoyed the flattery, even if I did not quite believe her. Not many boys had paid attention to me the way they did to Polya and it did not hurt to have it pointed out. But her joking around just then was downright inappropriate.

"Shut up, idiotic girl," I said. "He was just trying to help."

"Are you kidding? Misha is *so* in love with you. Now more than ever," she said.

"Who can think of love at a time like this?" I said, smacking her scrawny arm harder than I intended. "Silly girl, we could die any minute, and here you have your head in the clouds."

Her bottom lip trembled and I braced myself for the floodgates to open, but they did not. "I have to keep busy somehow, don't I?"

"Read a book," I told her, and then I reached into my bag and pulled out *The Idiot*, perhaps to justify hefting such a heavy tome to the mountains.

But she did not ask to borrow a book. She just crossed her arms and pouted for an impressively long time. She let me see her hurting, just to punish me. Eventually, she joined our grandmother, who was fanning her face and muttering, "This will not do, this will not do. . . ."

Polya put her arm around her and said, "We'll be fine, Baba, you'll see." It was strange to see my sister in the caretaking position, but perhaps that was why she liked being with my grandmother instead of me, feeling like the stronger one under these circumstances.

While those two carried on, Bogdan monkeyed around with little Yaroslava, for whom he always had a certain fondness.

"Of course dogs can marry cats," he told her. "Where do you think rabbits come from? They're as soft and fluffy as cats and as fast as dogs, naturally. It's science, silly girl."

"But who do rabbits marry? Do they marry each other?" the clever girl asked.

"Almost never," Bogdan replied solemnly.

Aunt Yulia was amused by his antics but pretended not to be. "Don't let him fill your head with nonsense," she told her daughter, who only giggled in response and turned back to her dubious mentor.

When the fathers were done conferencing, Misha patrolled the aisles, attempting to look helpful. When he could not find a function for himself, he stood at the window and watched the landscape for what seemed like eternity without even a twitch in his jaw, impressing me once more with his stillness. Mama and Papa returned eventually and crawled straight into bed though the sun had hardly had a chance to sink below the horizon.

The train traversed the distant land, which was far more remote than the fields surrounding the Orlovs' immense dacha on the outskirts of the city. I watched the wan grass, the occasional cracked huts, the thin-looking cows wandering here and there munching at the grass, the horses swinging their wild ancient tails.

Baba Tonya had fallen asleep and Polya returned to my side. She seemed to have forgotten our earlier fight and was only tired and frightened. Her stomach growled as she moved closer to me, tugging on my sleeve.

"I'm scared, Lara," she said, chewing on a strand of fiery hair.

"Well," I snapped. "Don't be!"

But this did not ward her off. She studied the dark fields as if they contained the answers she wanted. "What do you think will happen to us—out there?"

A tear fell down her pink, round cheek. I almost felt sorry for the girl. There were no suitors to ogle her here, and our parents were too busy to lavish upon her the praise and love she expected. Her other joy was hearing our grandmother's stories of soirees, and the old woman was too distraught to offer those. And her formerly gorgeous red hair was greasy and wilted. I considered noting that we were less likely to get blasted to pieces if we got the hell out of Kiev, but I didn't want to make her cry over her friends again.

"We'll just have to wait and see, won't we?" I said, patting her hand.

"I don't like the sound of that."

"This isn't about what you like and don't like."

I noticed something strange on the landscape, which I mistook for planks of wood and then understood were suitcases, strewn about without reason. Was it a sign people had been carted away and forced to leave their things behind—or had they decided to drop them because they were too heavy to carry?

My sister was sniffling beside me, and it was a sad sight to behold. I wiped the snot under her nose with the back of my hand. Across from us, the Orlov brothers rested facing the wall. The backs of their dark heads were identical from that particular angle, there was no telling who was who.

"Fine, fine, Misha might have a crush on me, are you happy now?"

She smiled the smile of a flatulent baby. "I knew it."

I shook my head at this ridiculous notion, but I allowed her this small victory.

"Come on, now, let's go to sleep," I said, and she rested beside me.

I wondered: was it true? Did Misha have any feelings for me, or was he just trying to help in a time of crisis? As I observed Misha's sleeping form rising and falling across from me, I tried to tell myself that our destination would not be completely bleak, because he would be there. Being near him during our evacuation and resettlement tinged the uncertain future with an aura of romance. It would be a thrilling adventure, not a descent into chaos. There would be an entire steppe just for me and Misha, whispering sweet nothings across a snowy divide.

When Bogdan sat beside me in the middle of the night, I was surprised but not annoyed. Hunger had gnawed away at all of us just a few days into our trip—our extra bread and honey and Aunt Mila and Uncle Igor's marmalades were long gone—and I would take any distraction that I could get. Everyone else was sound asleep except for us. I was wide-awake, sitting on my bed and staring out the window, fogging up the glass with my breath. I was hungry and hot, already feeling filthy, and there was no chance my body would relax. I was a poor sleeper in general, finding one thing or another to worry about long before the war began. Would I pass the chemistry test? Why was Anna so harshly punished for her love of Vronsky? Would I ever find such a love? Would Papa keel over from helping all those strangers? There was no relief from the onslaught.

"Too scared to sleep?" Bogdan said, his lips twisting into a mean smile.

"Of course not," I snapped. "Stalin will protect us from Hitler," I added, pointlessly echoing something Papa said to calm us down. "There's no reason to be scared."

He snorted. "You think Hitler is worse than Stalin?" he said, lowering his voice. He scooted closer to me, so our knees were touching. "Stalin knew Hitler was coming for us months before he did, but he was too proud to prepare his army to fight him. He couldn't believe his so-called ally would defy him. He felt so humiliated by this that he called any of his cronies who warned him traitors and had them shot. If it wasn't for him, Kiev, Leningrad—we'd all be safe. And now if any soldier doesn't want to walk into a German death trap, Stalin will have him shot and his family arrested. It's ridiculous."

"Be quiet with that kind of talk," I said, lowering my voice even more. He could go to prison for the things he was saying. And even if everyone around us appeared to be sleeping, you never knew who was listening. "What would your father think?" I added.

He shrugged at his sleeping father. "He can't hear me now, can he? Hitler, Mussolini, Stalin—all murderers and hypocrites. We just happened to be born under Stalin."

"Exactly," I said. "And that being the case, we must root for Stalin."

He patted my hand as if I had missed the point completely. "And that's just what we're doing, darling."

"As we should be," I said, but my head was spinning. I considered myself a patriot, and knew it was idiotic to voice any doubts about our government. From my parents' late-night whispers, I had the idea that they had found our leader less than perfect, but who wasn't? My parents would never critique Stalin at a regular volume because you could not trust the phones, the wires, your neighbors, your colleagues, or anyone who wasn't family. But what was this he was saying about Stalin, and where did it come from? He was taking it too far, much further than my parents ever had.

I wished I were sitting with the more serious, melancholy Misha instead of this rascal with slicked-back hair, who acted like a smug lord looking over the commoners. He had managed to dispel all the goodwill I had sent his way for playing with Yaroslava with this little speech. Besides, his favorite playmate had gotten sick the day before, so perhaps he was just bothering me out of boredom. Aunt Yulia was very worried, but Mama assured her it would pass, that the feverish child was just hungry, though I did not know exactly how it would pass when there seemed to be no hope of better food on the horizon. The girl rested in her parents' laps, and her hair was damp and matted to her head.

"How do you know all this anyway?" I finally asked.

"I hear Papa talking, that's how," he said.

"And does your father—share your perspective?"

"Of course not," he said. "You think you can learn everything from your books, but the only way to truly know the world is to hear what people are saying."

"I don't read to learn," I said, uncertain as to how the conversation had turned from Stalin to literature. I would often bring novels to our families' gatherings and would hide off in a corner to escape to my beloved pages. But I did not know Bogdan paid enough attention to see what I was doing.

"Oh?" he said, looking genuinely surprised. "Then why do you do it?"

"I like to read. . . ." I said, realizing I did not have a good answer. I knew it had something to do with making me feel less lonely, to connect me to lost souls from generations ago, many of whom came from the same place, but this was difficult and embarrassing to articulate. I said, "Because language is beautiful, even when it's ugly."

If Bogdan expected me to say more on the subject, then he would be sorely disappointed. I could not entertain him the way the little girl had, and I wasn't one of the neighborhood boys who called him outside to engage in mischief whenever my family visited. This was the longest conversation we had ever had. Until then, our talk had been limited to asking each other to pass the potatoes. He always had that look about him, of a person on the hunt for something more exciting to do, but for once he was calm, perhaps because there was nowhere to go.

I turned away, toward the window, where the vast fields were illuminated by a bright, nearly full moon. I had hardly been staring out for a moment before he pulled me toward him and shielded my eyes. I was so stunned by the gesture—we had not done so much as shake hands until then—that I stayed there instead of protesting. I did not know if I wanted to be held or to see. If the thing he shielded me from was so awful that it warranted shielding. I could feel his heart beating against my cheek. When he released me, the fields were as vacant as ever.

"What on Earth was that?" I said.

"Nothing," said Bogdan, but I could see he was ruffled, that his jaw was set and he was struggling to maintain composure. "Just a few dead cows. Starvation. It was very unpleasant."

"That's all?" I said. I most certainly did not believe him. Or, I mostly did not. Or perhaps I wanted to believe him so badly that I decided to. A few dead cows did not a tragedy make.

"That's all," he said, giving my arm a squeeze, not looking me directly in the eyes either. Had he looked me in the eyes to begin with? It was hard to say.

"We're the same age, you know. I don't need protecting. I'm not a child."

"I never said you were," he said, and he was quiet after that. I stared out at the vast emptiness, where I could detect no farms, which made the likelihood of dead cows quite low. Bogdan did not leave me, either because he felt I needed further comfort or because he did not want to be alone after spotting whatever dark thing had been lurking outside.

Soon enough my savior was asleep, tilting his head closer and closer toward mine until he collapsed on my shoulder. I did not move, wanting to shake him off but also not wanting him to wake up finding himself in this compromised position, so I sat there, rigid as a lamppost. From that angle, one that allowed me only to see his thick, haphazard hair and the top of his head, he was once again indistinguishable from his brother. So that was what I did then, I pretended Misha was resting his head on my shoulder and closed my eyes and leaned my head against his, at last settling into something resembling sleep.

Misha and I were reading *The Idiot* when the book began to quiver in my hand, and then the train shook violently. A siren rang through the cars and the train came to a halt, pitching us into the wall. Papa grabbed Polya and Baba Tonya's hands and Mama grabbed mine, everyone was grabbing everyone and the Orlovs and Garanins were shouting, too, come on, let's go, hurry up, hurry up, get off this train, take nothing with you, and even in the chaos it registered that there were explosions overhead coming from the formerly empty sky, making me question why exactly we were leaving.

"Come on, now, quickly, girl," said Mama, and we jumped out of the wagon and crawled right under the train, hid down in the warm darkness, scared white pupils blinking in the blackness, reminding me of the eyes of Timofey lighting up our courtyard as the dawn broke.

It was the Germans, of course. I did not need Papa to confirm this, though he did, or to explain to the group that though it may seem ridiculous to stay right under the train when the bombs were falling down on it, it was the safest place for all of us to be, since it was our only shelter in the vast steppe and the steel of the trains over our heads would provide more protection than the open fields could. We crouched in the muck, covering our ears; the Orlovs were silent and dignified while Polya and my grandmother whimpered. The old woman's boa was filthy and she looked so ridiculous that I wanted to choke her with it, or even to rip off her rubies and toss them out from under the train so she would get bombed while running after them. I was so terrified that it took me a moment to see that Papa was not beside us, that he had rushed into the fields to bring back a few rogue passengers who fled the train.

"Get back here, Fedya!" Mama screamed, but the sounds of the crashing bombs were so loud that I doubted if anyone heard her but me. But it was instinctual with Papa. He saw people who needed saving, so he went out to save them, forgetting that he had a family waiting for him under the train. Mama muttered that his orphanage instincts were kicking in again, this flagrant caring for others. But I was just glad he had returned to us.

Polya was crying and Baba Tonya was crying and Mama was comforting them both, while Papa met my gaze and nodded.

"My big girl," he said. "My stalwart."

"Let them just take me now," Baba was muttering. "Let this be it. Haven't I suffered enough?"

It got wearying after a while, though, the bombs, the hands on the ears, the thighs burning from all the crouching, the gravel and dirt digging into my knees, the hunger weakening my joints, the foul stench of the unbathed passengers. I opened my eyes and saw that Bogdan the rascal had stopped the assumed crouching position and even looked quite jolly for some reason, which turned out to be because little Yaroslava, who had not only grown weaker in recent days but who had also begun to chatter her teeth and look alarmingly pale, was looking at him with a trembling expression somewhere on the brink of bursting into sobs or hysterical laughter. Her golden pigtails mingled with the muddy ground.

Bogdan was amusing her by making a monkey face, and he reached into his pockets and pulled out two tiny teacups he must have stolen after a tea service and put them to his eyes and bobbed his head from side to side and stuck out his tongue. This image was so absurd, what with everyone else crouching and the bombs dropping from overhead planes, the sound of them raining down on our only mode of conveyance, that even I had to hold back a chuckle.

Yaroslava laughed first, and then, little by little, as others began to squint their eyes open, which had coincided with the sound of the bombs dissipating a bit, more passengers began to laugh, first Polya and then the Garanin parents and even Baba Tonya had a sliver of a smile emerge on her puckered face. Then Polya laughed completely, wildly, just as hard as Yaroslava, because she needed the release, and her laughter was so pure and singular that it even made Bogdan laugh at himself. Misha was the least amused. I could feel it from how his arm had stiffened around me, which was when I realized he had his arm around me to begin with. I did not know how long it had been there. His body emanated calm, unlike the manic energy that surrounded his brother when he had covered me in the train car.

"Enough clowning around, brother. We're at war," Misha said.

Bogdan removed the teacups from his eyes, offered his brother a goofy smile, and replaced them there. "War, what war? I don't see a war! Why didn't anyone tell me there was a war?" he said, pretending to search the ditch with the teacups still over his eyes, generating more rumblings of reluctant laughter. "Did you know there was a war?" he said to little Yaroslava.

The girl laughed hardest of all, and her weary parents were so grateful to him. I wondered if he could see something the rest of us could not, if perhaps he was the only one acting appropriately under the circumstances, embracing the absurdity of it all, understanding how badly the girl needed a bit of laughter. This feeling was only heightened the next day, when the girl was so feverish that she could hardly speak, whimpering in her mother's arms while Bogdan sat beside her father, holding her hand.

Yaroslava died and was buried the next morning, when the train made its next stop. I was not allowed to help, none of the women were, but as I watched Bogdan cover the girl with earth and tuck a teacup down there with her, I found myself having a strange thought I suspected was summoned by disorientation and hunger: that one day, this boy, who perhaps understood the world better than anyone else on the train did, would make a good and decent father.

A few days later, Mama shoved me and Polya awake in the middle of the night. At first, I thought we had reached our destination—we were supposed to get there any moment—but as I looked out at the barren fields, I saw this was not the case, that everyone else was asleep. What was going on—another raid? Did we have to run under the ghastly train again, and get caked in mud and dirt once more? No, no, this made no sense, it was not a raid, because it would mean everyone else would be up and alert. But only the three of us were awake while everyone else slumbered on, the train chugging its mean chug below us, the sky dark and unwelcoming above.

Mama helped Polya climb down to my bed and covered us with her shawl, an intimate gesture that trapped in our bodily stink.

"What? What is it?" said Polya, rubbing sleep from her eyes. Even in her dreaminess, even in the musk of the train, she looked like an angel and I hated her for it. Mama put a hand over her mouth and lifted the finger of her other hand in the air. Her face was solemn and purposeful, the same sharp squint I saw in her eyes when she sewed a button back on a dress for me late in the evening.

She reached into her pocket and took out a roll—no, two bread rolls! But she was not done. She ripped them open and took out a cloth napkin with a sliver of butter inside and rubbed the butter into the center of the rolls with her steady fingers. This was pure ecstasy, you understand. I took a bite of my bread, and Polya took a bite of hers. Only when I got down to my last bite did I see Mama looking at us with almost joy, as if she were the one eating the bread. I realized how hungry she herself must be, how hard it must have been for her to steal those rolls and that butter for us without saving a shred for herself.

I extended my last mouthful toward her but she pushed my hand away.

"Nonsense, kitten. You need to eat, you're still growing."

I expected my sister to glare at me for making her look like the selfish daughter she had always been, but she had a drugged, happy look on her face and even smiled at me, a faint trace of butter gleaming on her lips. As we shoved the crumbs into our mouths and licked our fingers, I felt as if my sister and I were allies, that maybe we even loved each other in our way. Perhaps that was what made Mama so fleetingly happy, more than the food. Or maybe she was just relieved her daughters were still alive, and it didn't matter what we did.

We returned to our bed, and I watched the mountains rising up before us, mountains that had long replaced the flat fields on the outskirts of Kiev. Then I heard the faint sounds of Aunt Yulia mourning her daughter, accompanied by the quiet whispers of her husband. Just as I began to drift off, a hand cradling my butter-filled belly, I heard a rustling and saw my sister tugging my grand-mother's hand and offering half of her roll, which she had managed to squirrel away. When Baba saw her small but significant offering, she clutched her bread-holding hand with her own shaking, sin-ewy fingers and kissed it before devouring it in two bites.

"You are my angel," she told her, wiping her mouth, but toward her lips, not away, so that any leftover rogue crumbs made their way in. "My absolute angel." And then she turned back around and retreated into dreamland.

Of course, I reminded myself, my sister and grandmother were as thick as thieves, would always be as thick as thieves for as long as the old woman lived. I would never come that close to Polya, even if we had smiled at each other over some butter. Though I knew that the majority of my lifetime was still ahead of me if I was lucky, I could not fight off the feeling that whatever had happened between Polya and me had already happened, and that it was too late to fix things between us, that there was no use trying, that I should save my reservoirs of hope for the horrors to come.

The train deposited us at a desolate platform at last. It was a warm day and it was a joy just to be outside, to be free of the bodies and their insuppressible stink. The platform was marked by a wooden sign with LOWER TURINSK written on it, heaps of dirt, branches, and bird dung. On one side of the tracks loomed the factory where the fathers would work, a gray building with tiny windows and three massive columns releasing smoke into the air; already, some workers were carrying the heavy equipment they had packed up from the Kiev factory off the train onto trucks to haul them to their new workplace. On the other side of the tracks stood a field leading to rows of apartment buildings. They did not appear all that different from the homes we had abandoned; I had expected a village, with huts and horses dotting the landscape as they had in the places the train had passed. Where was the steppe I had dreamed about? What was the point of leaving one place for another that looked just like it? There were mountains in the distance, sure, but I was otherwise unimpressed.

Grim-looking men in army fatigues spotted Uncle Konstantin and waved us over to the registration tent, gave each family our daily bread coupons, and told us we were living in Building 32. We were introduced to Uncle Ivan, a Black Maria–sized man with a rectangular, hair-covered face who was in charge of our building; he would take us and the diminished Garanins to our new home.

"Lower Turinsk welcomes you with open arms," he said, bowing slightly as the fathers introduced themselves, and I couldn't tell if he was joking or not.

As we followed him, he explained that the next day was Sunday, so we could settle in, but the following day, all men fifteen and older would report to the factory—so Misha qualified, but Bogdan did not. This pleased them both equally. Misha held his head higher, like the declaration had made him even more adult, while Bogdan pumped a fist in the air at being excluded from the hard labor. The women would work in the factory kitchen, while Bogdan, Polya, and I would go to school, like Mama promised. School! What a relief it would be to return to the land of learning.

Aunt Tamara tugged on Uncle Ivan's arm as we followed him down a paved road lined with poplars. "Is there a maximum age for the women's work?" she asked.

Ivan laughed and looked her over and said, "Don't worry, you'll do." Then he added, "Unless you are of unsound mind."

"I can certainly prove that if I try hard enough," she grumbled, but her husband silenced her with his gaze.

Baba, on the other hand, could easily be proven mentally infirm, and who knew what she would do all day. She followed us in a daze with a faint smile on her lips, her now-gray boa trailing her, thinking she was some kind of debutante, as if all the men in town were staring at her. Perhaps some were, but not for the reasons a woman would want to be stared at. Faithful Polya kept pace behind our grandmother, lifting her boa and draping it over her shoulders whenever it hit the ground. Maybe she hoped our grandmother would draw some eyes toward her in turn. There were men everywhere, but for once none of them were looking at Polina. I pictured Dimitrev senior, twirling his mustache while gazing at my sister—there was no one who had the luxury to do that here, and though her red mane was still somewhat beguiling, she looked a bit too haggard for wandering eyes.

I turned from all of them and gazed at the factory, which looked majestic and imposing from farther away. Papa caught me looking and winked. He put a hand on my shoulder and said, "I'd rather be in school."

"We can trade, then," I said, though of course I did not mean it. I thought school would be the highlight of my time there, though I was curious about the factory. Though I did not think making tanks and other instruments of war would suit my father, who was by nature a peaceful man.

"If school gets dull enough for you, I can take you for a tour. How does that sound?" Papa said.

I told him it sounded nice, but did not expect much. It was nearly impossible to get Papa alone, even during peacetime.

I was even more filthy by the time we reached the first of the apartments, my sweat mixing with the remains of the mud stuck to my body. The apartments weren't nearly as tall as the ones in Kiev; just three or four stories at most, with more poplars and orderly fences and wooden benches in their courtyards. In the center of the apartments was a row of functional buildings, which included a post office, a small, squat school building, the grocery where the mothers would get our family's daily bread with their coupons, which apparently was run by one famed Madame Renata, who lived in our building. "Get on her good side and stay on it," was all Uncle Ivan said about her. Other Ivans dropped other passengers off at their new homes, and it seemed ours was the farthest away. My grandmother was not pleased by the trek.

"I may faint at any moment," she warned us.

"Be our guest," said Aunt Tamara, rolling her eyes. My grandmother ignored her. The women had much in common, so naturally they had already become enemies.

I walked beside Misha, distancing myself from the complainers.

"We'll miss you in school," I told him.

"I'll be more useful at the factory, I'm certain," he said, but he gave me a little smile. "Though I will miss you when I'm working. We will all miss you, I mean," he said, clearing his throat and looking serious again, though I felt my face flushing, getting even warmer under the bright sun. Then he gazed ahead like a soldier like the parents were doing.

Bogdan was flopping his head around, looking at this and that like an overheated puppy, while my sister and Baba dawdled behind us with linked arms. We had reached the edge of the earth, the final apartment building, which had a few benches and a swing set out front and abutted a forest of pines, in front of which flowed a small but mighty stream. The long trek was worth it. I would take trees over more neighbors any day. I was drenched in sweat by then. The sun was high in the sky and there was no breeze to offer relief.

Our new home was on the second floor of a three-story building. Our families and the Garanins followed Ivan up the stairs, and the Garanins were the first to be dropped off in a one-room home next door to the apartment of Madame Renata. Aunt Yulia looked like a sleepwalker, the loose strands from her ponytail cascading down her shoulders like elegant seaweed. Though Bogdan walked near her, no one spoke to her, and her husband was equally vacant. Which was perhaps for the best in one regard, which was that, when they encountered the formidable Madame Renata, they hardly seemed to take her in. She was a nasty silver-haired woman with deeply arched brows who peeked her head out her door and gave us a once-over.

"I would shower now while the water is running," she offered, and then she returned to her lair.

If we hadn't been so exhausted, I might have exchanged a look with Papa and laughed at this woman's expense.

Instead, we parted with the diminished Garanins and followed Ivan down the hall, where he showed us our living quarters: two fairly large rooms with stoves, a balcony, and a shared kitchen for all of us. The apartments had minimal furniture, a few beds, a heap of blankets in the corner, a few dull lamps and landscapes, pale-orange wallpaper, and in one of the rooms, an empty bookshelf that broke my heart. The Orlovs were given the larger of the two rooms, though either room was substantially bigger than the one I was used to. In my opinion, my parents won out because their balcony looked straight out onto the pines.

This was a downgrade for the Orlovs. Once, when my family visited their massive apartment in Kiev, Polya and I pretended to search for the restroom and wandered down their endless hallway, counting six different bedrooms, such a tremendous number of rooms that I could not even imagine what could be done in all of them. Polina had even jumped on the Orlovs' bed and cried, "A whole family could sleep on this bed! An entire family!" We were much younger then.

Then, next to the bathroom, Ivan showed us another room that used to be a closet but which had a bunk bed in it, which we were welcome to use, if we needed it. Improbably, it had a tiny window. This was the room where Polina, Baba Tonya, and I would stay, it was decided. The brothers would sleep in an alcove in their family's room.

"We thank you. It is more than suitable," Uncle Konstantin said.

"It's the best we've got," Ivan said, bowing as he left us standing back in the main room. A mouse scurried past, and Polya and Baba Tonya shrieked while Aunt Tamara jumped.

"More roommates," Bogdan said, trying to ease the tension, but nobody laughed.

"This is where I will meet my end—I just know it," Aunt Tamara said.

"And I mine," said Baba, who was not to be topped in her misery.

"Enough with the theatrics," Uncle Konstantin told his wife. "This is home now. This is where we will serve our country, and there's no use in fighting it." He slammed a fist against the wooden coffee table by the stove and seemed almost human for a moment, capable of frustration. Even Misha jumped a little, at this. I had never heard Uncle Konstantin raise his voice.

His words lingered, but no one responded. We were all ready to collapse, too tired to think of Nazis or our strange new living arrangement. Mama paced around the main apartment, running her hands along the walls, kicking at the scant furniture with a strained, ferocious smile. "It is quite a nice apartment," she said with desperate near-cheer. "Much larger than I expected. It just needs a bit of attention, that's all."

Mama began settling in, which meant placing the clothes she and Papa had packed in drawers, putting the finery she would sell under their bed, and taking out a single framed photograph she brought of herself and Papa and placing it on the bookshelf near the stove. In the photograph, she and Papa stand in the kitchen of their first apartment, holding a pot of dumplings, looking impossibly young and wildly proud of what they had made. This must have been before I was born, because I had never seen such unabashed joy in my weary parents' eyes.

Papa ran a hand along the metal bunk bed in the corner and smiled grimly.

"Funny," Papa said. "These are the same beds we had in the orphanage. The exact same beds, it's like they've lifted them out of Kharkov and brought them here. Well, it wasn't as bad as I expected it to be there, and this will be more of the same. I made it through that and we will make it through this. If we stick together, we will do just fine here."

Polya and I exchanged a rare sisterly glance. Papa never mentioned the orphanage, though it cast a shadow over our family that no present-day joy or sunshine could dispel. This showed how desperate he was to create order, though I knew it was a false comparison: his orphanage was in the center of a real city during peacetime, not in the steppe during an unknowable war. And perhaps the one-roomed orphanage was the reason he had insisted our family live in such close quarters in the past—it might have comforted him, to have everyone in such proximity, as it reassured him now to see the cozy space where we would live together, even if we all did have separate rooms. Or at least I hoped Papa was mentioning his orphan past to calm himself and us, instead of a more troubling alternative—that he was already losing his grip, that he no longer cared about what he did or did not say, because the rules we were accustomed to had been thrown out the window the moment we boarded the train.

How I dreamed of food during those early days! Flaky Napoleon. Airy meringues. Salty caviar on buttery blini. Herring sprinkled with pungent onions. I did not even particularly care for herring, but those early evenings I dreamed that my tongue had become a salty slice of fish, that I could soak in its rich juices with every swallow. Most of the foods I dreamed of, I must admit, were delicacies we were served at the Orlovs' home, or even at my grandmother's before her fall from grace, instead of the potatoes and salami my family had eaten in the communalka. I was not alone in my fantasies. All of us spent our time dreaming about food, making our meals last as long as possible, or scheming up ways to procure it.

The Sunday market was one source. This was all Baba Tonya lived for, linking arms with me and my sister on our way there like we were going to a ball, her head high in the air in spite of the smelly, dirt-stained boa trailing her, as if she were balancing a plate on the tip of her nose. Polina flirted with the aged radish brothers and got us a bit more food, but not enough to make a difference. Aunt Tamara was used to being waited on hand and foot and mostly sat around the house fanning herself while Mama bartered the few pieces of finery she had brought.

Bogdan made a heartier contribution than the market, becoming our savior early on. He would skulk away after dinner and return several hours later with a folded cloth napkin of goods without explanation—a few slices of bread here, a jar of jam there, which kept us from falling into complete starvation. Aunt Yulia began working for the government store of the aging but still mighty Madame Renata, which served a brick of black bread for each family every day, though everyone knew it was mixed with glue and sawdust. To her credit, though Aunt Yulia ignored us during the week, every Sunday morning she came to our door with a burlap sack of salvageable food. A few times, Polya and I had even rattled her doorknob out of desperation when she was out, hoping to find some extra fare, but she kept it firmly locked.

So it was only natural that when I spotted the interloper about a month into our stay, my first thought was that we could not afford another mouth to feed. He was a sight to behold. Just as the mothers were making dinner, the kitty entered the room with his tail high in the air and sauntered toward us like he was an invited guest, or even a visiting dignitary. He was an ugly-looking thing. A mangy gray-brown ball of fur, dirt all over his face, golden brown fluff around his belly. His eyes were huge, honey-colored, and he looked like he had never seen humans before. He was squinting a bit, as if blinded by the dim lights in the apartment.

Polya's eyes lit up, but if she got any big ideas and tried to slip him any of our measly rations, I would yank all the hair off her head and stuff it in her mouth. Dinner consisted of what Mama managed to scrounge from the morning's market, where she had bartered her last porcelain plate. What did one plate manage to get us? Three loaves of black bread, a handful of carrots, and a stack of dried fish to split among the nine of us—adding another stomach to the mix was out of the question. But my sister was already enraptured. She put a hand to her mouth and knelt to meet the creature at eye level.

"What a darling," she said.

"A joy," said Aunt Tamara.

"A mouser," said Mama.

"A guard," declared Uncle Konstantin.

"A comrade," said Papa.

"A rascal," said Bogdan.

"A brother," said Misha.

"A toy," said my grandmother.

I alone remained quiet, seeing no need in making a vapid declaration about the creature. I hardly had the strength to be cruel to my sister, which meant I was in a dire state.

Polya knelt down and crawled toward the abomination. Bogdan joined her in welcoming the beast, proving once more that he, too, was a simple creature. My sister reached out her hand while Mama told her to be careful, that this was a feral mountain kitty, that he was no Timofey from the courtyard and was liable to bite her nose off, but Polya giggled as the kitty came toward her and licked and licked her trembling hand. My sister had become the weakest of all of us, since she had so little weight to spare to begin with, and it almost felt good to see her happy.

Our crew had been short on joy recently; Mama and Aunt Tamara would come home from the factory, reeking of cleaning supplies, and the fathers and Misha would follow after, covered in soot and sweat, utterly drained, Papa having long forgotten his promise to take me there. We could not help but laugh as the little fur ball explored the premises while we ate our meal as slowly as possible to make it feel more expansive than it was. Once he had sniffed all four corners and the bunk beds and curtains and circled the stove a few times, he settled by my sister's side and licked her hand again, and so she named him Licky.

"You be careful, now," Mama warned her, studying him more closely. "He's no ordinary cat. He's a bobcat. He must have wandered out of the woods, poor thing."

"He'll be a big boy one day, you'll see," said Papa, his lips spreading into a thin smile. "A baby lion. You'll be riding him all over town."

"Don't be silly, Papa," Polya said, batting his arm. I rolled my eyes at Misha and he gave me a small shrug to show he agreed my sister was senseless, but what can you do?

Papa loved indulging my sister's childishness. He spoke to her like she was about three instead of thirteen, treating her like the baby she wanted to be around him. He remained oblivious to how aware Polya was of her powers, how she batted her eyes at men if she wanted something, like an extra radish from the old radish brothers at the market, another day to complete a homework assignment from her teacher, or a flower from the groundskeeper's meager garden back home. Papa would never deign to make such witless comments to yours truly; he knew I was reasonable.

Of course Polya would never be able to ride the cat, no matter how big he got, unless she shrank considerably. She looked so blindly happy, getting licked by her new friend, teased by Papa, that it was hard to focus on nibbling my bread crust. That night, Polina carried her new pet into her bed above me, cradling him like he was a baby, but he did not protest, though he seemed more eager to ardently lick his mangy fur than to be rocked to sleep. I could hear the foul creature licking and scratching as I tried to drift off. At the time, of course, I only saw the beast as a distraction, a nuisance. I had not a clue he would be my family's undoing.

September turned to October, which was not the October I had known in Kiev. In Kiev, October was when the trees changed colors, when you could stroll through Mariinsky Park as the maples and chestnuts turned from green to majestic red and orange and gold. In Lower Turinsk, October meant the trees would change colors for a week or so before unceremoniously shedding their leaves. Papa and Uncle Konstantin rode to a neighboring village on horseback, returning with a sack of potatoes and two shubas, a white one for Polya, and a brown one for me, and by November, we lived within the confines of these thick coats. There was no use denying that we were in for a long stay by then, and the fathers' late-night grumblings about the state of the Red Army brought no hope. Millions of soldiers had died or been captured already, and the Germans were only fifty kilometers away from Moscow, advancing toward our capital.

I lived for my reading sessions with Misha in his family alcove after dinner, while Bogdan horsed around with my sister and Licky or went off to his food expeditions. I was breathless to find myself alone with handsome Misha, though Mama would "check in" on us once in a while. Misha's voice was firm and commanding, though his hands shook when he turned the pages, which pleased me because it suggested that I made him nervous. The shaking hands were his only weakness; since he started working at the factory, he seemed even more capable and grown-up, the soot behind his ears making him look like a true man.

And besides, reading with him gave me far more intellectual stimulation than I got from my new cruel teacher, Yana Nikolaevna, who was offended by the students who left class after the daily free lunch. "Filling your empty minds is more vital than filling your empty stomachs," she had declared, and followed this charming comment up with the fact that she would not bother learning the names of the new students until she saw who was going to "stick around."

By January, Misha and I were done with *Demons* and had moved to another favorite, *Onegin*. We had just finished the chapter where

Tatyana dreams of being chased by a bear and entering a party where Onegin stabs Lensky and wakes up scared and confused. I recited my favorite part of the dream for good measure:

But suddenly a snowdrift stirs,
And what from its recess appears?
A bristly bear of monstrous size!
He roars, and "Ah!" Tatyana cries.
He offers her his murderous paw,
She nerves herself from her alarm
And leans upon the monster's arm,
With footsteps tremulous with awe
Passes the torrent but alack!
Bruin is marching at her back!

Misha gave me an unreadable smile. The weight he shed gave his face an older, more dignified look, which suited him.

"What?" I said.

"Nothing," he said, shaking his head.

"What is it?"

"I just find dreams in literature to be a bit silly, don't you? I mean, if it didn't really happen, then why write about it?"

"None of it really happened. The dream is what makes *Onegin Onegin*. The rest of the book—the duel, the spurned love, none of that is so very unique, is it? Of course, the narrator has a sharp wit—but in this passage, he abandons that wit, and yes, perhaps he's mocking Tatyana a bit, but he must believe in it on some level, or he wouldn't describe it so vividly."

"He can't help himself. He's a writer. I'm just saying—I find the dream a bit frivolous, far less interesting than the outcome of the duel between Onegin and Lensky."

"Can't it just be a beautiful interlude?"

"I didn't know you were such a dreamer, Larissa."

"Some occasions require it."

Misha just shook his head. "Pure silliness."

"It's not silly at all," I insisted, but there would be no changing his mind.

He gave me an intense look that made me uneasy. Did our argument stir some passion within him? Of course I had been trying to will him to kiss me for months, but I was uncomfortable, afraid. He looked at the book and back at me and his lips drew a straight line. Had he kissed girls before? He always seemed so competent and knowledgeable that until that moment, I never considered that perhaps he had not, that he was just as clueless as I was when it came to romantic matters. He kept looking at me, waiting for me to say something that would direct him, one way or another.

I looked down at my enormous shuba and recalled the bones and knobs and blue-green veins on the body inside it. Would anyone really want to kiss someone in my awful state? I hardly felt like a woman anymore. My womanly visitor had not returned since we arrived in the mountains. Mama had to stitch Polya's and my pants to keep them on our waists. Hairs sprouted on my chest to keep me warm and my voice was so weak, I didn't sound like myself. My clothes floundered on my body, reminding me of a happier time when Polya and I paraded around in Mama's enormous dresses when she and Papa left us home alone.

Misha turned away, the intense look gone, and he was quiet, gazing out the one tiny frosted window in his alcove, where a light snow was falling. By then I understood that his staring fits were not a mere indication of his solemn, poetic soul. His stillness could be attributed to melancholy, not simple awe at the wonders of the world. I never knew what to do when he disappeared like this. Should I leave? Try to bring him back to Earth? Ask what was on his mind? I was relieved when I did not have to find a solution, because Bogdan entered the room. I could not help his brother, but I could ask for a second opinion.

"What do you think of Tatyana's dream in *Onegin*?" I asked.

As the smile curled on his wily face, I had a feeling that of course he would agree with me. How could he not? The boy was a bit of a dreamer, and he would have been taken by the imaginative interlude.

"It's the best part," he said. "Naturally." I nearly gasped, putting a hand to my chest, and then he laughed wildly. "I tricked you, didn't I? I don't think I got that far in *Onegin*. There was a dream? I must have been playing hooky."

"Don't talk nonsense, brother. You must have read *Onegin*," said Misha, who seemed more annoyed by his brother's cavalier declaration than was justified.

"Then I suppose I don't remember," Bogdan said with a complacent shrug.

It was time for bed. By then, we had all given up on our individual beds and slept on a blanketed pile by the stove in the center of my family's room, any need for privacy trumped by the flames flickering near our thawing limbs. We hunkered down by the stove and I found my usual place, next to my parents. I put a blanket over my shuba and relished the warmth, knowing I would wake up sweating the next morning but that I wouldn't care, that it was a pleasure to know my body was capable of producing sweat. Just as I closed my eyes, somebody poked me in the back. Bogdan was looking right at me. His brother was sound asleep to his left, and my sister was dozing on his other side, her head resting on Licky's haunches.

"The dream was pretty wacky," he said.

"So you did remember after all."

"No. I just read it over. Some wild stuff."

"Indeed," I said, and I was more touched by the fact that he had read it over than I cared to admit.

"It wasn't much of a burden. There isn't exactly a lot to do," he said, patting my hand, making certain that he had not made me feel too important.

I closed my eyes and shifted closer to Misha, who had already fallen asleep, and felt his breath on my neck as I tried to settle into a slumber as wild and beguiling as Tatyana's. But I woke up in the cold light of morning, my stomach rumbling, not having remembered a single thing I dreamed about.

Papa remembered his promise to take me to the factory by the dead of winter. It was a brutal time. Any minute I spent trudging to school or gathering wood was the cruelest torture, the frigid air stiffening my bones as my boots crunched through the snow. The windows were frosted with ice and the balcony door was sealed shut.

Twice, I had seen my father grab onto a piece of furniture to steady himself when he was on the verge of fainting. Aunt Tamara and my mother were shedding hair like summer pets. At dinner, I caught Uncle Konstantin squinting into his food like he could not remember how he got there. Baba Tonya took to sleeping with her eyes open, making me think she was dead the first few times she did it. As for Misha, when we delved into *Karamazov,* I understood that his hands shook due to hunger, not nervousness. Bogdan maintained his spirits and nighttime excursions, but he was as pale as a frozen lake. My sister's body was deteriorating so fast that Mama had to wrap twine around her forearms to keep her arm meat from sagging. She no longer walked but drifted. I was fading, too, though nobody held me up. My fingertips were numb even beside the stove; my teeth chattered all day long.

I forgot all that as I followed Papa out. We bumped into Ivan, who was knocking the icicles off the front doorway. They had been hanging on the eaves of the apartment building like deadly dragon teeth for months, and recently Ivan had made the fatal mistake of slamming the front door hard enough to make one of them careen down and stab his forearm, turning it a ghastly black and blue. Now he was trying to protect the rest of us. He was accompanied by Snowball, a big white ownerless dog he regaled with garbage scraps and potato peels once in a while, whenever he came around.

I offered him my usual greeting. "Is the war over yet?"

"I'll keep my ear to the ground for you," he said with a mock salute, and winked at Papa as we walked on.

I was so thrilled the cold hardly stung me. I was used to it by now, having my limbs assaulted by the mean, relentless air. My heart skipped as we approached the factory, our boots crunching through the nasty snow. Going in would be a true privilege for a girl. Mama once told me that the only woman who ever went inside the actual factory was Marina Ivanovna, the old cook, to call the men for their lunch, and I would soon be among her sacred ranks.

But when Papa opened the central steel door to the monstrous edifice, I saw there wasn't much to get excited about. It was not a magical, wild, and violent chamber of science and destruction but a dingy, dark room cramped with steel machinery, grime and oil, and rows and rows of greasy old tanks, which might be rendered obsolete by the new tank Papa and Uncle Konstantin were working on. Papa held my hand as I gazed at the high, sooty ceilings.

I knew factory life was no picnic, of course. The other day, I'd overheard Papa telling Mama that many of the younger men were practically begging to be sent to the front. At least at the front they would be given three substantial meals a day and would hardly be expected to work for twelve hours straight. And if they died, they would do so with honor in their hearts and food in their bellies. The factory had already lost two dozen men to hunger and exhaustion; one of them was Uncle Nikita, Aunt Yulia's husband, whose death kept the new widow at home for one week before she returned to Madame Renata's food store with glazed eyes; it was strange not to see Uncle Nikita, the former third in command, returning home from the factory between Papa and Uncle Konstantin. But I knew better than to mention that.

"This is where you spend your days?" I said.

He let go of my hand and looked defeated by the question. "What choice do I have?"

I followed him to the center of the factory, where a single tank stood in between a series of work benches. This one looked larger than the others, and several half-completed versions stood behind it. Papa ran a hand over the top.

"Here it is," he said. "The T-34."

The tank was dark green, with five wheels on each side and a long, narrow stock in the center and cylinders on either side. It didn't look like much to me, or rather, since the only time I had seen tanks was at a distance, during state military parades, I couldn't quite see what made this machine of destruction different from the ones that came before it, other than its more impressive size.

Papa's eyes lit up as he explained how Uncle Konstantin had helped invent a process that allowed Soviet tanks to be made far more efficiently than the German ones. Previous methods of tank making led the tanks to be brittle because of the air that remained between the parts; Uncle Konstantin had the idea of plugging up these air holes with sand, which made the tanks come out hard and strong. Germans kept their tanks strong by using chisels, but this took ten times longer than the sand procedure.

"And that's how we will triumph," Papa said. "Uncle Konstantin's tanks are going to end the war, once we build enough of them." He patted the tank like it was a well-behaved child, but the light was extinguished from his eyes. I did not understand why. The quicker we killed the Germans, the sooner we could all go home. Then I recalled what Bogdan had said on the train, that we could have easily been living under Hitler or Mussolini instead, that war was a nasty thing with no winners.

"Do you believe in war, Papa?"

"What a silly question," he said, putting an arm around me. "Do I love the thought of using these machines to end the lives of men not much older than Misha or Bogdan, men who did nothing but get born in the wrong country? Of course not. But do I believe in doing what I can to keep my family safe, which means keeping my country as safe as possible? Of course I do." He ran a hand over the tank again and then led me back outside, out of the factory, our white breath escaping into the cold air.

"Family is everything," he said, his eyes filling as he put an arm around me. "Everything else is just wind through the trees. One day, you'll see."

I knew he was right: that one day I would have a family of my own. But I had to admit that my one example of solitary life, Papa's brother, Uncle Pasha, made it quite appealing. When he visited us in Kiev, he always seemed more like a carefree older brother than an uncle. With his feathery hair, slighter frame, and narrow shoulders, it was difficult to see him as an adult, as my father's near peer, especially when he slung me over his back and cried, "I've saved the princess! I've saved the princess! Back to her castle she goes. . . ." before depositing me on the balcony. Uncle Pasha had no family to speak of and didn't seem to want one. But this didn't seem to be the time to bring this up.

"I am trying my best to take care of you all—your mother, your grandmother, your sister . . ." he said, and when he mentioned Polina, his voice cracked. I was also struggling, but I was older and appeared sturdier, so no one pitied me the way they pitied her. And now here was my father, getting emotional because there wasn't enough he could do for all of us.

"You're taking good care of us," I told him. "Polya and I would have frozen to death without the coats you brought back for us," I said, running a hand along my furry shuba, reminding him that he rode a horse to a distant village just to keep us fed and clothed, but this rolled right off him, and he just nodded vaguely. "Are you all right, Papa?"

"Perfectly fine, darling. Just a bit worn out, that's all. We've been working so hard."

"Thank you for showing me the factory, Papa," I said, and I turned away, understanding that he needed to be left alone, though he could not stay out in the cold for very long.

I tried not to cry as I began the long walk back to our apartment. I felt sorry for my debilitated father, but I was overwhelmed primarily by self-pity. The day had been a terrible disappointment. It was far from fair. All I wanted was for Papa to take me by the hand and show me his man's world, one of drama and violence and machinations against the Nazis, filled with elements of far greater interest than my stinky school, and what I got was watching the grown man I loved more than anyone crying like a child.

One morning, my sister and I had a chance to remedy some of our pain. When the adults were out, we checked Madame Renata's door again and saw that she had left it unlocked. It was a weekend. The women were at the market and the men were conferencing at Uncle Ivan's. It was so quiet I could hear the distant drip of a faucet downstairs. We crept down the dark hallway, which felt endless, a plank over a raging sea. I knew the penalty: if we were caught, it would mean the end of Aunt Yulia's supplementary parcels.

"My God," my sister said, when we stepped inside. "All this time . . ."

"And we were so grateful for her sacks of onion and moldy bread."

The place was a veritable grocery store. I could not believe its bounties. She seemed to possess everything: sausages, batons of bread, potatoes, onions, tomatoes, bunches of dill, bowls of individually wrapped chocolates and even chocolate bars. I never had much of a sweet tooth, but in that moment I would have died for chocolate. I looked at Polya and saw that this was what had also caught her eye.

"We're starving under the woman's nose. And she doesn't care for us at all!" she said.

"I don't know how she can live with herself," I said, reaching a trembling hand toward the chocolate. I didn't care that the woman's daughter and husband had died. If she had walked in at that moment, I might have tried to end her life as well.

"Lara," Polya whispered. "There is so much chocolate in there. They will hardly miss it. . . ."

"Stealing is wrong," I said uncertainly. "We could get in trouble. What if she stops giving us extra food?"

"There are no rules during war."

My sister said it so stonily that the words sounded utterly right, making me feel like she was the older one, though she was likely echoing something she had heard Bogdan say.

Wherever her words came from, it was hard to argue with them. There was an unconscionable amount of chocolate in that apartment.

We grabbed two pieces of chocolate from the bowl, and then we carried them to the main apartment and ate them slowly, luxuriously, like careful birds. When we finished, smacking our lips and smiling like lovesick fools, I briefly adored my little sister. She wasn't perfect, but who was? We were blood, after all. We fell asleep holding each other, but this sweet moment did not last, because I woke up to screaming.

"They are thieves! Thieves! They stole my chocolate. I know they did! There were twelve pieces in that bowl when I left—now there are only ten!"

Aunt Yulia's eyes were filled with venom; she had run in from outside and brought the chill with her, her cheeks still rosy. This angry woman had nothing in common with the soft woman I remembered guiding her daughter onto the train, yet there she was. Apparently Polya and I were not the most sophisticated criminals; we had left her door open. Mama and Papa stood beside her, looking troubled, while the Orlovs were near the balcony, gazing at the floor. Bogdan looked particularly upset by this turn of events, since he was the closest to Aunt Yulia on account of her daughter. Misha stood beside him, his hands by his sides, and I wanted him to rush over to protect me, but he didn't do a thing.

"Is this true?" Papa asked us. I could hardly look at him.

I said nothing. Polya began to cry, instantly giving us away like the dimwit that she was. Once she nodded, I saw no use in denying it.

"We are starving, and you have all the food in the world. Have you no shame?" I said to Aunt Yulia.

Mama smacked me across the face, my cheek stinging wildly. "Are you mad, child? If it were not for Aunt Yulia's generosity, we would be cold in the ground by now!"

"Thieves! Thieves!" the woman kept crying, ignoring my accusation.

Polya tried giving her the expression that predated our stay in the mountains, a certain batting of the eyes and pouting of the lips that typically worked like magic.

"Don't look at me that way," Aunt Yulia said to her, shaking her head. "I have seen you give that look to every man in your path. But you know what, child? Look in the mirror. That doesn't work here. You don't have your looks to fall back on anymore—none of us do. You need your brains, child, and you have not used them!"

Baba Tonya gasped. No one else had dared mention my sister's waning appearance directly up to that moment. Aunt Yulia had diagnosed my sister perfectly. Polina could not forget the fawning gaze of Dimitrev senior, of her schoolboy walking companions, and she hadn't yet accepted that she was just another starving girl. Bogdan was the only boy who noticed her, but their relationship was not romantic.

"You disgusting woman," my grandmother said to Aunt Yulia. "She is hardly more than a child!"

"There are no children among us," Aunt Yulia said, softening a bit, and I nearly pitied her, recalling her sweet daughter.

"Please, Antonina Nikolaevna," my mother said to Baba Tonya, who stood behind a trembling Polya with her hands on her shoulders. "My deepest apologies, Yulia," Mama said. "I promise you, my girls will be punished." She gave her a roll of bread, which was to constitute most of our dinner, and the vile woman snatched it up and walked out, pivoting on her heel. How could she live with herself—walking out with her fat rear while two girls starved in her midst! Bogdan hesitated, and then he followed her down the hall. They spoke in low voices, but Polya's cries drowned out their conversation. I hated my sister for being so weak.

Mama grabbed a rolling pin and raised it over our heads. She did not often hit us, and when she did, we usually deserved it. Mama smacked the pin into her hand several times. Polya did not seem terrified. In fact, she stepped closer, wanting to get the punishment over with. She even held out her hands, palms up.

"You are both hopeless!" Mama said with a sigh, tossing the pin on the floor. Her face contorted and I did not realize what was happening until a tear escaped her eye. Papa put a hand on the divan to steady himself, like he was going to faint. The moment was over before Mama could notice, and he put his arm around her and stroked her hair. He looked so small compared to her, and it seemed impossible that he could bring her anything resembling comfort.

"That Garanina woman is a tyrant," muttered my grandmother.

"Nasty," agreed Polya.

"Hideous," I added, just for sport.

"Ruined," said Mama.

"Broken," Papa said.

"Doing her best to get by," Bogdan said quietly from the doorway, venturing back into the room.

The Orlov parents stayed quiet, not certain how to weigh in. Of course the woman was a monster, but she gave us food. Even Misha still said nothing, which disappointed me. Did he care at all about how Polina and I were treated? Bogdan was close to Aunt Yulia, but what was Misha's excuse? And yet, in spite of his twisted alliances, Bogdan put an arm around my sister. My grandmother stood on her other side and put a hand on her head.

Just then, Licky trotted in from the outdoors and nuzzled my sister's legs. He was her biggest protector, and he continued to grow larger than any domestic cat I had ever seen, nearly reaching our waists, as if he were gaining all of the weight my sister had lost. Though Polya did not ride the creature all over town, as Papa had suggested, I was certain she could have. When he walked beside her as she weaved her way through the apartment buildings, he was truly her protector. Sometimes, old white Snowball would trot along with them, and the three of them painted quite a picture. And now she knelt down and wrapped her arms around him, like he was her prince, the only one who understood her.

Mama had stopped crying and collected herself and Papa followed suit.

"Foolish girls," Papa said. "Nobody is angry with you, all right?"

"Nobody but your mother, it seems," said Mama, toughening up now.

"Please, do not do this again," said Papa. "There could be real consequences for all of us. We must maintain cordial relations with that woman, don't you understand?"

I understood nothing. I mumbled an apology and marched to the door with my sister. The adults seemed so defeated that I knew the discussion was over, that "there are no rules during war" would not impress at that juncture. I passed Misha on my way out, and I did not realize how angry I was with him until he reached out his useless hand and put it on my shoulder.

"Why didn't you do anything?" I said.

"If there was something to do, I would have done it," he said. "The best course of action was not to act, so I followed it."

"You're a coward."

"Not at all," he said. "It takes bravery to know when to restrain yourself."

Polya wiped her face and laughed meanly. "That's the dumbest thing I ever heard," she said, and Misha lurched back, but he said nothing more. He looked away from me, down at the floor. My sister laughed darkly as she linked her arm through mine and led me away from him.

When winter finally released its icy grip on us, the brothers, Polina, and I celebrated by dueling with sticks near the woods. The government had given each family a sack of potatoes to plant after the final frost, and Mama and Aunt Tamara were planting their allotted share behind our building; however, Aunt Tamara had gotten it into her head that if she cut her potatoes in half, her family could eat half now and more would sprout when harvest came.

Though Mama tried to dissuade her, there was no reasoning with the woman, and the mild air put everyone in such good spirits that she did not push the issue. The fathers were also out, smoking and muttering about our losses in Crimea and Kharkov; Licky and Snowball circled us as we played. We knew we were too grown for these escapades, but we were too happy to be outdoors to care.

Spring was almost upon us; a few bits of grass had clawed their way through the earth, still soggy from the melted snow. I was relieved to be outside, but I was still hurt that Misha had done nothing to defend me against Aunt Yulia, though I did not say anything about it; after all, he was my only companion, and what was I supposed to do? I knew Polina judged me for it, but she preferred the company of her cat, the dog, our grandmother, Bogdan, our parents—basically everyone's over mine, so who was she to tell me who to spend time with?

"Fyodor Mikhailovich takes too long to get to the point," Bogdan was saying, while fighting his brother. Though Misha and I had finished *Karamazov* just last week, and Bogdan snatched the book away from us afterward. And now he was claiming to have read it already. There was no way he could do it without skimming.

"You're a dunce," Misha said, but his brother was making him laugh. "He needs to take his time because his ideas are complex."

"They seemed pretty simple to me. All that suspense over whether or not Father Zosima's corpse would stink—I knew it would stink to the high heavens all along!"

"Aren't you clever?" I said, switching off from fighting my sister to fighting Bogdan.

"I didn't say I didn't enjoy it," he said. "I just said it took too long," he said, flashing a smile.

"Dostoevsky has more to say about family and art in one sentence than you could ever say in your whole life," I told him.

"I don't know about that," he said with a shrug. "You and your beauty of literature. Maybe I'm just too pedestrian."

I stopped stick fighting him for a moment because I was stunned that he remembered what I said on the train so long ago.

"Perhaps," I said, and I could see Misha watching the two of us, not liking what he saw.

"Besides, there weren't any dream sequences," Bogdan said with a wink, and now my sister was confused, feeling left out.

"All of it is boring nonsense," she grumbled, and then she shoved me out of the way to fight Bogdan, leaving me to fight Misha.

"Everyone is entitled to their own opinion, even if that opinion is wrong," Misha said, and we hit sticks, kicking up dirt. His nose was red and there was dirt in his hair, and I was still so very angry with him for not defending me, and for not even apologizing for it afterward. Meanwhile, Bogdan talked to Aunt Yulia and made her promise to continue giving us her extra food at the end of every week. But I had aligned myself with Misha. It was too late to turn back, but I had been hoping for some confirmation that I had made the right choice.

Now my sister was whispering in Bogdan's ear and his lips curled into a smile as he absorbed whatever secret message she was imparting to him, likely something related to me and Misha. That was the first time I wondered if they were more than friends.

"Our opinions are just fine," she told me, when she caught me staring. "I'd rather watch a lake freeze than read that dull book again."

"You're too young to understand. There's nothing dull about it," I told my sister, and she rolled her eyes while swatting her stick.

"Of course, Larissa," she said, almost singing the words. "You know everything by now, don't you?"

I got distracted and forgot to defend myself against Misha's attacks. He jabbed his stick into my palm. I cried out and pressed my hand to my chest, and Misha threw down his stick and ran over to me to see the blood blooming on the inside of my hand.

"I'm so sorry, Larissa," he said, putting an arm around me. "I didn't mean to hurt you."

I could see it in his brown, brooding eyes—he meant what he said, and this was it, the most he would give me, and I could either take it or continue to hold a grudge, which was no easy thing in a time of war.

"I know that. I know you didn't," I said, and then he put an arm around me and led me back to his alcove, where I avoided my sister's gaze. I didn't owe her an explanation for my alliances any more than she needed to tell me why she, Bogdan, and Licky were running up and down the hallway like schoolchildren while Misha and I pursued higher matters. He picked up my Tsvetaeva tome, though we had not read much poetry together, and it was a bit subversive to be reading her at that point.

"Are you ready, Larissa?" he asked, and I could not resist him.

At the beginning of the summer, the government gave our families a crate of food as a reward for the fathers' continued work on the T-34, which they claimed would end the war any day now; by fall, our family harvested our potatoes, sharing half with the Orlovs, because of course Aunt Tamara's sliced potatoes did not sprout a lick. Though Papa called her "our Gregor Mendel," he was not angry, reasserting his claim that we were all one family. The crate of food and potatoes helped us make it through the summer, but we would not have survived without Bogdan, our main supplementary source.

One day, in the fall, he brought home three eggs, a tiny onion, and even a live chicken, which Mama carried onto the balcony and decimated with one swift twist of the neck, a familiar gesture from her childhood days, when she would routinely kill chickens to help out her mean old restaurant-owning aunts.

The stew Mama and Aunt Tamara made afterward! I can still taste its warmth coating my shivering tongue. We were in the highest of spirits after that particular meal. The food had even relaxed Baba Tonya enough for her to fall asleep with her eyes open, a state of hers that always unsettled me; she sat with her hands on her lap, but from her glazed eyes I could see she had temporarily left us. Even my sister was cheered, though she was still the weakest among us, her sagging arm flesh still held together by twine.

I was feeling bold. Though it was against our unspoken rules to ask Bogdan about the source of his bounty, I was so drugged from the food that I could not help myself, so I tugged at his sleeve and asked him where the eggs had come from.

He winked at me, reminding me of the fuller-faced boy he had been, not this gaunt man before me. "Eggs come from hens," he said. "Don't you know that? I thought you were the smart one around here."

"Such a joker," I said, and he laughed. I thought I saw Mama's face harden, though it was impossible to be certain because she had taken on such a permanently stony visage. Bogdan shook his head, smiled, and returned to playing with the kitty. Licky was the only one thriving among us, scarfing down mice and other rodents left and right. Many times he had trotted up to my sister with a bloody offering she would make Bogdan throw out—on one occasion, he even honored my sister by depositing a mouse on her pillow.

My question about the food seemed to awaken my grandmother. She rubbed her eyes and narrowed them at me. "Do they taste good?" she asked.

"Of course," I said.

"Then why does it matter?" she said, adjusting her boa like she had somewhere to be.

"Can't a person be curious?" I said.

"Not here," Baba said. I could not remember the last time I was reproached by my grandmother. It was like being chided by a baby.

"Enough," Mama said.

As the women cleaned up, Papa and Uncle Konstantin spoke grimly of Leningrad, how the starving, surrounded city could not possibly make it through another year. Uncle Konstantin tried to offer some optimism, saying that surely the war was turning in our favor, hoping that we would stave off the Germans in Stalingrad any day now. It was hard to believe his patriotic claims because he kept pausing to catch his breath, to stave off the dizziness that plagued him. He was a few years older than the other parents, and it was showing. Misha listened intently to the men's talk and quietly chimed in when appropriate. It became clear that no one would answer my pressing question about Bogdan's missions.

I didn't get an answer until that evening, and the truth came from Polya, of all people. She told me when we gathered firewood from the edge of the woods. Or, rather, when I gathered wood and too-weak-to-help Polya and her faithful cat tagged along. A witchy smile flashed on my sister's caved-in face. Licky trotted at her side, and I swore I could see the same expression on his stinky cat mug.

"I thought you knew everything," she said, almost singing the words.

"What do you mean?"

"Oh, nothing," she said, smiling still. "I just assumed you knew where Bogdan got those eggs—and everything else."

There was a mean edge to my sister that evening. The scraps of eggs and chicken had not sated her. She struggled to get them down, as if she were making a great sacrifice for the benefit of us all, when in reality we all would have killed for a bit more food.

Now she stroked Licky's head and turned toward the apartment as I filled my arms.

"Isn't it obvious?" she said. "He gets them from the women in town. And the ones in the villages nearby. Women whose husbands are at war or at the factory or just plain dead, what-have-you. He does them favors."

The firewood was impossibly heavy. I wobbled and set it down. "What kind of favors?"

My sister laughed sharply. "He's not a bad-looking boy. He's nearly fifteen. Close to being a man. Close enough for them anyway. Certainly better than nothing. . . ."

My eyes filled with wild, dirty tears. So this was the thing my sister and all the adults, even my half-insane grandmother, knew as clear as day. Who was I to think Bogdan was paying attention to old bullfrog-looking me, with his winks and innuendos about beauty and dreams, when he was off servicing half the women in town? And how did I think he convinced Aunt Yulia to continue giving us extra food? He must have thought I was as chaste and idiotic as a little girl. If I wasn't attempting to pick up my woodpile again, I would have smacked the remaining fat off my sister's face. I tried to mirror her smug look, to give it right back to her and her idiot beast.

"Thank you for telling me the truth," I said. "I don't know how I could have missed it."

I didn't get a chance to ask Bogdan about the eggs until the next time we were alone together, after the winter had truly set in again. We went to the edge of the pines to gather wood and Licky followed along; my sister had stopped gathering wood or doing housework weeks before, after she disappeared, leading us on a goose chase all over the village, thinking she had perished. I found her passed out in a snowbank in her white coat, hugging her beloved white dog, Snowball, not far from the woods, while Licky circled the pair.

The snow had stopped falling and we had to rescue the least soaked branches from the white morass. But the wind was fierce and it blew large chunks of snow out of the surrounding trees, which fell on our heads periodically. We stepped across the small frozen river to get to the forest, Licky leading the way with his wagging bushy tail. Bogdan walked ahead and only then did I notice how much he had grown in the past year. I had never really stopped to take a look at his figure. He was truly becoming a man, though I remembered what my sister told me about him being an "almost man" and my eyes smarted. And since he had recently turned fifteen, he was following the other men to the factory, though it seemed he found excuses to leave his post.

I felt shaky before him, and he moved slowly, like he was waiting for me to say something. I could not come up with much.

"Winter is endless," I said.

"I have a feeling we'll make it through," he said, winking at me. "We're a hearty lot."

"Some are heartier than others," I said, again baffled by the stupidity of my comments, or the fact that I was nervous before Bogdan, babbling like a dimwit.

I can't explain what happened next. Maybe it was because the moon was full. Maybe it was because a little boy from school had died that week and my feelings about mortality and the senseless brevity of life were eating away at my weakened brain. Whatever the case may have been, as if driven by an external force, some kind of madness out of Dostoevsky, we dropped our wood in the snow and regarded one another. A smirk rose on Bogdan's face.

He was not, I reasoned, more handsome than his brother. He was not nearly as hardworking or kind or sophisticated. He fit in more with my sister's frivolous nature than with my own. And yet, I felt myself moving toward him in a way I had never felt compelled to move toward Misha, in spite of the comfort I felt in his presence during our late-night reading sessions. Under the moonlight, Bogdan's blue-tinged skin seemed particularly blue, but that did not deter me either. I wondered what would. I knew I was being ridiculous, that he was not at all my type, but I let the feeling overtake me.

Licky meowed again, knocking me back to reality. Reminding me of his own fate and of Polya and the things she had told me about Bogdan. I did not want my first kiss to be with a man who had slept with half the women in town—I wanted to be wanted singularly. I ignored the breeze, the glowing sky, the strange energy between us, the snow that kept sputtering out of the pine branches. I took a step back.

"Thank you," I said. "For the eggs. They saved us."

He smiled a disappointed smile and took a step back as well. "It is my pleasure to serve," he said, saluting me like a cadet, and it was clear that there would be no more romantic opportunities.

"Naturally," I said. "We all do what we can."

He bent down and scratched Licky behind the ears. "And soon, this one will play his part, unless our luck turns."

His words were more shocking than the electricity between us. I tried not to look like I had been run over by a Black Maria. As my breath settled around me like a fog, I understood everything. Why Mama did not forbid Polya from playing with her pet, or why, when Licky wandered into our apartment, Papa mentioned how big he would be, one day. The meat on his haunches. How Mama was more worried about Polya than ever, and what it meant when she looked from Polya to the cat and back to Polya again. This was yet another truth that had been lost on me, like Bogdan's escapades, and I wondered if everyone but me, and in this case, Polya, also knew the score. The cat was not just useful as a mouser and a soother of Polya. He was also an emergency food supply, and we had far surpassed emergency status. I aggressively patted the cat on the head and tried to maintain my calm.

I recalled helpless Polya resting in a snowbank in her white coat, her face placid until I shook her awake, keeping myself from yelling at her for being so weak, wandering out with only her dumb animals for company when she was feeling so dizzy already. Mama sat beside her as she recovered by the stove, telling her that there would be more food soon, that it would make her big and strong, though what grounds did she have for these words, unless she was thinking of the family pet? Likely it wouldn't be long before Licky met his fate.

I met Bogdan's gaze evenly. I was not going to let him see how clueless I was.

"A shame what has to happen," he said quietly, as if the cat could understand us. "Your sister will be devastated."

"We have no choice in the matter," I said. I tried to hide my surprise that he knew about the cat all along. What didn't he know?

"It can still be a shame, can't it?" he said.

I threw our wood on the pile and agreed, feeling like I had lost something I could never get back. Licky was nuzzling the side of my leg, as if he were begging me to reverse his fate. He didn't seem to want to go back inside the stuffy apartment and neither did I, in spite of the windy bluster. Another blast of snow fell from the branches, landing at our feet. And then, I began to feel a sudden pull toward Licky, which felt as unexpected as my attraction to Bogdan.

"I think I'll stay out with Licky for a little while," I said, stroking the cat behind his ears. "He wants to roam."

"We all want to roam," Bogdan muttered, and then he grabbed his pile of wood and walked away with purpose, as if to make it clear how little I mattered to him, and how whether or not we kissed was of supreme indifference to him, a man who had certainly done more than kissing.

He left a stick behind and I kicked at it. It was hard to believe that not that long ago, Bogdan, Misha, Polya, and I had played at swordfighting with those same sticks. That had turned into a fun and frivolous afternoon, even when everything felt so serious here. What did he expect from me now? To break all decorum and embrace him in the moonlight, with the ill-fated cat as our witness?

Licky was oblivious to my struggles and that was why I loved him, right then. He nuzzled my leg until I moved and found he was happy to follow me. He had never followed me before the way he followed after Bogdan or Polya, and I was moved to tears. I pulled him into my waist and stroked either side of his mangy face. I met his gaze and his white-blue eyes seemed to contain all the sorrows of humanity, I don't know how they fit in there.

"Come, now," I said to the doomed kitty. "Let's walk along the river."

The market had finally opened for spring and Mama managed to get Polya to leave the apartment with me and Baba. My sister had already quit school and spent much of her day in bed with the cat, but the unexpectedly mild weather had lured her out. She had given up her arm twine for aesthetic reasons, and the stray skin clumped around her wrists, but she didn't care. I knew why we were taking her away. It wasn't because we expected the market's sad wares to save us. Licky was resting on the balcony, in a lake of sunlight, and did not seem inclined to move anytime soon. He rolled around on his back, collecting dirt as his belly wiggled in the sun. I was tempted to stroke him one last time, but I did not want my sister to get suspicious. As soon as we were gone, Mama would open the balcony and strike.

The market had already sprung to action when we arrived, the weather-buoyed townspeople milling about even though the selections were as spare as ever. Onion Man Oleg was faithfully stationed at his post in the middle of the rows of blankets; he gave me a wink and threw an onion the size of a large grape at me, which I gladly accepted. Polya did not flirt with anyone besides Bogdan anymore, except she perked up a bit when she chatted with her favorite ancient radish brothers, two of the three of whom were present, which suggested that the third did not make it through the winter.

Baba Tonya was doing her usual routine, flitting about, picking out a wilted cabbage and winking at the vendor to say, "I expect more from you next time, darling." By that point, no one found her strange, or at least not worth staring at. She and her dirty boa and worn coat were just part of the scenery, like the factory blowing gray smoke in the distance and the dirt on either side of the train tracks.

"A lovely day," Baba Tonya said. She paused to gaze into the tracks for a moment, and I worried she had drifted off to her own sad and distant world, thinking about her chance to leave this godforsaken country a quarter of a century ago and all the choices that had got her to where she stood, but then I realized she was just buying Mama time. "Let's take a stroll, shall we?" she said, and again Polya did not protest or declare that she'd rather be back in bed. With the sun on her face, she did seem slightly cheered, even if she was determined not to look that way.

We followed Baba along her preferred path, which ran by the tracks, behind the factory, and then toward the stream that would eventually connect with the back of Building 32. My grandmother was delusional, but she understood what had to be done with Licky without hesitation, just as Bogdan did. Yet my sister seemed oblivious as ever, having no inkling that her beloved pet was being slaughtered for stew.

"His name was Count Bikovsky," Baba was telling Polya. "He had fiery red hair, which was surprisingly charming. He was also an incredibly talented dancer. You should have seen him waltz! He had perfect rhythm. He asked for my hand, but Papa rejected him because he said he was frivolous. Though he was a successful official, Papa didn't trust a man who spent so much time dancing, and that was that. . . ."

"I thought all men knew how to dance in those days," Polya said, but she was amused by the silly story.

"Far from it, my child, far from it."

"You found others to waltz with, I'm sure."

"Did I ever!"

As we approached the apartment and their conversation grew increasingly idiotic, I was weighed down by dread. How could they be talking of balls, petticoats, and suitors at this moment? But when I looked up at my grandmother, as if she could answer this question, I saw that her chin was quivering as she spoke, that she was making a conscious effort to soothe my sister, and I felt the urge to take her by the hand, though I did not follow it.

When we returned to the apartment and presented Mama and Aunt Tamara with our lone cabbage, Polya went straight to the balcony, oblivious to the rich scent of stew filling the apartment. The small lake of sun had spread to twice its size, making the balcony feel twice as empty. Licky should have been rolling on his back by then, showing off the white of his big belly, but of course he was not there. Bogdan followed my sister out, looking troubled. Papa, Uncle Konstantin, and Misha, who was allowed to stand in the adult circle now, were under the trees smoking with a few other factory men, talking their man talk. This was how Papa routinely spent his days, though I had a feeling he made a point of leaving the house to avoid the return of his disappointed daughter.

"Where did Licky go?" Polya said, staring over the edge of the balcony. "Did he go out without me?"

"I haven't seen him," Bogdan said quietly.

"Who?" Mama said when Polya tried her, shrugging and turning back toward her cooking. "Oh, the cat? He must have wandered off, child. He'll be back," she said, vaguely waving her ladle toward the pines.

I saw the worry mounting on my sister's face and wondered if she would care that much if I was the one who had gone missing. Though the cat went off without her occasionally, she seemed more worried than she usually would be under these circumstances, and I wondered if she could sense what was coming. Bogdan ran a hand through his hair and joined Polya on her fruitless search for Licky. I met the gaze of Mama and Papa and the Orlovs and saw that everyone knew what was coming, but no one else cared because we were all so hungry that the smell wafting up from the pot was not completely unappealing.

Though I knew Licky was going to meet his end, until that moment I did not consider the particulars. What did Mama do to snuff out his short, pathetic life? As she continued to stir the pot, it dawned on me with a startling clarity. Licky must have gone the way of the chicken Bogdan had brought back earlier, and the chickens of her childhood—Mama probably broke the cat's neck right on the balcony with one swift gesture. Did the others bear witness to this sad act? Did Papa help Mama hold down the innocent beast, or would that have been too much for him?

Once everyone wandered back in and Mama began to serve the stew, all my dark thoughts were replaced by the scent flooding my nostrils. Though Polya and Bogdan returned looking dejected, my

sister's blotchy face did not keep me from sighing happily when
Mama pushed my portion in front of me.

"He never just . . . wanders off like that," my sister said.

"He will be back any moment now, kitten. You'll see," Papa
said, but he could not meet her gaze. I had never heard my father
lie before, and it would have startled me if I wasn't so mesmerized
by the stew. I took a breath and closed my eyes, issuing a silent
apology to the cat and trying to swallow the memory of our goodbye walk by the river. And then I dug right in to my tin bowl. Bogdan did the same and nodded at me, and I tried to ignore him.
Polya sighed, took a reluctant spoonful, and then, liking the stew
in spite of herself, she kept eating and eating.

"You are getting your color back as we speak," Misha said,
squeezing my arm.

"Liar, liar," I said, but I was pleased. It was nice to be back at his
side. Our relationship had clear terms and was not like the confus-
ing mess that swirled between me and Bogdan. He was a handsome, dependable almost man, a kind, agreeable person, but not so
agreeable that he had a penchant for frolicking with desperate
older women.

"Delightful," said Baba Tonya, and Aunt Tamara made a noise
of assent, which might have been the first time the two women
agreed on anything.

Nobody spoke after that. We gobbled our fare until it was gone
and we were sated. And not only sated but temporarily calmed by
the fact that there would be enough stew to last us a week at least,
if we distributed it carefully. Only after Mama carefully covered
the stew pot did an image of the innocent cat float before me. I
studied Mama's face to see if she had broken under pressure, if it
had hurt her to kill and cook the kitten, but neither her nor Papa's
face indicated that anything untoward had happened. It was busi-

ness as usual, only we were all a bit less starving, and even a bit friendlier with one another as we cleaned up.

The rest of us sat around the stove while Polya and Bogdan left to search for Licky once more. I didn't know if it would be more kind to stop her, or let her think her kitten had truly run off. They returned a little while later, and Polya's face was blanched, showing no signs of the nutritious benefits of the stew.

"Where did—the stew come from?" she asked. She looked at me and I looked away, thinking of the time I asked about the origin of Bogdan's eggs, though this question had a far more sinister answer.

Mama looked up from her stove seat. "Aunt Yulia brought some scraps of beef," she mumbled. Then, when she saw that Polya was unconvinced that Aunt Yulia was capable of this act of kindness, Mama turned away from her and said, "What you are given, you will eat." Papa walked toward her and put a hand on her shoulder and stared at the ground.

"No," Polya said, truly horrified, looking at all of us. Bogdan, too, stared at the ground, Misha pretended to read, the Orlovs were preparing for bed, and I was left staring at my sister. This was my big chance. I had been waiting since the day she told me Bogdan had serviced the neighborhood ladies like a know-it-all. I was, after all, the older sister. It was my place to if not deliver, then to confirm the bad news.

"Licky did a good thing for all of us," I told her. "He saved us from starvation. You should be proud of him."

I thought I would have some joy in telling her this, but I only felt defeated. For a long time, I had been waiting for this grand revelation to dawn on Polya, to show her that she wasn't as smart as she thought she was. But now her bottom lip trembled, and she looked so weak that I was surprised by the volume of her cries.

"No!" she shrieked. "You couldn't! You didn't! How could you let me—"

"Foolish girl," Mama said. "You needed to eat something. Take a look at yourself."

"Your sister is right," Papa tried, putting his other hand on her shoulder, but she flung him away. "Licky was a true patriot. He served his country."

"All of you are disgusting!" Polya said, putting a hand to her throat and making a retching noise. "Disgusting pigs. I don't know how you can live like this."

"We live however we can," Aunt Tamara said. "You think it makes us happy to slurp up the meat of a bobcat? You don't have to be so vulgar. This is undignified enough as it is."

Baba Tonya observed the scene with her hands on her lap as if she were listening to the radio or hearing a story, genuinely curious to see what would happen next.

"I, for one, feel quite dignified," Mama said. "There is dignity in honesty, is there not?"

"I will never forgive any of you," Polya said, and then she clutched her stomach and ran out to the balcony, shrieking like a harlot. I watched her heaving right over the rail and almost felt bad for her, but I was too content with my dinner portion, in spite of its source. Bogdan gave me a mean little nod. He considered going out there and so did I, halfheartedly, but in the end it was my father who went after Polya, my dear father who rubbed her back and kissed her hair, and when they returned to the apartment, my father who promised her that he would do everything in his power to make her happy again, even if he'd have to risk his life to do it.

We were all silent as he promised her that he would send a letter to Uncle Pasha saying he was ready to venture out to a neighboring village to bring back food for everybody; Uncle Konstantin was too weak to go, and it was high time he saw his dear brother.

"We'll leave as soon as possible, kitten," Papa said.

"Whatever you think is best," she said, though she didn't care where he went or how much food he brought back. He held her gaze, willing her to care, and she managed a smile for him after all. And I'm convinced that this smile was it, the thing that tipped him over the edge and made him decide to venture out into the vast nothingness.

I was alarmed by his proposition. Papa had been particularly weak lately, though I was of course intrigued by what he could find out there. What did my father think he could bring back that would resuscitate the girl? Dainty cakes or watermelon or roasted pigs? Polya seemed unlikely to be brought back by anything other than the sight of her deceased cat, yet Papa was convinced the trip would save her. I thought of him breaking down at his factory again, weeping over his inability to take care of his family. This was more about settling something within himself than making up for what he did to Polya.

It was merely symbolic. Polya was beyond caring about food. Papa felt guilty for his daughter's suffering and was determined to redeem himself. I watched Mama's face as Papa and Polya finished this exchange and she did not seem too pleased about Papa's offer, but she did not stop him, either, though I trusted that tomorrow, she would tell him it was not a good idea. But she did no such thing. The next morning, Papa got up to mail a letter to Uncle Pasha, and nobody did a thing to stop him.

I sigh and stare into the computer, where Natasha is rocking her baby and Stas still looks as if I have not given him the story he is after. Well, why should I care for him? I didn't even notice when he returned to the scene. But Natasha is my guiding light, my savior. I want to reach through the computer and hug her, to erase my foul memories. She is my everything, though in this moment she looks forlorn, caught up in the dismal scene of my ailing sister, acting as dramatic as Polina herself, all because of a dumb dead cat, not even caring that my father had to put his life on the line for the girl.

She wipes her face one more time to emphasize how much my story has touched her. Always such a sensitive girl! When she was a child, she cried at everything, everything. Homeless people on Kiev park benches. Cartoon rabbits dying on television. Rain spoiling a good walk. I should have known my story would undo her, but she was the one who asked for it, and how could I deny her?

She and Stas are touching shoulders, leaning closer to the screen. Their long hair mingles and they resemble a two-headed beast. Yes, this Stas is a typical homosexual, looking nearly as feminine as my Natasha, with his slick long hair and thick lashes.

"Eating her poor cat," Natasha says. "That's so awful." She looks around for nasty old Sharik, but he is nowhere to be found. Honestly, I would not mind if someone put that boy in a stew.

"Of course it was awful. But we had to survive somehow. If only my sister could have understood that, everything would be different. Stupid, spoiled Polina!" I say, a bit surprised to feel such anger unfurling from me. Though my outburst was alarming enough that it sent Stas running off to the balcony, and good riddance.

"She wasn't all bad," says Natasha.

"Excuse me?"

"Your sister."

"Easy for you to say. You never met her."

"She just wasn't as tough as you, Baba. Most people aren't."

"I suppose that is true," I say. Of course she would defend Polina when she has so much of the girl in her. Any room she steps in is filled with light. Anywhere she goes, men turn their heads. All that time wasted, crying for pitiful beasts. And though Natasha is not a full redhead like Polina, she does have that auburn tint to her hair. If things had gone differently, perhaps Polina would have tried to pursue acting herself, who knows? But I do not intend to spend so much time thinking about Polina.

"Plus," Natasha goes on, "she defended you when Grandpa Misha didn't."

"Oh," I say, feeling my stomach tighten. "That was nothing."

This was not the first time I revisited the day my sister and I stole that chocolate, when my dear Misha had said, "The best course of action was not to act, so I followed it." Over the years, as he never brought up the topic of my loyalty, I wondered if this had become his mantra.

"It's okay, sweetheart," says Natasha, but she is comforting her baby gremlin, not yours truly. For a moment, I think it might be nice to give in to Natasha's requests, to come out to visit my new great-granddaughter, perhaps even to help her mother find her former spirit. But no one can help a new mother, not truly—and she does look a bit less disheveled than she did a week ago, when I began my story, and that is the most I can hope for. After all, even the thought of resettling in Sevastopol wears at my bones, especially since I refused to let Misha's driver take me, insisting on taking the train like a good soldier. How could I possibly cross the ocean—all for the sake of a little nothing who won't even remember me? Yet the girl smiles right then, and I can't help but smile back.

"I have changed my mind about the girl," I say. "She is not *so* ugly."

Natasha laughs. "That's very generous of you, Baba."

"Of course, she does not hold a candle to you as a child," I say, but I see her making a face, that her patience on this subject is wearing thin. Still, I see her as the beautiful young girl dancing by the water, reciting lines from her latest school production. "How's work, darling? How was your audition?" I say.

She laughs a mean, dark laugh. "It was pointless," she says. "But I have another one in a few days—kind of."

"Oh? Something interesting?"

"Sure, Baba. Something interesting," she says.

"Good for you, darling," I say, but I sign off feeling uneasy, like there's something she isn't telling me. Then again, why should I be surprised? There are plenty of things I have kept from her.

My screen is frozen on the image of my exhausted granddaughter blowing me a kiss, and for a moment, stuck in place, she resembles her former gorgeous self, it is something unbelievable. In all my years I have never seen such beauty, and it nearly gives me enough pride to die on, even if we share few physical characteristics. My poor, darling granddaughter. The girl deserves so much more than the world is giving her, even based on looks alone. It must be said that I speak with the utmost objectivity. Anyone who saw Natasha in her former glory would agree. Not even my idiot sister was so beautiful.

Natasha

"So are you a prostitute this time, or a spy?" Stas says as I check my hair in the mirror once more.

"Actually, neither."

"Making moves, Sterling."

Though I didn't get called back for the *Pen & Sword* role, my agent sent me a consolation: an audition for a horror movie called *Sinister Sister* about a girl who was separated at birth from her twin sister when her sister was adopted by Americans, leaving her behind to be abused at a Ukrainian orphanage. When Ukrainian twin me grows up, her now-American sister tracks her down and gets her to come to the States, but when the girl arrives, it becomes clear that something is wrong with her. She's out for blood, on a mission to kill or maim all the creepy men in L.A., where her sister lives, and there are plenty of them. In the end, she realizes her sister's husband is abusing her and decides to kill him and leave her sister for good.

I knew it wasn't exactly *Citizen Kane*, but the important thing was just to keep going, and besides, all I had to do for this one was send in a video of myself. Stas would film me while Tally slept in her crib, which she has been getting better at, thanks to Baba's recommendation. Baba who traveled halfway to Siberia on a train and nearly starved to death—whose problems make my disaster of a career seem like a hangnail. And how about old Tonya, whose sad story is coming into focus, who seems to be smirking at me from her photo today, what would she say if she knew her great-great-granddaughter made it to America, where she spent her days trying to book a role as a hooker or murderer to solve her problems? When I try to explain the role to Stas, he just laughs at me.

"So you're still playing someone from Ukraine, but you're a killer now?"

"I only kill the men who deserve to die. It's empowering!"

"If you say so," he says, snorting. "Have you ever tried to audition for a role for something that wasn't Russian or Jewish?"

"With this nose?"

"Your nose is fine."

"I was on three episodes of *My Husband the Mobster*, until I got strangled. And I got close to a speaking role in *My Big Fat Greek Wedding 2*, but that's about it. Look, my agent mostly sends me to auditions for Russian parts because that's where I have the best chance. I can't just make up the parts I want to play. I mean, look at the Borsch Babies, putting on a play about fucking *Chernobyl*, as if anyone would give a shit about that! It was, like, thirty years ago. Where is that going to get them, exactly?"

"That depends on where you want to go, I suppose."

Now he's just pissing me off, acting like a naïve idiot. "I'm tired of playing all those suffering Jews. I mean, my grandmother wasn't Jewish but she fucking suffered, and if I'm going to play some old Soviet person who suffered, then I might as well play her."

He claps his hands. "That's not such a terrible idea, Sterling."

I nearly trip over the cat when I see he's being serious. "You're crazy," I tell him.

"Why not go for it? It's a good story. So far anyway."

I roll my eyes. I need to get ready to be this killer instead of talking nonsense. "And who would play all the other parts, genius? Where would I put it on?"

He shrugs. "That would be for you to figure out."

"Can we not? I need to focus."

"Fair enough. And so, *Sinister Sister*."

I don't like the little smirk on his face. "What?" I say.

"I didn't say anything."

"You don't have to."

Stas acts all pure about his supposed writing, but it's hard to take him seriously. Like most artist-waiters, he seems more waiter than poet, and he never shows me a word of whatever he's been furtively scribbling in his little notebook, reminding me of how I would rant in my diary about Mama only to slam the book in her face when she walked by. When I asked if I could see a poem of his the other day, he just said, "I don't share my work until it's ready. And it's never ready."

"I'd rather die having lived purely than having whored myself out," he says.

"Good for you. You're a coward."

"For not putting my work out there? I'm not like you. I want to improve as a poet for myself, not so the world—or let's face it, with poetry, so the eighty people who still read—give a shit. I don't think there's anything cowardly about that."

"Suit yourself."

"Don't mind if I do. You ready to be this killer?"

"Of course I am." I settle in my chair, feeling all frazzled, but try to shake it off.

He picks up his phone to start filming, but then it rings.

"Shit," he says, turning it off. "Sorry."

"Your—sister?" I say, nearly asking if it's his mysterious ex.

"Yeah."

I don't think he's lying, but I'm getting more and more curious about the woman he left in Boston. Yuri claims to know nothing about it. I'll get it out of him eventually, but not today.

He's furiously tapping into his phone, and old Sharik jumps on my lap and I scratch him under his chin. The big guy is twenty years old, the last of all my pets—I had two other cats, Elvis and Yanina, along with a parakeet, seven tropical fish, a guinea pig, two rabbits, and a snake named Igor, all my treasured beauties from over the years that I took to the vet and sang to and fed lovingly and mourned when the time came. Only Sharik remains, and though I love my sweet boy, he does have a defect: he loves sucking his own dick more than anything. I knew he was that way when I found him at the pound—I was told his mother died in childbirth and he was found sucking on the dead thing's teats and never recovered from the need to suck for comfort. Who could turn down such a pathetic creature? Though today he's being a good boy, and I am grateful for that.

Stas puts his phone down and meets my gaze and I can tell he doesn't want to talk about the sister anymore, but I can't help myself.

"Why don't you talk to your sister, then?"

"I'll catch her later."

"If you love her so much, why don't you go back to Boston to see her?"

He sighs and looks at the phone again. "Because I'd rather die than see my mom."

"Because?"

"Because she just spends all her time in bed, taking pills."

"She getting help?"

"That is the help she's getting. She sees doctors, and the best they can do is put her on a bunch of antidepressants. My sister just sits in front of the TV, doing her homework or drawing. Usually she makes dinner for them both. It's not dangerous, I mean she can take care of herself, she has her act together enough to go to work, but it's just depressing as fuck in there. It smells like death. I can't stand it."

"You must miss your sister."

"Of course I fucking miss her. But I can't see her in that house. It's too much. My sister and I used to hang out at my place across the city, but that's not an option anymore," he says. I wait for him to elaborate, to explain why he moved out and what this mystery girl did to him, but I can see he wants to move on. He starts tapping his foot and running a hand through his hair.

He starts acting all agitated, so I feel like it's my turn to talk. "My mom had her problems too," I tell him, though I never talk about my mom.

"A depressed addict?"

"She barely drank—a glass of wine or two might have helped her to loosen the fuck up, actually. No, she was just a hardass. But I didn't really even know who she was, up to the day she died. I thought she hated anything artistic. I didn't know she wanted to sing. She only sang in front of me once."

"Oh?" he says, raising his idiot eyebrow.

"One time I caught her singing, in the middle of the night, not long before she died. I had no idea she sang," I say. And then I sing a few bars: "My heart bleeds and bleeds for you, darling, my heart bleeds rivers of the darkest blood. . . ."

"Ah," he says. "*Heartsongs for the Drowned.*"

"You know it?"

"Mishkin wasn't exactly Viktor Tsoi, but he was pretty famous."

"Were you even born when Tsoi died?"

"I didn't say that," he says, getting defensive. "I got into Soviet rock because of my dad. Or, at least, his rock CDs were some of the things he left behind when he left us, and I got this idea that I would get to know him just by listening. Anyway, it's stupid."

"That isn't stupid. I wish my mom left behind something like that. I didn't know her at all," I say, and suddenly I feel too exposed, wondering how we got on this topic anyway. What the fuck is wrong with me?

"Why didn't she sing in front of you?" he says, but I don't want to talk about it anymore.

"She didn't want me to know she had artistic tendencies, I guess."

"Who could blame her?" he says, and I smack him across the chest.

I study his greasy blond hair and neck tattoo and tattered, oversized long-sleeved shirt, and think, *She would have hated you*. But then I feel it, just a little bit, that old stirring, maybe even *because* I thought Mama would have hated him. I didn't even think I had a real body anymore, not one that wanted things, but here I am, feeling shy all of a sudden. And who could blame me, when I spend all my time either with a baby or this fuckboy? That's it, I decide, I need some time with Yuri before I go crazy. As soon as Stas leaves, I'll go to the bathroom, get myself off, and forget about it. And besides, I'm pretty sure the weirdness is just coming from me, that he doesn't think of me like that, and shouldn't.

He clears his throat and looks all serious and takes two steps toward me. I freak out until he picks up his phone to film me and I remember why he's here. "Are you ready?" he says. "You're gonna kill it, sis."

But I'm not thinking of *Sinister Sister* right then. I stumble through the audition, but I'm thinking of Mama the whole time. Why did I tell Stas about her singing to begin with? I never even told Yuri about that strange night, or what I learned about her after that.

———

After Mama died, I celebrated the New Year at home with Papa in front of the TV, eating stale Russian chocolates and snacking on the blini and chicken cutlets some family friends put in our freezer after the funeral. Mama had been gone what, three weeks? A month? For the first year it felt like it had happened the day before, so it was hard to say, but it was fucking recent, our wounds were wide-open and gangrenous, and yet there we sat, Papa saying he was feeling hopeful about my college applications, though the look on his face, which was completely gray, his eyes just two swollen little mounds, did not exactly signify hope. And who was I to tell him that those apps were all for Mama, that I would turn them in just to delay the inevitable but that there was no fucking way I could make it through four years of school?

Though I had kind of been suppressing the memory of that night on the back patio, maybe because I had convinced myself I had dreamed it or because it felt so much like it didn't belong to this world, that bringing it up would make it combust or something, I couldn't think of anything else to say to my father. I needed to say something, because though he had been pretty depressed since I could remember, since Mama's death, he had reached a new low. He had stopped taking care of himself and it was amazing he had managed to grade final papers, with my help. Maybe I thought asking him about it could distract him, in a good way.

"Hey, Papa? How come I never knew Mama was such a good singer?"

"Excuse me?"

"I heard Mama singing a few months ago. And it was so beautiful. But when I asked her about it, she acted like I was crazy. What was that about?"

Papa sighed and unwrapped another chocolate. "You must have been dreaming."

"That's what Mama said. But I'm not crazy. I know what I heard."

"Your mother could sing," he said slowly. "There was no doubt about that." And then what he said next was so shocking that I would have been less surprised if he had revealed Mama had been a mermaid all along. "When I met your mother, she wanted to be a star," he said. He even managed a thin little smile when he said it. "Can you believe it?" he said, and I just sat there with my mouth hanging open. "You should have seen her then—thick mascara, long flowing dresses, earrings with heavy fake jewels . . ." I had never seen such a photograph of my mother. All the ones I saw featured her looking stern and makeupless, her hair pulled back tightly, a matron by the time she and Papa married when they were twenty.

Papa told me that Mama had tried to make it as a singer, back in Kiev, but it never quite worked out. That maybe it was bad luck, maybe it was just a tough business, or maybe, as she suspected, she was just too Jewish for the job, that her big nose, while I thought it was the most striking thing about her, made her look too distinct, too un-Russian, so nobody wanted to hear her voice. "But then you were born, darling, and she went to school and became an ac-countant eventually, and that was that. Do not feel sorry—she loved you, you were the greatest joy of her life. But when she saw you trying your acting business, well, you can imagine, she did not want you to have your heart broken."

"Why didn't she just tell me that?"

"Because you and your mother are of a kind, darling. Too stub-born for your own good," Papa said.

The ball had dropped while we were talking and we didn't even notice. It was after midnight, and we both knew there would be a cold, long year ahead. I had so many questions for him, but I knew it was not the time to ask them, that there would never be a good time to ask. Maybe, even, I was better off not knowing the subtext of all my fights with Mama, who, with her stylish but conservative clothes, tamed hair, and sharp eyes, could not have seemed less like a former aspiring singer. Maybe because she had tried to seem as unartistic as possible to discourage me from trying to be anything but ordinary, to keep me from the onslaught of disappointment that would come when my big, bloated dreams fell flat.

"Too stubborn," Papa mumbled, his eyes growing heavy. "Too beautiful."

Yuri and I barely manage to make it out for our first real date night, which is, of course, at the Lair. He had some fancier ideas, but I turned him down, insisting that we didn't need to go to some dumb new sushi place in the Village we couldn't afford anyway; I just wanted to get out of the house, with him, and would have been happy going to Gray's fucking Papaya. When we walk in the door, dripping with early July sweat, the scent of the Devil's Lair takes me back to a time when I was exhausted but excited about the big, glowing world. I'd get off work at three, four in the morning, and walk five blocks home in Toms, holding my heels, feeling like I was doing something big, like I was part of something. And now here it is: the scent of old red wine and the greasy kitchen food, and then Mel, who hangs up his towel and walks over to our side of the bar and gives me a big hug—it's only the second time I've seen him since Tally was born—and then shakes Yuri's hand.

"Big Mama," he says. "How are you?"

"Tired."

"Well, you look good."

"Don't flatter me, Mel."

"I'm doing nothing of the kind, girl. I have four myself, so I know how it is," he says to Yuri. "Drinks?"

"Please," I say, and then we take a seat at the bar and shoot the shit as he pours a glass of wine for me and a beer for Yuri, but Mel knows to leave us alone. I spot two regulars: Scotty, a retired elementary school teacher and alcoholic, and Isabella, who works at Yard Sale, a bar a few blocks away, but refuses to drink in the place where she works on principle. I'd been at the Lair for the last four years, and it was by far the classiest of the bars where I had worked, a place with frayed red lamps and paintings of women in lingerie and fake candles and soft pop in the background, a place to take your mistress. I got the job when I moved in with Yuri to the rent-controlled apartment he'd lived in for a decade and I never looked back. Before that, I worked at Tequila Predator in Murray Hill, a post-college douche bro bar with a table for beer pong and even an N64 setup in the back to boot, and I hated it almost as much as the endless subway ride to Inwood. But that wasn't nearly as bad as No Satisfaction, a place true to its name in Astoria where I worked after I dropped out of NYU after one semester, where the manager didn't care that I didn't have my license but knew it would make it hard for me to leave and cupped my ass one too many times as a result. Compared to all that, the Lair was basically heaven. I was sad to quit when I got too pregnant to stand on my feet for that long.

"This is a nice place," I say, and Yuri laughs. "What?" I say. "I mean, it's nice, for a bar." When he keeps laughing, I say, "I'm sorry. We should have gone—"

"No, no, who needed to schlep downtown? I don't care, I just want to see you. I'm just laughing because you just said it like— like this was Versailles or something."

"Maybe it was, to me," I say, though I have never been to any country but America and Ukraine. I'm already feeling the first glass hitting me, hard, and I order another round and some food because it takes about an hour to get even a grilled cheese. When I

take a few sips of my second drink, the room is practically spinning, though that is likely from exhaustion and not the fact that I
haven't had more than one glass of wine in about a year.

"Man, I am so fucking tired."

"Me, too," Yuri says, cheersing me with his beer. "Though not,
of course, like you."

"No. Of course not."

He sighs, looking hurt. "Hey, ouch."

"Ouch yourself."

"I just feel like I still do thirty percent of the work and am
treated like I do zero." And it's true, he does do some shit around
the house, like cleaning the litter box, hauling all the diapers to the
trash, and so on, but it hardly registers.

"I think you do twenty percent of the work and I treat you like
you do ten."

"How about we agree I do about twenty-five percent and you
treat me like I do fifteen."

"Deal," I say, taking another gulp of my wine. "I can't believe I
actually thought this would be kind of like taking care of the cat. I
mean, I know I wouldn't just, like, brush her and feed her and
change the litter box once a day. I'm not an idiot, but I just thought
babies nap the whole time, and I don't know, I thought I'd just
get—a moment to breathe. And people are like, It gets better, it
gets better, but I feel like the longer she's here, the worse I feel,
because my gas tank is running more and more empty. . . ."

"About that," he says, taking a cautious sip of his beer.

"Oh no. I should have seen this. When I said I wanted a date
night, I thought you got excited because you wanted to see me, not
because you wanted to *have a talk*."

"Can't we have a date night that includes a talk?"

"A talk on the theme of . . ."

Yuri sighs. I don't think I've ever seen him drink more than two beers in a row, so he must also be feeling it. "Look," he says, "I don't think it's too late for you to go to school. I don't mean this fall, but maybe in the spring? You've always loved taking care of animals and, well, I'm not saying you should go to vet school, but you can get an associate's degree, you can work as an assistant to a vet or at a pet daycare—"

"Why can't I go to vet school?" I say, and he smiles, because he thinks this line of questioning, instead of *What the fuck are you talking about,* shows that I have some interest in his idiot plan.

"What?"

"You said, blah, blah, associate's degree, so why not vet school?"

He smiles. "Well, first you need a bachelor's degree to apply, and then, it's very competitive—"

"You don't think I'm smart enough."

"No, no, that came out wrong. It would just take, what, at least eight years before you made any money, and it's a lot of long nights studying—"

"You're not helping your case, Shulman."

"Then please help me take my foot out of my mouth. Okay, forget what I said about vet school, and just listen to me. I just think it would be good for you, for us, to have another plan that doesn't involve going back to the Lair. You love Sharik, you loved all those other pets, you even cat-sat to make some extra money in high school, no?"

"I love the Lair. What's wrong with the Lair? On Friday and Saturday nights, I'd walk out of here with a couple hundred bucks in my pocket. And I made that and more doing voiceover work. How much does it pay to—take the temperature of some cat up the ass? Probably a lot less than that."

"Definitely less, but it's a path to a more stable future. Do you want to work at the Lair when you're fifty?"

"I would fucking love nothing more than to work here right now, instead of changing diapers and getting my tits ravaged," I say, and my voice is so loud that Mel even raises a brow. "And I can always do voiceover work."

"When you can find it."

I close my eyes, willing myself not to cry. So fine, *The Americans* is over, and nobody else has been begging me to speak Russian in the background of their show for thirty bucks an hour, but I'll get another break eventually. I think of my poor mother again, singing in the fucking backyard during her last months on Earth. And then I think of Stas, who is back at home while Tally is sleeping. He would never tell me to clean cat shit for a job.

"I know you've given up on me having a career," I say. "But I haven't, all right? I'm just in a low period because of the pregnancy and the baby, but I'm not ancient yet."

"I didn't say I've given up. I believe in you. I'm not trying to be the bad guy here. But I'm just saying—think about it, all right? If not this year, maybe the next, when things are more stable with Talia?"

"Sure," I say, hoping my eyes communicate how pissed I am, because I don't want to make a scene. "I'll think about it."

He gets up to go to the bathroom, knowing I need to be left alone for a minute, and I really do, I need to remember why I'm on this fucking date to begin with, remember why Yuri is the love of my life, instead of just someone who seems to want to bring me down, to turn me into some boring person I didn't sign up to be. How did this happen?

Yuri had been about as far from my life of acting and bartending as you could get, a physicist, a former student of my father's and his favorite companion. They went fishing together on Lake George during the summers, fucking *fishing*, a weird, boring-seeming activity I didn't criticize because it gave my depressed father a kind of peace, because he would come home after these trips looking a bit lovesick, so why make fun of him? Papa made courtship-related hints about Yuri, though he was aware he was not exactly my type; it was obvious Yuri had a crush on me, that anytime we made eye contact, he would blush and stutter and once, when Papa invited him to dinner and even made an elaborate lasagna to try to stimulate romantic feelings between us, Yuri clinked his wineglass so hard with mine that it shattered, shards scattering into the meal and dispelling any potential love feelings on my end, though I did feel plenty of pity. But on the afternoon of Papa's funeral reception, when I saw this actually quite handsome man in his ill-fitting suit approaching me with love and pity in his sweet eyes, it was like stepping into a warm lake after spending decades getting manhandled by tidal waves.

"I'm so sorry for your loss," he had said, extending a bouquet toward me. "Your father was an incredible man. I wouldn't have survived graduate school without him."

"I wouldn't have survived—well, anything, without him. Though I guess I have to now," I said, feeling awkward for some reason, though I never felt awkward around Yuri before, I always saw him as a cousin, someone I could go braless around. Maybe it was because he was dressed up, I don't know. Maybe because I was at the beginning of a life without my dear father. My poor bumbling father, whose hand I could still feel at the top of my head, sometimes.

"I can help you, you know. If you need someone to—take you back to your place at the end of this," he said.

I paused, impressed by his boldness. Finally, some life! Was he really hitting on me at this moment? But he tried to walk it back.

"Only to help with the flowers, of course," he said. "I don't mean to say that I was trying to, well—look, I know what you think of me, of course I'm not attempting anything, what I mean is, you have a lot of flowers here and I know you don't drive and I'm sure you've had a very long day. . . ."

"Don't be so sure," I said, "you know what I think of you. I myself may not be so sure."

He looked stricken for a hot second, but then he smiled and said he'd find me later. It had been a year or two since I saw him. Now he was a real professor at a community college in the Bronx. He just got a tenure-track job, which was impressive, according to my dad, who never got tenure, in the end, and maybe this made old Yuri more self-assured. Hours later, he did drive me home, all those flowers in the backseat of his little Buick, which was not fancy but clean and respectable. And he stayed for a while, we even drank some wine. I knew he was a proper man, that he would not come on to me after my father's funeral, so I had to do all the fucking work. So when we drained the bottle, actually a very nice bottle I had been given by the unfunny comedian as an attempt to patch things up after I complained he never spent any money on me, I forced myself on him, kiss-wise, and he gave in to it, and it was a nice, chaste but not unpleasant kiss—if his Buick could kiss, that's what it would have felt like.

He said good night after that like a proper boy, but he asked if he could take me out when I was ready. I remembered something Papa said about Yuri dating a nice Jewish girl, though I might have imagined it, but when I asked if he was seeing someone he said he was not. I called him a week later, and he continued to surprise me with his wit and sexual competence and sweetness throughout the impressively long—for me—one-year courtship that led me to move in with him, the longest I had ever dated anyone before moving in. A year after that, we were married, and then three years later, which was the longest I could stave Yuri off, I got pregnant with Talia at thirty-six. So after all the fighting with Mama and the drummers and musicians and older men I would torture her with in high school and the binge drinking and everything else, I was married to a respectable university professor and had a daughter on the way, living the life she would have wanted for me, and it was too bad she wasn't there to say *I told you so.*

But now, sitting at the bar of the Lair as my cranky husband returns to me, I feel like I'm the one who should say *I told you so* to Mama, that I knew what I wanted all along, and it was not this, not at all.

Does Yuri even fucking remember who I was when he met me? I was hot, I wore heels, I was a regular on CBS prime time and drank like a fish. Who was the person he fell in love with, if not her? I can't get started with all that, so I open my phone and scroll through Instagram, looking at all the likes and comments on my post about my audition—and it's kind of nice, having dozens of people I don't care about cheering me on while my husband basically told me I was washed up.

I check my more recent post—baby Tally smiling up at me from her crib, where I wrote *We smile now! #HeartfullAF #tanksoempty #ActressMama #nailedit #shesnotacting,* which I can't help but notice got three times as many likes as my post about my audition. People don't really give a shit about the almost two decades of blood and bullshit I've given to make it as far as I have, but as soon as I got knocked up and pushed a kid out, everyone acted like I solved global warming.

Still, I think as I look at my audition post again, I would have been better off staying at home tonight, preparing for yet another audition in a few days, another bullshit part as an Uber-driver-slash-spy with five lines on a less-prestigious-but-still-not-bad TV show, instead of sitting here hating my clueless husband. I keep glaring back at the kitchen, though I know the score there. Frankie's the only cook, and though he's damn good, he's always high and takes his time. My stomach feels like an enormous empty balloon that's gonna pop if I don't eat something ASAP.

"There you go, talking to your real friends," Yuri says, shaking his head at my phone. He is of course above it all and does not use social media, not even Facebook.

"Maybe I am," I say, kicking him under the bar.

Finally, Mel comes over with the cheese balls, wings, and nachos, but I have lost my appetite. Yuri and I have drained our glasses but we're too defeated to ask for more.

"Smile," I tell Yuri, taking a picture of him looking miserable over the food. It's a terrible photo, but I post it anyway: *#Datenight!*

"Please don't post that."

"Too late."

He reaches over for a cheese ball, and those things are way too hot, you have to wait at least five minutes before touching one, but I don't warn him.

"Jesus," he says, spitting the thing out. "I think I just burned my tongue off."

"My grandmother nearly starved to death, but she never really complained. She even had to eat a cat, once. Did I tell you she had to eat a cat?"

"Now you're just being mean."

"So what if I am?"

We wait for the too-hot food to cool in near silence, mostly out of principle, because this is our fucking big night out and I'm not going to go home and sulk and eat Trader Joe's chana masala, not tonight. When we try to settle, Mel just gives me a wink and says, "On the house."

"See?" I say to Yuri. "Nice place."

"How was the audition?" says Stas.

"It was shit," I say, tossing my bags by the door of my shit apartment. Shit, shit, shit. Everything is shit, and has especially been shit for the past three days since my botched date night. Except my baby girl, who evidence says is sleeping in her crib in the next room—yet again not needing to fall asleep in my arms to drift off. Though I'm relieved I don't have to immediately go into mom mode when I walk in, it would also be nice to see her little gremlin face for a moment, to be reminded that there is still some good in the world, even if that good is slowly making me go insane. Alas, she's not up to remind me that I shouldn't care that I definitely did not book the Uber-driver-slash-spy role, which would have given me twenty seconds on prime time, ten of which I would have spent saying, "Please, I am innocent! Give me another chance!" and the rest sliding down a flight of stairs with two bullet holes in my head.

I say, "They basically flat-out said I was, like, too American for the part. Which is bullshit because my Russian accent was perfect."

"They really said that?"

"Basically." He raises a brow and I continue. "They just kind of gave me this *look*. I know what it meant."

"You sound a bit paranoid if you ask me."

"I didn't ask you."

"No, you just asked me to watch your baby," he says, but he's not done. "If it's so stupid, then why do you keep doing it?"

"What do you mean, why? This is my life. I need to get back into the game. What else am I supposed to do, stay home?"

"Aren't there some other options?"

"Such as?"

He looks at me blankly like this is obvious. "You said it yourself—you might as well put on your grandmother's story as a play. . . ."

"I was joking before. I'm not going to make a damn play of Baba's story. How the fuck could I even pull it off?"

"Why make it so complicated? Can't you just do it all yourself?"

I laugh at how stupid he is. "Sure I can. I'll just do a one-woman show and will get the stage ready and write the fucking thing and promote it all by myself. That's a great idea. I have all the time in the world to do something like that. Why don't I ask you for advice more often?"

He laughs. "Maybe you should. I think it would make you happy."

"I don't want to be *happy*, you moron. I want to be successful. Putting on this play isn't going to get me noticed again."

"Ah," he says, looking so smug I want to smack him. I move closer to do just that, but I second-guess myself. Maybe I'm better off not touching him at all.

"It must be nice, to be so above it all. And how many poems have you published, Mayakovsky?"

"Hey, hey," he says, lifting up his hands. "I'm on your side, remember? I think it's amazing that you put yourself out there, Sterling, really, I give you props. I don't think I could ever do it."

"Then why write?"

"Have you heard of this whole 'art for art's sake' thing?"

"But who came up with that anyway? Some famous person?"

He laughs. "Probably."

"I can barely function as it is. And what, I spend the summer trying to make this thing work—I find a stage, I promote the event,

I write the fucking thing—and then, if I even do convince her to come, she'll see the wreck I've made of her life during her last trip to America? Then I can say I've actually done something meaningful as an actress, even if nobody gives a fuck?" I realize I'm tearing up. I need to sit down. I need to breathe for about a year. And yet, I feel excited for the first fucking time. Whenever I close my eyes these days, instead of thinking about my next audition, I see my grandmother as a teenager before my eyes. Those cold, far-off mountains. Her sweet, tired, father. Her sister and her beloved cat. Her shifting affections for my grandfather and his brother. "It would be completely ridiculous," I say, but I see the slow smile spreading on his face and I know that he knows me for some reason, and now that he's got me sinking my teeth into this idea, he won't let it go.

He smiles and goes back to his book. "Sounds pretty doable to me."

"Fuck off."

We have a standoff. I don't know why he's so up my ass about this, or why he cares. But he's standing pretty fucking close to me so I move away and get kind of nervous, so of course I ramble on and on.

"The last time I wrote a play was like, ten years ago, when I wrote *Diddler on the Roof*, a play about a Hassidic child molester. Some of the Babies thought it was in poor taste, but it was hilarious! It nearly broke the group up, but the committed people put on quite a show. Then some Jews got all offended and spoke to the *Times* about how today's youth was ruined, calling me out by name! I was just so excited—never in a million years did I think I would be in the *Times*. And guess what? I got a better agent after that."

"You're a credit to your race."

"I thought so anyway," I say, tapping my foot.

I think I hear my daughter, but it's just the stairs. Then I hear the key grumbling in the lock. Yuri walks in, in a wrinkled shirt, looking tired but happy. I give him a hug and rub a bit of marker off his cheek.

"How was the audition?" he says.

"It was shit," I say again.

"I'm sure it wasn't."

"But it doesn't matter because she's going to put on a play about her grandmother's life," Stas says, and I kick his foot. I didn't expect him to blurt it out like this, not when I don't even know what I really think about the whole thing. Yuri gives me this kind of blank look and I think, why not test him out?

"A one-woman show at that," I say. "What do you think?"

He laughs and kisses me on the forehead and only after he drops his bag does he realize I'm not kidding. Or, rather, the alarmed look on his face, as if I had said something truly crazy like that I was thinking of going to medical school or that I was pregnant again, or thinking of scaling our building makes me see that maybe I am not kidding after all. And Stas, twenty-eight-year-old, pony-tailed Stas, is more on my side than my husband is. He's the one who gets me right now.

"And when would you get that done, exactly?" Yuri asks.

"When do I get anything done? When the baby is napping," I say, all defensive all of a sudden when moments ago I didn't even take Stas's idea seriously.

"Are you serious?"

"Serious as a heart attack," Stas says.

"Shut up," I tell him.

He lifts his hands like, *Don't shoot,* as if he's so innocent.

Yuri looks from me to him and back to me again. "Interesting," he says.

"Listen, I'm going to go," says Stas. "Sorry, man," he says, looking at Yuri, not me, like I'm the one who's fucked everything up instead of him. He tells us he's off to see about a server job in Harlem, the first I've heard of it. As he puts on his shoes and then the coat he doesn't need, I think, *No, no, don't go.* But what good could come of him staying? What's he going to do, take me in his arms and declare that I should be able to put on this play if I fucking want to? Tell me I'm beautiful and talented and make sure Yuri knows it? He leaves and it's quiet, quiet. I pick up poor neglected Sharik and stroke his hair, and then I look up at Yuri.

"Are you really serious about this?" he says.

"Let's say I am," I tell him. "I haven't really done anything for myself since Tally was born. Or even since I got pregnant, really," I say.

"Look, I know you think I have all this time to do my own thing, but when I'm not here, I'm in teaching hell, trying to get students who don't care about science at all not to drop out of my class or leave me RateMyProfessor reviews saying that I'm 'boring and dense,' and sucking up to my bosses so I can get tenure and a decent chance at a normal salary. I'm not just trying to screw you over here."

"I didn't say that. I know it's not all fun and games when you leave the house. But I would actually like leaving for a few hours every day to do some work. And auditions don't count," I say.

"That's because you actually like your work."

"Some of it."

"I wish I got to do some of the things I liked more."

"Like what?"

He's quiet for a minute. "Like," he says, "I haven't gone fishing in a million years."

"Fishing?" I say. "Fishing? You haven't fished since my dad died."

"I haven't really wanted to."

"You do realize it's not the same thing?" I say.

"Yes, I know fishing is not my passion. I don't know where I'm going with this, I'm so fucking tired, Natasha."

"Me too."

"You know I love you," he says. "I'm not the bad guy."

"You've said that a number of times."

"Which makes it true, obviously."

"Is that how that works?"

"Mm-hm."

He gives me a long, tender kiss, but after a moment we both stop to crack up because we can hear Sharik behind us, sucking his little cat-dick, which doesn't sound all that different from Tally sucking her pacifier.

"Sharik! Foo!" I say, swatting him and pulling him out of his seated position until he meows and walks into the kitchen, defeated. "Bad boy," I say, though I know it's pointless.

Yuri laughs again. "I think he's on to something."

"Is that so?" I say, and this time, when I kiss him, it becomes very apparent very quickly that we were going to fuck for the second or third time since my baby girl came into the world, that soon, there would be something much more welcome between my legs.

"Come here, you," Yuri says, reaching for my dirty shirt.

"Always."

"This," he says, "is our real date night."

He takes off my shirt and unsnaps my stupid nursing bra, and I'm anxious about having my new mom tits out like that, but he doesn't seem to mind. I unbutton his workshirt and pretty soon his pants are off, too, and we're down to our underwear and I feel almost, almost shy. I take off my bra and try to ignore how heavy my tits are, and run a hand across his chest while he strokes my hair.

It feels exciting, unfamiliar, to fuck again, since we didn't exactly fuck all the time when I was pregnant, except during these crazy bursts of horniness I would get. But now, feeling him inside me, reliable and warm and not so different from before, I remember the early days when we couldn't stop fucking, and am also relieved to confirm that apparently I'm not a complete cave down there. When we're done, I rest on him for a while and even briefly drift off and I wake up to him stroking my hair. I check my phone to see my *#Datenight* post from a few days ago had racked up a shit ton of likes, too, more than the one about my second audition, but I can't say I'm surprised.

"I miss you," Yuri says, and I kiss him.

"I miss you too," I say. "I'm sorry I've been so out of it."

"What are you sorry for? I'm sorry for you. You should do whatever you want to do, Natashka," he says.

"I'm just—I'm not ready to give up yet. My mom wanted to sing when she was young, but then she just became an accountant. I don't want to die wishing I had really given it everything I had."

He stops stroking my hair and turns to me. "Why didn't you tell me that before?"

"I don't know," I say. I don't even know why I'm telling him now. I hate talking about my mom. "It was kind of a family secret, I guess."

"Well, we're family," he says, and then he gives me another kiss. He can tell I don't have anything else to say on the subject and I love him for it.

"I just don't want to clean up hairballs for a living," I say, and this cracks him up.

"I didn't say you had to, darling. I was just making a suggestion. Haplessly."

"Okay," I say. "All right."

I even consider going for round two, which would be ambitious after a bunch of nothing, months of it, but then Talia stirs, and for once, I don't mind going into the room to pick her up in my arms and guide her to my breast.

It's crazy, how much she looks like Yuri. Stephanie told me it goes back to the cavemen, that babies are born looking like their dads as proof of paternity, so they keep going out into the bush to kill meat for the family instead of abandoning ship. Well, there's no doubt here—the square jaw, the horizontal brows and big blue eyes and protruding ears, it was like she came straight from him, like I had nothing at all to do with the reproductive process. I, however, look like my mother, but not as pretty, though she seemed determined to hide her beauty. When Talia was born, I kept straining to find myself in her face, coming up empty.

My daughter's blue eyes are getting bigger every day, or maybe her big ears are just getting smaller, whatever it is, she's starting to look just a bit more human, and I'm even pretty sure two tiny tufts of hair are getting ready to sprout on the back of her head. After I nurse her, she doesn't settle right away, and I don't mind that either. I take her into the living room, and onto the balcony, and though the streetlights shine down on her almost-bald little head, she does get back to where she needs to be, her sweet little eyes closing as she lets go completely, and for about one delicious minute of my life, I feel like I know exactly what I'm doing.

I lower a sleeping Tally into her crib and climb into bed next to Yuri, but I can't turn my mind off. I stay up all night sweating and shivering, those damn postpartum hormones raging through my body as I remember how good it felt to fuck my husband, but then it gets all mixed up with Stas, who returns to the apartment at some point, with spending all that time with him arguing about art and how he stood up for me doing my play while Yuri thought it was a waste of time. And then I think more about my grandmother's damn story, of how she obviously had a thing for my uncle Bogdan over my grandfather, but she was with my grandpa because he was a good guy, because he liked books and didn't rebel against his family. Was that what I did—sign up to spend the rest of my life with a guy who thought all I was good for was walking dogs just to avoid throwing wine bottles against the wall once in a while?

Who could say my grandmother did the right thing? When I was a kid, I didn't understand who the random men were who came to the sea with us; I thought they were cousins, and only when I was maybe eleven did Baba tell me that it was best I didn't mention uncle this or that to my grandfather, when I understood what was happening when she told me to "explore the beach" on my own one evening. Though the men visited less often as she got older, the last one I remember was the summer after Mama died, when Baba had the nerve to invite one of them over even though it was supposed to be the summer of grieving and Papa was sleeping in the next room. That was the only time I addressed it, waiting up for her at the kitchen table like my mother had done for me: "Do you have to right now?" I had asked, trying to look strong, to keep my face free of Mama-related tears. She gave me a long, resigned shrug and said, "People die, the heart wanders, life goes on," and marched toward her room, filling the cottage with her snores almost instantly while I stayed up, furious with her and missing Mama hard.

The sun is already peeking through the window, and Tally starts whimpering, which means it's six and time to start my day, though I'm pretty sure I haven't slept a wink. As I nurse her, I'm thinking pointless thoughts like how long did Mama even nurse me for, why don't I even know this most basic thing, would Baba know, why did it matter how long she stuck it out for when she's nearly twenty years dead? And I can't help but wonder: how would Mama take it, me putting on this play? Would she tell me to start shoveling cat shit instead, or would Mama—the late, final-days singing version of Mama, not the cold, college-application-focused Mama I remember from most of my days—be proud of me for trucking on?

Then again, Mama was always opposed to my pursuits of anything vaguely artistic, or even literary, and wasn't particularly thrilled when Baba gave me a stack of books every year on my birthday and set a date for when I would discuss each one, from the plays of Chekhov to Tsvetaeva. Mama found this to be a distraction from my studies, not understanding that they would be neglected anyway. She would see me reading Baba's books and would raise a brow, saying, "For hours you'll read Chekhov, but you can't be bothered to study for your biology exam. . . ." "Chekhov was a doctor," I told her once, which actually got her to laugh and even stick out her tongue at me, throwing her hands up at the situation, one of the rare times anything I said to her was met with approval.

After Tally's done nursing I do my mom things, trying not to wake up Stas, I down a banana and take my girl out for a stroll, my head in a fog the whole time. Tally is sleepy and full and smiling at me, so utterly content from something as simple as milk from my boobs. When we get back, Stas is having his breakfast cigarette on the balcony, preparing to listen in on my Baba call. I put Tally down in her crib while Yuri still sleeps like the dead, and curl up for a bit next to him before it's time for Baba, though I need to brush my hair, at least. But there's no time, my Skype is dinging already, so I just run a hand through my hair and sit at my little desk and answer, ready to spend some time away from my own shit.

Baba looks put-together as usual, her hair in a long braid and pearls on, and she squints at me, like she has smelled something foul beyond the cigarette smoke around her.

"What's the matter now?" she asks.

"Nothing," I tell her. "I couldn't sleep last night."

"Who can?" she says, and this manages to make me smile.

I'm already emotional as fuck and seeing my grandmother at that kitchen table makes me want to weep, especially because she's leaving Kiev for good tomorrow, and the furniture will be gone for good too. That wobbly little table is the only plain piece of furniture in her apartment, where I would sit with her and Dedya whenever I visited, eating our kasha and eggs, though there was a big dining room with a glass table around the corner my grandfather liked more. My grandmother insisted the little table was more cozy, and I didn't mind, I liked it, how we all knocked elbows as Baba pushed more sweets on us, all that morning light flooding our faces. "More sweets for my sweet," my grandfather would say, while I would wrinkle my nose and tell him, "It's too early." Would it have killed me to eat a jam-filled pastry or two instead of being a surly, weight-obsessed teenager? It would have made my grandfather so happy, though I guess it doesn't matter now. "Never too early for dessert," my grandmother would always say.

"Are you ready for your big move?" I ask her.

"As much as one can be, I suppose."

"You won't miss the apartment?"

"There is always something to miss about a place," she says, and I know she means the kitchen in particular.

Tally's crying again, and I take her out of the room where Yuri is blissfully sleeping; he wouldn't bat an eye through Armageddon, that bastard. I sick her on my boob and stroke her cheek as I watch Baba watching us. Stas is on his phone on the balcony, but I won't wait for him.

"A good little thing," Baba says, gesturing at my girl.

"You could see her in person," I try again. "You can see what a good girl she is. You can see me and Yuri too. That would be nice, wouldn't it?" I know it's pointless, but you can't keep me from trying. And if I really do put on this play, then she really has to come.

She smiles slowly. "It would be something unbelievable," she says, but she's not really listening.

Then her face relaxes, her eyes softening as she looks away from the screen, out her kitchen window, easing into remembering.

PART III

HAPPY WIFE

Larissa

Uncle Pasha arrived about a month after Licky's death to embark on his journey to find food in a neighboring village with Papa. Two years had passed since I saw him, and he was, of course, greatly diminished. I'd always thought of him as a diminished version of my father, but now he was objectively smaller, like a boy playing dress-up in a man's clothes, his broken nose even more severe because the rest of his face had sunken in so much. Papa clung to him for a long time when he and I greeted him at the station, and as they spun and hugged, for a brief moment, they were restored.

My uncle arrived to our apartment in a buoyant mood, and all of us were cheered in his presence. Even Polina deigned to leave the bed where she had been moping ever since Licky died to join us. My uncle could see the dire state my sister was in. "My darling princesses are more radiant than ever," he tried, gesturing at us both, but my sister barely mustered a smile.

Polya hardly spoke to any of us except my grandmother since the Licky incident. While the rest of us fattened up on her cat's meat, she spent most of her time curled up in bed, vomiting air, moaning, clutching her stomach, and pulling at her hair and sweating as if the spirit of her cat were still contained within her body and she was desperate to exorcise every last bit of the creature. Occasionally, she would step out on the balcony, as if she spotted her resurrected cat wandering out of the woods once more, eager for another trot around town with her. But since her cat would not come back from the dead, my sister did her best to avoid the living.

Uncle Pasha got her to eat her dinner, at least, and she seemed genuinely amused when he jumped up and down like a child, demonstrating a performance he and my father had put on when they were kids in the orphanage. But Mama was not amused by his antics, for once. She was quiet that evening, pulling out strands of her already-thinning hair. She was worried about their trip.

"We had the whole dance perfected," Uncle Pasha said, jumping around and clicking his heels, oblivious to my mother's fragile state. "We could have taken it on the road."

"You should have," Polya said, giggling as he danced like a nincompoop, shocking all of us with her laughter.

"The reward was seeing the joy on the children's faces. There was no price on that," Papa said, and then he laughed sadly. I understood it: he had a better time in the orphanage than he did here, because there, he was able to help the other children by cheering them up. Or at least to feel like he had done something for them. Now he hardly felt equipped to help his own family.

They continued to laugh for a long time while the rest of us watched and even tried to join in, though the thing between them, their brotherhood and their memories of orphan times, was impossible to penetrate. And this act of theirs was perhaps their way of gearing up for the journey ahead.

As they spoke of the war, Uncle Pasha was on edge. This was because though his city of Kharkov had been recaptured by the Red Army, the Germans, though depleted, were knocking at his city's door yet again. My grandmother tried comforting him about his adopted city, putting a hand on his knee, but he just shook her off. He didn't address her directly until the very end of the night, as the adults were preparing for bed. "Exhausted, Mother?" he said with a cruel smirk, and she told him that indeed she was.

That night, I couldn't sleep. I tried reading Tsvetaeva by candlelight, but it did me no good, reading about another woman's obsession with the abyss and sleeplessness. I snuck into Mama and Papa's room, where Mama and Uncle Pasha were sound asleep, while Papa was missing from his bed. I went to the balcony and spotted him outside, standing under his favorite linden tree, staring out at the dark woods. I threw on Mama's coat and stepped out. I didn't realize it was still so cold in the middle of the night, this far into the spring.

My father looked small from a distance, not like anybody's husband or father. His breath clouded around him and for a moment I thought he was smoking, though Papa did not smoke. He did not look like he wanted to be disturbed, but I could not help myself.

"Larissa," he said. "You should be in bed."

"I'm having trouble sleeping."

"Your father is also having some trouble, I'm afraid."

He put an arm around me and kept staring into the woods like there was something in there I couldn't see. Papa had aged considerably since we arrived in the mountains. He looked at least ten years older than he did on the day when we arrived and he compared our new home to his orphanage. He looked almost like a grandfather, the gray roaming in his still-thick hair and the skin sagging under his eyes and neck.

"Papa?"

"Yes, darling," he said, his voice heavy.

"Are you all right?"

"Of course," he said, but then he lowered his head in his hands.

"Lara, dear," he said. "When I look back on my life, do you know what makes me the most proud?"

Papa's eyes made me think I was not expected to answer. What, that he rose out of the nothing of the orphanage to become second in command to the most powerful engineer in Ukraine? That he did not let his mother defeat him? That he married a strong woman like Mama?

"It is not my work on the T-34, I will tell you that," he said. He patted the top of my head. "You," he said. "You and Polina. Of course your mother is my world, but I am most proud of the girls we have raised. Everything else is just wind through the trees," he said, repeating his favorite expression.

"What if I'm happy on my own, like Uncle Pasha?" I asked, this time unafraid to challenge his declarations about family life. My dear uncle, who was peacefully sleeping inside while my father fretted, always seemed lighter on his feet than Papa.

Papa stopped in his tracks. His eyes brimmed with terrible longing. "Your uncle is missing the greatest joy of life, dear Larachka. One day, you will have a family of your own, it's no question," he said. "And you must be true to them. And when it comes down to it, you must forget everybody else. Life isn't long enough, the heart isn't large enough, to contain love for all of humanity, even if that makes you a bad Communist," he added with a lowered voice. He nodded toward the apartment. "Your sister is struggling," he said. "She needs you. You may not see it, but she does."

"Why can't you and Mama take care of her? She hates me," I said, crossing my arms, but he already looked so defeated on the eve of his journey that I didn't want to complicate matters. I wanted to take him by the hand and lead him back to the stove, where I could nestle against his chest like I did when I was a little girl, drifting off to the sound of his calm, even breath.

"She loves you deeply, Larissa. She's your sister. It's plain as day. Just do your best to be kind to her, little dove. Do you promise?"

"I promise," I said, though I didn't mean it, not truly. I squeezed his hand and added, "You're doing all you can for our family, Papa. And so much more."

But this brought him no comfort. He just shook me away and lifted his head back up, in the direction of the forest. I wondered if he, too, wanted to run away like the partisans, but begging him to stay would do no good, I knew. I kissed him on the cheek and gazed into those woods one last time, as if I could see whatever it was out there that haunted him so much, but there was nothing, just dark pines under the moonlight, clouded by Papa's white breath.

I fell into a cold panic after the third day passed without Papa and Uncle Pasha's return. I was certain they were not coming back, that they had contracted a fatal illness or got killed by Nazis or hit by bombs or had met their fates in some other tragic manner. Misha and I were revisiting *Onegin* during that period—by then we had memorized most of it—and while imagining a frivolous life of country soirees and petticoats had helped me through the dark winter months, it felt like an absurd indulgence after Papa had left. After a night of distracted reading, Misha put a hand on my wrist and said, "We don't have to do this right now." I thanked him and got up, and when he tried to follow me, I told him I'd like to be alone. I kept seeing Papa at the edge of those woods, wondering if there was anything I could have said to dissuade him from making the journey, to keep him at home, with us, where he was needed.

After Papa had been gone for five days, I went out in the middle of the night, after Baba Tonya and Polina had finished another round of nonsense. I stood under the linden tree and stared at the dark sky. I did not believe in God, of course. Nobody in my family or in the apartment believed in God or anything ludicrous like that, but I could not help but wonder where people go when they are no longer on Earth. It seemed cruel and unusual for us to turn to dust and corpses, to be reduced to memory and anecdote, and I longed for something more. I wondered if my father and Uncle Pasha were somewhere up with the moon and the stars, not with gods, but just, I don't know, floating around.

"What are you thinking?"

Bogdan materialized beside me. I wasn't really surprised to see him. He was coming back from one of his late-night exploits. I tried not to get close to him, to avoid the scent of another woman's sweat or perfume.

I sighed. "I can't take any more of this waiting."

"I can't imagine," he said. He moved closer to me, but I did not smell the smelly ladies of his trysts. He grabbed my hand and said, "If you need anything, I am always here."

"How so?" I said. I could not take his kindness. "What, you think I am one of your middle-aged ladies? I don't have any eggs for you."

He was quiet for a beat. I had never acknowledged his ladies before, though I assumed he knew I knew by then. He said, "I am only doing what I need to do to help the family. You think I enjoy myself out there?"

"I don't want to think about what you do out there."

"Well, it's not exactly something I look forward to," he said, shaking his head. Then his face broke into a playful smile. "Just very occasionally. There is one number—" he began, and I punched his chest. He had so much vigor I did not expect him to be so bony. He saw I was in no mood for jokes and continued on. "If we make it out of here alive, I'm getting the hell out of Kiev."

I didn't really believe him, but I indulged him anyway. "Where will you go?"

"Far from the Soviet Union. Somewhere more—civilized. This

place is shit. Do you even know what's going on back home? Half of Leningrad has starved, and most of the Jews have been wiped out by our own people. Even the children, they don't spare anyone."

I looked out at the empty field ahead, searching for my father's figure. Of course, in theory, I felt very sorry for the people who were even hungrier than we were in Leningrad, though it was hard to picture them. And I was sorry for the Jews too, especially my downstairs neighbors, if what he said was true, but the fact remained that my stomach was groaning and my father was missing.

But he went on. "But things are taking a turn for the better. I wouldn't be surprised if we took Kiev back any day now," he said, and this was so shocking to me that I could not even fathom it. I didn't bother asking how he knew all this; I didn't want to hear him mysteriously whisper "my sources," with an added wink. I didn't want to give him the satisfaction of thinking he knew more than I did about anything.

Bogdan put an arm around me and I shook him off. Polina was the one he preferred and touched, not me.

"You don't have to be nice to me," I said. "Why don't you go comfort my sister instead?"

"Has it ever occurred to you that I'm not just being nice to you? That I might even prefer you over your sister?" he said. I was startled by his rising voice. He was finally angry. I was horrified and thrilled that I had managed to produce this effect.

"Why would you do that, now?"

He shrugged. "It's just a feeling."

I looked away, my eyes smarting, missing my father, still convinced Bogdan was only saying these things to cheer me up. What gave him the nerve to declare this now? I thought once more of how different he was from his courteous, conscientious brother, who would never overstep his bounds or bring on this emotional assault during such a turbulent time, who was waiting for the perfect conditions to declare his love.

I said, "Your timing is lacking."

"I say what I feel when I feel it."

"So you didn't feel it earlier?"

"Of course I did. But you didn't notice because you were occupied with your reading companion."

"I don't need your pity," I said.

He sighed and put his head in his hands. "For heaven's sake, Larissa, I read all of *Karamazov* to impress you. What more could a man do?"

I laughed, feeling truly flattered, not understanding that this had been his motive. But I quickly righted myself.

"I don't feel—close to you like that," I said slowly.

"Are you certain?" he said.

I felt ridiculous. Of course I had always preferred his brother to him—so why did I feel so short of breath, right then?

"I'm not certain of anything right now," I said.

He gave me a triumphant smile, but I stepped away from him, signaling that our conversation was over. We turned away from the woods, toward the path through the apartment buildings to the center of town, the path Papa and Uncle Pasha had taken to get to the village, and one from which I knew they would not emerge. I knew that none of us would emerge from this place unbroken. And that I would never open myself up to a person like Bogdan. It was too risky. I waved him off and sank against the base of the linden tree.

"Go on, now," I told him. "I've had enough. Please go to sleep."

I stayed up every night, staring into the woods from my tiny window, as if I could summon what? Papa and Uncle Pasha riding out of the dark abyss? Licky resurrected, crawling back to me like nothing had happened, lapping the dirt off my hands? My former meaty body, the heft in my haunches I had once hated? The curve of my sister's buttocks? A hearty summer meal? Misha and I plowed through *Quiet Flows the Don* but I could hardly read a word; all those fighting, violent Cossacks and the poor women, who were either raped or beaten or both, did not suit my mood or level of concentration. I tried to picture my former kind teacher, Marina Igorevna, patiently sitting beside me as I read to help me focus, but I could not summon her.

I tried not to think of Bogdan's ill-timed declaration. Surely he just felt sorry for me. He continued to favor Polina and I kept reading with his brother like nothing happened. School was the only suitable distraction. At that point, only a handful of students remained, and I began helping Yana Nikolaevna in the classroom, delivering lessons when she was too weak to stand. "Spring can be just as brutal as winter!" my teacher would cry during these spells, though she did not explain how. Nights were harder. My sister started climbing out of bed in the late hours. When I followed her, I found that she would go to Mama's balcony, to stare into the woods during the brisk nights, awaiting our Papa in her own way.

About two weeks after Papa and Uncle Pasha had left, a figure appeared on the horizon one morning. I spotted him first because I left the building early, to help my teacher clean the schoolhouse. For a few precious moments in the pink near-darkness I hoped and believed I was looking at my father. But as the figure continued his approach, there was no mistaking my father for his brother, whose frame was slighter, and whose careful gait could only mean one thing. His crooked-nosed face and clothes were dark, covered in soot, as if he were already preparing to mourn. He saw me approaching, nodded, and took his cap off his head and held it to his chest, and I howled and sank to the ground.

Mama came running out next, trailed by Polya and the Orlovs, all four of them still thick with slumber, because it was a Sunday and they did not have to report to work. By the time Baba Tonya lumbered out in her nightgown, so disoriented she did not remember to cover her ruby necklace with her boa, Uncle Pasha was convulsing before us, as if he were caught in a windstorm.

"Papa," Polya kept saying. "What happened to Papa?"

I wanted to smack the girl. Did I have to explain this to her too? I thought the death of Licky had hardened her, but here she was, innocent all over again. Her eyes were wilder than ever, though they had retreated deep into the caverns of her face. Even Baba Tonya understood what Uncle Pasha's solitary arrival meant, and she grabbed Polya and pulled her into her dirty skirts, and my sister was the first of the group to sob. She whispered that she was her princess, her angel, all the useless epithets, but they fell on deaf ears.

Misha put an arm around me, and Bogdan kept looking at me, waiting for a reaction. But I turned to Mama for inspiration. Mama was a statue, and I tried to mimic her.

"Out with it, already," Mama told Uncle Pasha.

"I am so sorry," said Uncle Pasha. "So profoundly sorry."

"Come inside," Mama said. "I will make tea."

He nodded and followed us in like a sleepwalker, and Aunt Tamara even took over making tea and let Mama sit down. We sat around Uncle Pasha and he began to speak once he clutched the warm cup in his hands, which had stopped shaking quite so much.

He told us what happened. They spent a day just getting to the village because they had to stop so often to rest their tired horses. At last, they arrived in the village, but something was off. An eerie quiet hung in the air, followed by a massive noise in the distance that made them fall to their knees. Finally, an old woman emerged from her hut and told them they were crazy, they needed to run away. She said some of the villagers had caught the plague and the Soviet soldiers were going to burn down the place. "You're still healthy," she said. "You get out while you can, find a way to escape!" They tried to turn away, but at that point the flamethrowers had the village surrounded, and they would burn down with the sick ones if they did not find another way out. They dropped their horses and followed a path on the outskirts of the village until they found a cave.

"It was filled with young, healthy boys," Uncle Pasha told us. "Their parents had caught the sickness but told them to run off before they caught it too. We had no choice. We had to stay with them and hope they were not infected." The boys were hardly teenagers, he said, and did not know how to fend for themselves. There was one young boy named Slavik who reminded my father of a friend from the orphanage, a helpless, scrawny child for whom he quickly developed an inordinate fondness. As the village went up in flames, they searched for mushrooms in the woods and even cooked a few squirrels, waiting for the soldiers on their side of the village to beg off. "Finally, we found an opening. It was the dead of night. The tank that had blocked our path had disappeared. Slowly, we crept away, holding hands in a chain. Fedya was in the back, making sure everyone got out. But then the shots were fired. The soldiers were shooting at us. The boys were screaming and shouting for mercy and running as fast as they could, but the young boy tripped and fell."

Mama put a hand to her mouth. "Oh, Fedya," she said.

"Fedya couldn't help himself," said my uncle. "He ran back for the boy, and they were both shot at once."

"Of course they were," Mama said, her head in her hands.

"You know Fedya. He could not let an innocent boy die," said Uncle Pasha.

I stared at my lap and wished I, too, were holding a cup of tea. I understood that I should not have heard this story, that Polya, my grandmother, Aunt Tamara, and everyone but Uncle Konstantin and my mother should have been removed from the scene. But we were too weary to sort this out. I couldn't believe it. My poor father, killed by his own people.

"He could not let the boy die," Uncle Pasha said again, crying into his hands, and I could see him as the small, weak child he once was, back at the orphanage with Papa, who did everything for him, no doubt, who tied his shoes and sliced his bread and tucked him in and helped him navigate the cruel, dark world. When my father and Uncle Pasha visited their mother's fancy home, my uncle tripped over the polished parquet and broke his nose. My dear father was too sturdy to slip in the same shined shoes. And yet—

"Fool!" Mama said again. "My darling fool," she said more quietly, and then she began to cry the only tears I would ever see her shed in her life. Misha put an arm around me, while Bogdan put an arm around Polya, where it belonged. I wanted to touch and comfort Mama, but I was too scared to move toward her. But I finally did. I hugged her and so did my sister, and as the three of us embraced I thought of the long-ago time Mama had given us the buttered bread in the middle of the night, when I thought she could solve everything. My grandmother stood at our periphery, clutching her necklace. My sister opened her arms to welcome her into our circle, and together, all of us wept. I didn't even care when her filthy boa fell over my face.

"I am exhausted," my grandmother said.

The days after my father's death were hideous and long. We dragged about our apartment without purpose, like bugs trapped in a jar. Even Uncle Konstantin was diminished by the news, and paced around on the balcony, though he was prone to dizziness. I was fairly certain I even saw him wiping his face, at one point. Aunt Yulia and Madame Renata came by with a sack of food a few days early. "You look awful, the lot of you, you need to eat," said Madame Renata, and we thanked her while I held my tongue and did not point out that we had looked awful for a while now and she didn't care until one of us died. Aunt Yulia even held out a handful of chocolate, but Polya and I said we didn't want it, agreeing on something at last. "Suit yourselves," she had said, pivoting away on her heel.

Since there was no body, we couldn't hold a proper funeral, but something needed to be done. I couldn't take much more of our collective anguish. I came up with the idea of burying the framed portrait of Mama and Papa under his favorite linden tree behind our building. Mama was in no state to make decisions, but she did not protest. In the photograph, where my parents held a ridiculously large pot of dumplings, laughing at some private joke, my father looked nothing like himself. He was young and smooth-skinned and full of hope, and so was my mother.

I did not want to bury the man in the photograph. I wanted to bury the tired man who spoke about the importance of family the last night I saw him alive under that tree, so a newer, more energetic Papa could be resurrected, though this plan was as likely to work as Aunt Tamara's failed scheme to grow potatoes from the sliced seeds. And so it was that all of us and Uncle Ivan and Snowball stood over the small pit where we had buried the portrait on a cool, breezy morning, the grass just starting to sprout from the earth. It was difficult to get started.

"A brilliant mind," Uncle Konstantin managed at last.

"A loyal friend," said Aunt Tamara.

"Commander," Misha said.

"Guide," Bogdan said.

"Dearest brother," said Uncle Pasha.

"Sweet husband," said Mama.

"Kind father," I said, speaking for me and Polya.

My sister wouldn't look at the Papa pit, or anything else besides her feet. She stood with one arm around Mama and the other on Snowball. She and my mother had been fused in their sorrow, while I was left out, standing with Misha's dutiful arm around me. During the days, my sister either cuddled with Mama or my grandmother or roughhoused with Bogdan and the stupid dog; at night, she wandered the balcony in the main room to stare at the dark pines, as if she could summon Papa that way. I sensed that she no longer looked for Licky out there, that at least she had forgiven us for that. But I had failed to take care of her as I promised Papa I would do. I tried hovering around her, even hugging her on one occasion, but she didn't seem interested. Besides, she had enough people caring for her already.

Since I had spoken for me and my sister, we all turned to Baba Tonya, waiting for her to complete our recitation by stating what kind of son Papa was. We hoped to hear just one kind word bestowed upon our patriarch, but what did Baba Tonya do? She watched a flock of birds flutter through the cloudless sky.

I couldn't believe her. Of course she was in shock, but her silence made me livid, for some reason, while Polya's did not. She was the elder, after all, batty or not, and it was her turn to dredge the corners of her mind for a scrap of kindness toward her first-born boy. But this was just the kind of thing she got away with because she was weak, like my sister. I would never be able to pull off such a thing. Aunt Tamara even put an arm around her in sympathy, as if it were a badge of honor that she was so troubled that she could not speak. No, the honor came in being maddeningly overwhelmed with sadness and standing upright and saying something in spite of it.

"Caring neighbor," said Ivan at last, just to fill the silence. "Comrade."

He put a hand on my shoulder when our ceremony ended. "Is the war over yet?" I asked him, and he just shook his head, unable to find a clever retort.

As we walked away, my grandmother began to speak at last. But she did not intend to be heard, no. She was muttering to my father. "Oh, Fedya," she said. "You used to have the rosiest cheeks! You were such a beautiful, healthy boy! Who would have thought I would outlive you?"

"What right do you have to speak to my father?" I said, but she barely seemed to hear me. I expected one of the adults to admonish me for causing a scene, but they did not, not even Mama. Misha stood at my side in solidarity but did not touch me.

"A healthy, beautiful boy," my grandmother muttered again, but I was not impressed.

"If he was so healthy and beautiful, then why did you let your husband send him away?" I said.

She laughed a frightening laugh. "Silly girl," she said, even putting a hand on my shoulder. "Going to that orphanage was the best thing that ever happened to your father."

I pulled away from her. She was talking utter nonsense, and there was no use in trying to reason with a madwoman. Perhaps I should have felt sorry for her, but how I hated her then! Spouting those lies when she couldn't even bother to speak at Papa's grave, when she was the one who sent him to the orphanage, a place where he became so selfless that he died over a stranger. Though I had not paid her much attention as of late, in that moment, I became utterly convinced that everything that had gone wrong in the mountains was my idiot grandmother's fault: Papa's death, our hunger, Licky's demise, Polya and Bogdan's long embrace, the dead villagers, Hitler invading Russia, and all the injustice in the wild, cruel world.

My grandmother's extreme eccentricity had tipped toward downright insanity by the time summer arrived. I reminded myself that my father had been her son, after all, no matter how poorly she had treated him. Even though she did not care for him much when he was alive, his death must have meant something to her, something I could not understand as daughter instead of mother. After I berated her about talking to my father directly, she turned to the other dead.

"Shura," she would tell her sister, "your hat is all wrong for the occasion, all wrong!" Or, "Husband Dimitrev, why so much red caviar and so little black, people will think we're slipping!" And to her first husband: "Arkady, I need my back rubbed, and soon!" Once, I even heard her talking to Emperor Nikolai. "You are a dignified leader," she had said. "Not without your flaws, of course, but so much more civilized than Comrade Lenin!" Sometimes, she would wander out in the middle of the night to Papa's linden tree to have these conversations, until my sister escorted her home. These were disturbing developments, yes, but with all of us barreling forward after Papa left us, who had time to notice?

The only time any of us truly paid attention to my grandmother was one morning when she woke up to find that her necklace was gone.

Her cries knocked me out of a dream about my father I could not quite grasp, and I woke up thoroughly perturbed.

"Where is it? Where is it?"

My grandmother stood upright beside her bed like a soldier. Sunlight was streaking in through the window of our tiny room. It was a Sunday, the only day when everyone was allowed to sleep in, when even Uncle Konstantin afforded himself a bit of rest. Or we all would have been allowed to sleep in, anyhow, if my grandmother did not fill the apartment with her hideous cries.

"Where is it?" she said again. "Who has it? Where did it go?"

It took me a moment to understand what she was raving about. At first, I thought she was referring to her boa, but the black thing was in a heap on the ground below her like a vanquished cobra. But she was pawing at her neck, which was bare: the necklace, the ruby necklace given to her by her mother, a supposed gift from the wife of Alexander III, was nowhere to be found. She ransacked our bedroom and then pounded on all our doors until everyone was reluctantly awake.

Aunt Tamara was first to respond. "Calm down, Antonina Nikolaevna," she muttered, still groggy, as we all convened in Mama's big room. "It must be here somewhere. If we all search, we shall find it in no time at all. . . ."

Misha and I dutifully searched the ground on our knees, while Polya and Bogdan combed through the furniture. Since Bogdan's declaration, he hardly looked at me, but I did not believe it was because he felt rejected. He probably forgot all about it and had moved on to my sister for good. Mama searched every cabinet and drawer. Aunt Tamara and Uncle Konstantin searched the other rooms, the bathroom, and the hallways, as if the necklace could have ended up there.

Once we had all given up on finding the necklace, we returned to the main apartment, where Polya settled next to my grandmother and stroked her back. My grandmother looked truly crazed. Her face was as pale as death and her temples were soaked with sweat.

"We'll find it," Polya said. "You probably just set it down and forgot where you put it. . . ."

"Impossible. Everyone here knows I never take the damn thing off."

"Maybe it slipped off, Antonina Nikolaevna. If it's not in the apartment, then the boys can search the perimeter," Aunt Tamara said.

I saw my grandmother's stony eyes settling on Aunt Tamara. It was a logical conclusion. Not only was she her sworn enemy, but she was also the most likely of us to long for such luxury.

"I know it was you," my grandmother said, grabbing Aunt Tamara by the collar. "Tell me, what will my necklace get you at the market? My life's inheritance for a handful of potatoes? Is that all I'm worth to you?" she said, shaking her with a mad fury.

"Please," said Uncle Konstantin, pulling the women apart. "Do not cause a scene."

"It's all right, Babushka," Polya said. "We don't steal from each other here."

"Of course we do. We do anything to survive. That is why . . ." Baba Tonya said, her lip trembling, "that is why we took your precious cat. This is no different."

It seemed quite different to me, but Polya burst into sobs regardless. Mama and Bogdan comforted her before I had a chance to consider doing it. Instead, I kept searching the floor in vain. It was a relief Papa was not here to see what had become of us all— this ugly cacophony. Then again, if he were still around, we might not have fallen apart.

"I know she took it! I know she took it! Shura told me in my dreams last night," said my grandmother, returning her boa to her neck. But Baba was probably bluffing: she never spoke of her dreams. It was considered bad luck to report them, because they might come true.

Baba shook Polya off and marched toward Mama. "But maybe it was you, eh? You never liked me, you little prig."

Mama stepped away from her and began to sweep, as if this would solve the problem. Though she was far from her industrious self, she had returned to work, and had enough strength to ignore my grandmother then. Thankfully, my grandmother did not linger on my mother for long and turned her vitriol to me.

"You don't like your grandmother much either, do you, Larissa?" she said, grabbing me by the collar. "Are you the one who slipped it off my neck, nimble one?"

Before I could protest, a wild laugh escaped Mama's lips, the first I had heard from her since Papa died. Everyone else stopped what they were doing and stared. Aunt Tamara dropped a bowl that did not break. Mama laughed again and again. The maniacal glee in her eyes chilled me to the bone.

"What use?" Mama cried. "Tell me, old woman, what use would any of us have for your dumb rubies now? They can't bring him back. They can't save us. Your necklace!" she said again, throwing back her head and cackling wildly.

"Please," said my grandmother, her voice heavy with desperation. "It is the oldest thing in my family—in our family. An heirloom. Not to mention its price. We all need it, don't you see?" Her eyes were wild as she looked for others to accuse, but Misha and his searching-the-ground father were the picture of innocence, and Bogdan seemed far too involved in caring for Polya to bother with stealing.

Baba had lost the energy for her campaign and did not accuse anyone after that. As she lowered herself to the ground, into Polya's arms, I felt a pang of pity for her. I knew she did not see her jewels as just another piece of finery. I understood it, her desire to maintain her connection to her long-gone mother—and perhaps, in some twisted way, she saw it as a way of maintaining the thread between her and my father, a genetic lifeline. She put a hand beneath her boa and continued her raving quietly. "It is irreplaceable. It is beyond value," she kept saying, until Mama gave her some valerian root and returned her to bed.

———

Baba Tonya had officially gone mad by the time we took our next trip to the market a few weeks later; and without school to keep me occupied, I wasn't faring much better. Mama, who was basically back on her feet by then, insisted we take her out with us. Though we were in the middle of a gorgeous, almost life-affirming summer, Baba hadn't left the apartment since her rubies were taken and spoke of little else. Polya was docile but functional. She continued wandering to the balcony in the middle of the night from time to time, and nobody stopped her.

My sister and I linked elbows with Baba, and the Orlov brothers dutifully walked two paces behind us, like bodyguards, though I did not know what we could possibly be protected from anymore. I kept a firm grip on my grandmother and looked out for obstacles. Aunt Yulia and Madame Renata had already wandered off with linked arms, having satisfied themselves that their product store was faring far better than the threadbare market, and good riddance.

We faced the usual bustle. Onion Man Oleg handed me an onion the size of my fist for nothing, and the rest of the vendors, mostly women, peddled their sad, green-hued potatoes, cloves of black-spotted garlic, and wilted lettuce, as if they were doling out rare gold. The empty train tracks stood stolidly behind us, a gash among the dirt and trees. My grandmother looked far off, a slow smile sliding on her face. "I suppose one dance won't kill me!" she said to an imagined suitor, tossing back her tangled hair. "But take it slow. Already I feel a bit dizzy. . . ." Then she sucked in her breath and took my hand. She had not held it a single time before.

No one else made note of this fantastic gesture. Bogdan and my sister were already searching for the least green of the potatoes, their heads leaning together like the beams of a steeple, while

Misha inspected the onions. When I looked up at my grandmother, the grimace that had settled over her face since she lost her necklace had been wiped away, replaced by a steely calm.

"Here it comes," said my grandmother, loosening her grip on my hand. "My train."

"What train?" I said, peering into the distance. "There's no train."

She smiled and nodded. "You just don't see it yet, little one. It's coming, I promise. Coming to take me away. I should have taken it long ago."

There was still no evidence of a train, but my grandmother was convinced. She moved closer to the tracks, until her toes were touching the platform, her black boa billowing about her like the feathers of a deranged raven.

"Larachka," she said sternly, "I need you to let go of my hand."

I could not explain it. Though holding her hand was giving me the chills, I could not bring myself to let it go. I took a step forward and joined her at the edge of the platform. Down below, not terribly far, a colony of ants swarmed over the body of a dead bird.

Baba was right. I felt the ground vibrating first, then looked out to see the train approaching in the distance, its bright lights piercing through the morning fog. I should have thrown my tiny body in front of my grandmother's, I should have pulled her away or asked for help, but I just stood there, not knowing what to do, feeling like I was watching something that had already happened play out.

Not all of the trains stopped to deposit passengers. In fact, it had been months since the latest shipment had been sent to the village. Uncle Konstantin's optimistic opinion was that this was yet another sign that the war was reaching its conclusion and we would not be dragging it out in the mountains all that much longer. His wife's more pessimistic view was that there were simply no more men to send. Whatever the reason may be, this train would not be slowing down.

My grandmother had finally wrestled her hand out of mine and lifted her boa arms in the air, a bird ready to take flight. The burst of air from the oncoming train made her stole flap in the wind. In one swift motion, it got caught in the gears of the train and pulled Baba underneath it and a deadly rumble rang through the market as the train plowed on. I should have screamed, I should have jumped down into the tracks once the train took off, but I could not move, my feet were rooted in the ground while I heard the commotion, the rush of footsteps storming the tracks.

"What happened?"

"My God, where did she go?"

"How did it happen? Did she jump?"

"Who is it?"

"It's her, it's her—the old woman with the boa!"

The villagers were peering down to where my crushed grandmother was collapsed in a bloody heap of feathers and gristle. Before I could jump down there, Misha draped an arm around me and folded me into his chest, as his brother had once done on the train. I pretended to hide into his chest like a good girl should do, while I peeked and saw the state my fallen grandmother was in. The wild gashes along her middle, the bloody patches of hair sticking to her forehead, while her face was nearly untouched except for a gash along her lip. Her eyes were wide open, staring at the heavens. Having gotten her bloody peace at last.

"What happened, Larissa?" Misha said quietly.

"She just—got caught up," I said. "Her boa . . ."

He nodded and asked no further questions.

A shrill cry told me that Polya had stopped flirting with Bogdan and had noticed the commotion. She screamed and started clawing toward Baba, while Bogdan ran toward the edge of the tracks with her and took her hand. But he did not shield her as Misha had shielded me; perhaps he was beyond shielding anyone, having learned that it did no good. He let her stare down into the bloody gristle while I continued to look out while Misha thought my eyes were closed, having wrapped both arms around me like the gentleman that he was. Misha tried to pull me away, to get me to go home, but I released myself from his arms and moved toward my sister, though I knew I could offer her no comfort. She met my gaze with soft eyes.

"All of that over a necklace," she said, and I flinched at the steeliness of her voice.

Her whole body was shaking, but her jaw was firm, and something was happening inside her then, as she held Bogdan's hand and then hopped down and fell over my grandmother's body. Bogdan locked eyes with me only for a second before returning to my sister, putting an arm around her as she wept silently. I shook Misha off and continued to stand at the edge of the platform. Misha gave up on trying to shield me, and he, Onion Man Oleg, and one of the potato vendors jumped down and dragged Baba's body out and up onto the platform, or rather, they dredged up a bloody and mangled mess that must have been my grandmother's body, black feathers flying up in its wake. I looked at her up close, the white exposed meat of her neck and belly, and did not look at her again. I stood alone, hugging myself.

What happened next? Ivan ran up and fashioned a gurney from a blanket and a vegetable-stand base with the onion man and radish brothers and I followed the procession as Baba was carried back to the apartment and left outside our door. She was immediately buried in the local cemetery, and only Polya and Aunt Tamara lost their composure that day. I nearly lost mine, too, but it wasn't from the horror I witnessed so much as the fact that, somewhere between the market and home, Polya and Bogdan had become completely intertwined.

That night, Bogdan entered our room and climbed into my sister's bed, taking over Licky's role. I was victim to their sweet murmurs and the sounds of their limbs settling into sleep and knew there was no chance I could rest under these circumstances. This just proved that Bogdan did not mean all that business about preferring me over my sister. I pictured him standing at the edge of the tracks with Polya, not shielding her from the darkness. I wondered what the look he gave me then meant—was he thinking of what I was thinking of now, the long-ago evening when he held me on the train, protecting me from some nasty truth? And if so, was he finding that it was easier to win over my weakling sister by letting her stare at her dead grandmother, to show her he knew she could handle it, after all?

I was not naïve: I knew it was likely Bogdan was not thinking of me at all, that he had been hardened by the war and was more interested in reality than comfort. I knew I needed to get out of there, that it was untoward to stay below them. Mama had a big, empty apartment all to herself now, and I could have joined her, but I stayed in my closet room out of stubbornness. Night after night, after my reading sessions with Misha, the only bright spot in my days besides the news that Kharkov and Kiev had been taken back by the Red Army, I would return to my post below the non-lovers, just to unsettle them. But as the days wore on, I heard fewer sweet murmurs, and more of Bogdan's criticism of our dear government.

"Stalin is a madman and a narcissist," he'd whisper. "He's no more a man of the people than a chimp; his cronies are as fat as cows before the slaughter, while we're starving to death. Once the war is over, I want to get out of here—to go somewhere enlightened." My sister would mostly just murmur, but she never disagreed with him. "That sounds nice, darling," she would say. "Quite nice." Part of me wondered if he was babbling on for my benefit, to provoke me to defend our fathers, to remember the T-34, the importance of winning the war, of being on the side of Stalin and not some foreigner's.

As far as I could see, only kissing and Stalinist critique went on above me; lovemaking wasn't in the picture yet. My sister, who was once entertained by my grandmother's talk of balls, now heard Bogdan talk about the peasants, the Famine of the '30s, which was caused by our government, the purges, anti-Semitism, party corruption, and seemed even more engrossed in what he had to say, and who knew why; perhaps it was because he let her see the state my grandmother was in, because he felt she could handle anything and wasn't as weak as she appeared, perhaps confirming this on the nights when he would get back to the room late because of his wanderings and my sister didn't seem to care, understanding it was for the good of us all. He continued to sleep above me with my sister for months, swiftly claiming my grandmother's role as Polya's nighttime companion and entertainer as summer caved into fall and eventually yet another winter, and that was how we slept until one fine morning, when Uncle Konstantin burst through the door to tell us that though the war was not quite over, it was time to go home.

I pressed my head against the window of the train car, wondering what going home would mean. It was the beginning of January 1944, thus far a hopeless, freezing year. The workers of the Institute packed up their things, leaving the factory in the hands of the local workers once more. Kiev was safe, but the war raged on. Who knew what condition the city would be in by then, or if our apartment was even standing? I wasn't thrilled about returning home with Mama and Polya. Mama was functional but never showed weakness; sometimes, I'd catch her gazing out the balcony with longing and expect her to mention Papa, but she would just turn to me and say something like, "The dishes need a bit more scrubbing." Polina was also a near stranger to me. At night, I heard the wet smacks of her and Bogdan's kisses, so they had progressed from friends to lovebirds. Not only did I feel a million miles away from Mama and Polya, but the thought of entering our communalka without Papa would only widen the hole in my heart.

It was hard to believe this was the same train that had carried us to the mountains over two years earlier, when I was just a girl. The train brought back more innocent memories, of trepidation but also the sense that nothing could be too terrible because Papa was beside me. Now Misha was holding my hand in his warm, comforting one, bringing some solace. Evening was turning into night and everyone was settling in to rest. But I was not yet tired. I was content watching the barren fields roll by, their patches of snow catching the moonlight.

Our car was emptier now, courtesy of the dead as well as Aunt Yulia, who had taken a different car home. What was I to make of this wreck of a coterie? I had always believed, perhaps from Tolstoy, that the strong survive, that character means something, while weakness is what gets you thrown under a train. And perhaps that was true in my grandmother's case, but then why did Uncle Pasha survive over my dear papa? Why did a wench like Aunt Yulia survive while her sweet husband and daughter perished long ago? No, no. Life was random and cruel, and none of us would get out alive. We were all its playthings.

Misha understood me. He knew I wanted quiet. I did not want to read or discuss what had passed or even quietly mock our siblings. I could feel him studying my face, as if to divine the contents of my mind. Or, perhaps, to find the right moment to speak to me. He cleared his throat but said nothing, though the sound did make me turn to him. He tucked a folded piece of paper into my hand. I unfolded it slowly, slowly, so the sound of the rustling paper did not wake anyone up. It was a poem of Tsvetaeva's we had read together. He had copied it on a thick piece of parchment, in fine ink. I wondered how he had the means to do such a thing.

A kiss on the forehead—erases misery.
I kiss your forehead.

A kiss on the eyes—lifts sleeplessness.
I kiss your eyes.

A kiss on the lips—is a drink of water.
I kiss your lips.

A kiss on the forehead—erases memory.

It was meant to be a sweet gesture, but the poem unsettled me. Why write so much about kissing instead of doing it? Though it was hard to build up much romantic momentum after everything we had been through, of course. And why end on the bit about erasing memory? What is it that the speaker wanted to so badly forget? All of us could stand to forget a thing or two, but surely this was not what Misha had hoped to communicate. I didn't have a chance to ask before he opened his mouth.

"You and I make a suitable match, Larissa Fyodorovna," he said. "You are my equal in spirit and mind. You are a serious, studious woman with a sense of proportion. Once order returns, I have a promising future ahead of me at the Institute and hope to take over one day. You have a promising future ahead of you as well, and I would be honored to have you by my side. Together, we can achieve greatness."

Though I watched his lips as he spoke, he hardly looked at me. He delivered this speech with a wavering voice I had never heard before, staring straight ahead. His hands were shaking, but I was certain it was from nervousness, not hunger. We were passing an icy lake, one of the few bodies of water along our route.

"I would like you to be my wife," he said, and then I laughed, because it was clear this was what he was after, and then I kissed him. I knew the poor boy had been planning to kiss me at last, and he seemed so scared that I wanted to take some of the pressure off him. His kiss was warm and comforting—it was like holding his hand, only better. I had never been kissed before but I could tell he wasn't exactly Vronsky—it wasn't the world's most romantic display of affection, but it was hardly the time for romance. And besides, if Vronsky was to be a signpost, then I knew where too much romance would get you.

"I would like that very much," I said.

He smiled and kissed me once more and squeezed my hand. He seemed utterly exhausted by the effort and soon settled into sleep.

But I had been wrong about one thing. Not everyone in the car had been asleep that night. Not long after Misha climbed into his bed, Bogdan turned around from where he had been resting with Polina in his arms and gave me a wicked wink. What did it mean? He had heard the entire clunky proposal and wanted me to know that he knew? That scoundrel. But what was I supposed to do with this knowledge? I shook my head at him and closed my eyes and pretended to drift off until I was certain he had turned back to my sister.

Misha was eager to announce the happy news the next morning, insisting it was the good and proper thing to do. I told him we should wait until we were all settled back in Kiev, but he believed the news would bring some necessary joy to our otherwise bleak lives. I didn't see the point in fighting him; everyone would know eventually, wouldn't they? I didn't mention that his brother already knew, which likely meant that Polya did also. After everyone finished their tea and black bread, he stood, cleared his throat, and clasped my hand in his.

"We're getting married," he told everyone. "Once the war is over, of course."

"It's true," I added.

It took everyone a moment to collect themselves, proving that I had been right, that it was not the time for such information. My face flushed as I saw the self-satisfied grin spread on Polya's face as she confirmed her belief that I was under Misha's spell; she thought he was spineless ever since he failed to defend us when we stole the chocolate and nothing he did could change her opinion of him. Bogdan stood completely still, for once, like the information did not reach his ears, this time around. He didn't look at me or his brother, though I continued to stare at him, hoping for a smile, another wink, any kind of acknowledgment of the news being made public, until the first of the adults reacted.

"A joy," Mama said, clasping her hands together.

"A wonderful union," said Aunt Tamara.

"Many happy returns," said Uncle Konstantin.

"Welcome news," Polya muttered, as if she were forced under torture to say something.

"A useful alliance," said Bogdan, so very pleased with himself.

No one else seemed to care that it sounded like he was talking about Hitler and Mussolini instead of two teenagers in love, like he was going to jump into more governmental critique then and there. Everyone took turns hugging us, but Polya barely touched me when hers came, it was like hugging air. Bogdan hugged me tightly,

far too tightly, just to make a mockery of the entire thing. He released me at last, giving me a nod to make it clear he did not take
my engagement seriously. But again, no one else seemed to notice
anything awry. Perhaps I was just imagining things, I told myself,
and tried to focus on the promising developments in my threadbare life. Not only had I become a woman, but I would soon be a
wife.

I was restless the night before our train was to arrive in Kiev. While
everyone else slept, I looked out the window near the empty bed in
our car, not knowing what I was looking for. The farms slowly
ceded to villages and hints that a city was looming on the horizon.
Though I had been longing for Kiev since we left, I was terrified to
return, though comforted by the fact that I would be doing so as
Misha's lifelong companion.

"It is hard to believe we're only hours from the city."

I did not jump at the sound of Bogdan's voice. I had been waiting for him all along, though I did not know it until that moment.
He had been the one I was searching for as I observed the dark
night.

"As if our years in the mountains were a bad dream," I said.

"A nightmare," he added, "with some bright moments."

I searched his face. He was gaunt but had grown nonetheless.
His hair was long and greasy and I wanted to push it out of his
eyes, to make him look more civilized. What did he want from me?
Certainly he was not planning to congratulate me on my engagement.

I had the urge to ask him something, though I wasn't sure what.
Had he really meant it when he said he preferred me over my sister? Did he still feel that way, even if his actions suggested otherwise? Was he jealous of my "useful alliance," or was he just being

ornery? What were his designs on my sister? Would he continue his nightly escapades in Kiev, or were they truly a means to an end? What would the future hold for us all?

I gazed at the landscape again, a row of houses facing the station, a tractor gleaming in the distance, as if it could tell me what to say to him.

"That night when we were leaving Kiev on this very train—what were you shielding me from?"

His face fell. Clearly he had been expecting a question of a different nature, perhaps a romantic one, not for me to remind him of whatever darkness he had seen long ago. I must admit that I, too, was a bit shocked by my line of questioning.

"A pile of corpses," he said.

"A pile of corpses?" I repeated, too loudly though no one stirred, and even surprised myself by laughing. "Is that all?"

He swallowed and took a step away from me. "It was something at the time."

Then he seemed to reconsider. He grabbed my face with both hands, and planted a big, mean kiss on my lips. He even jammed his tongue in my mouth, which was the first time I had ever tasted a stranger's tongue. I let it linger for a moment out of curiosity before pushing him away. The kiss did not exactly repulse me, but it angered me. The fact that he had gone from discussing a pile of corpses to kissing me showed that he was compelled by aggression, not affection. Additionally, he knew I was marrying his brother and didn't honor our union. And he was entangled with my sister—disrespect all around. I pushed him away and kicked his ankle.

"What fire," he said, putting a hand to his cheek and shaking his head, as if I were some coquette, as if the whole thing had not been his idea.

"What gall," I said, but he just turned away and climbed back in bed with my sister.

He left me standing there, facing the window, confused and not knowing whether to laugh or cry at the prospect of my second kiss trailing my first by only a day. After a while, I was fairly certain I had hallucinated the kiss, that Bogdan couldn't have possibly kissed me then, just like he couldn't have possibly declared his feelings for me when my father had gone missing.

But this was all nonsense, to be put behind me at once. I pledged not to think of his sneaky, dirty kiss just as I told myself never to think of poor Licky once he was converted into stew. I also pledged not to think about my poor father, or even my wicked grandmother. And so I pressed my face up against the glass thinking about all the things I promised myself never to think about again until I saw Kiev looming in the distance and realized it was morning.

What else is there to say? Mama, Polya, and I returned to our communalka, which was largely intact except that some Germans had lived there and left with the Dimitrev cabinets and Stella and Ella, having taken them for brides. Aunt Mila's husband went the way of Papa, and the Kostelbaums from below fared much worse. Even our groundskeeper, Maxim, who had once told my sister she could be a film star, had been purged. The empty rooms in my family's apartment were quickly filled with other families who returned from the war whose homes had been blighted, and Aunt Mila resumed fighting with them over her territory as she had done in a previous life, which lifted her spirits. But thankfully, I did not have to spend long in the apartment, which would never feel like home again.

Over a year after our return, Hitler was defeated, Misha and I were married, and I shed the Volkov name for good, becoming an Orlov and severing my tie to my dear father. Courtesy of Uncle Konstantin, Misha and I moved into a commodious single-family apartment on the Khreschatyk. Though it lacked a parquet or chandeliers, it was a palace compared to my old apartment, and I never felt quite comfortable in it. I visited Mama and Polya several times a week, where things were quiet but companionable, as they drank tea on the balcony and listened to the radio and brushed each other's hair without any need for conversation. Though once, I walked into the house to hear my sister singing one of my grandmother's ditties to Mama, the two of them laughing; I would have been less shocked if I had found my grandmother herself sitting on the pink divan.

Though I was relieved my mother had fallen back into her work and housework routine, my sister was more unknowable to me than ever, looking even more alien when she decided to chop off her pretty red hair not long after I married Misha, as if she hung on to it as a favor to me to avoid ruining our wedding photos with images of her short, boyish bob. When I first walked into the apartment to find my sister looking like a deflated asylum escapee, I backed up against the wall and took a deep breath before I offered my compliments.

My sister was still weak, prone to bouts of dizziness, and could hardly make it through her schooldays: the famed three Annas were just fine, it turned out, healthy-looking, even, but Polina showed little interest in reconnecting with them, and they stopped coming around. She was as lean as a birch tree, while I generally began to resemble a woman again and even had my monthly visitor return to me after a while, that reminder of my body's purpose—I had not the slightest inkling over whether my sister ever menstruated at all.

When Polya wasn't with our mother, she was either volunteering at a center for stray dogs run out of some abandoned schoolhouse or attending revolutionary meetings with Bogdan. It seemed that all of his late-night whispering after my grandmother's death had its desired effect, and she was fully consumed by his impulsive ideals. If he had whispered that they should be trapeze artists and join the circus back then, then she would have been practicing her routine instead of criticizing the government by now. Her prewar indifference toward me had moved into slight hostility as she believed I was becoming frivolous, just because occasionally Misha would take me to the theater, a man whom she refused to truly acknowledge or respect, seeing him as the boy who stood by and did nothing when we were chastised over chocolate in the mountains, way back when. Other times, I wondered if it had nothing to do with Misha or my new lifestyle, and if she had seen me kissing Bogdan on the train, but I doubted it, and reminded myself that we were just falling back into our old ways. We were never friends, and it was as much my fault as hers.

But who needed Polina or Bogdan? I had my dear, sweet Misha. No matter how long the days were, we would read in bed at night, in a far more comfortable environment than the alcove of our mountain days. Our first year back in Kiev, we blew through *Oblomov* and *War and Peace* and *Crime and Punishment,* and I loved him more than ever, wondering at how, just four years earlier, I fantasized about him in my tiny home and now had him all to myself in a big, warm bed. But a few months after we were married, he put a stop to our nightly ritual. After a long day at the Institute and a quiet dinner, he asked if we could listen to the radio instead.

"I thought you loved reading as much as I did," I said. He kissed me and said, "I liked it, of course. But I am so worn out with work that I need to unwind in the evenings, not stir myself up with literature. Besides," he added with a twinkle in his eye, "reading was what got me close to you, and now I have you." I could not tell him it was not a matter of having or not having but of renewing that having day after day, and so there he went, severing the thread that tied us together. I tried to be sympathetic to the immense pressure he felt at the Institute, knowing he would one day follow in his father's golden footsteps—if listening to the radio at night helped him relax, then so be it. He was still prone to the bouts of melancholy that would leave him staring at the ceiling while I read in bed, as if the answers to the world's ills could be found there. I did not offer any choice passages to him as comfort; I did not conjure Akhmatova's own suffering and cry, "It drags on forever—this heavy, amber day!/How unsufferable is grief, how futile the wait!" because I knew it was best to leave him alone. At first, I used the folded parchment with the Tsvetaeva poem he had used to win me over as a bookmark, until one day, it disappeared, and I did not go searching for it.

I did, however, go searching for my pretty former teacher, Marina Igorevna. After Misha's betrayal, I was desperate to see her. I found her in the same classroom where she had taught me after school, and she gave me a bewildered glance when I knocked on her door, taking a moment to place me, which stung. "Of course," she had said eventually. "My little reader." I told her I was a literature student now, that reading all those books out in the mountains had kept me from going mad. She said she, too, had evacuated with her family, and from the look in her eyes, I had the sense she had lost someone or everyone. She looked out the window and then back at me, and patted my hand. "I'm happy you're still reading. Keep your chin up now, dear Lyudmila," she said, and I thanked her and walked out, understanding she would not be my reading partner either.

I stopped brooding over Misha's betrayal eventually—I had more pressing concerns. I was expecting. Soon I would have a little child on my hands with whom I could read for hours every night, filling the void my husband created. But almost eight months into my pregnancy, I had an unwelcome distraction from my enormous belly. When the Orlov family and mine sat down to dinner for

Uncle Konstantin's sixtieth birthday, Bogdan stood under an enormous chandelier and said he had an announcement. We all assumed it was that he and Polya were getting married, but instead, he said that their papers finally went through and they were moving to Rome the following week. I felt like I had been kicked in the stomach. "It'll be an adventure," said my sister, flashing a big, dumb smile. I had to restrain myself from bursting into tears or slapping my sister—I was already a puddle of hormones—for being such a thoughtless, selfish girl. I didn't care a lick if she or Bogdan stuck around, but what about our poor mother?

Rome! A place of such unimaginable romance that I could not picture it at all. It belonged to the list of lush, Western cities that my grandmother might have fled to during the Revolution, so remote from the snowy Kiev landscape that they might as well have been moving to Jamaica. Bogdan said he knew some people there, which meant he had revolutionary buddies, of course. His parents acted as if a demon had possessed their son, but Mama just wiped her face with a napkin and said, "Whatever makes you happy, dears." I should not have been as surprised as I was. Bogdan was the one who stood under the moonlight with me and Licky when he revealed the cat's fate to me and said, "We all want to roam." And he did whisper to my sister that he wanted to leave the country, but I believed it was just fantasy; the son of the director of the Industrial Engineering Institute could not stray far from home. But what did I know? Uncle Konstantin moved toward the gold-railed balcony. "I don't know you," he muttered, without turning around to face his son.

A week later, I was at the station to see my sister and Bogdan off with the rest of the family. The Orlovs stood with Mama, who had convinced them to come in spite of their anger at Bogdan, as well as Aunt Mila, Mama's favorite non-Polina companion; the parents had already hugged the defectors goodbye and took two steps back, ceding the stage to me and Misha, though I didn't have the faintest idea of what I was expected to say. I tried to ignore Mama's stony face, the face of someone who had lost her husband and now her daughter, and told myself I should end things on a good note. Who knew when Polina and I would see each other again?

My sister was pale and dead-eyed, with her short limp hair wilting below her ears, though its fiery color could not be denied. She looked like a bedraggled, slightly unstable boy. I recalled the old Polina with two braids in her hair, hugging the three Annas goodbye in our courtyard the night before we left for the mountains, looking absolutely lovely as she wept for them, a porcelain doll in mourning. When her friends parted, she sank to her knees to emphasize her struggle, in case any stray men were watching. I never denied her beauty, though she drove me mad with her vanity, but now I wondered if she could have used just a bit of it.

I cupped her pale face in my hands. "You are still beautiful," I told her. "Just—take care of your hair a bit more. . . ."

"Beautiful?" she said with a cruel little laugh. "You think I still care about any of that?" She gave me a steely gaze, studying the new shoes and sturdy wool coat Misha had procured for me; I was eight months pregnant, for heaven's sake, not some elegant starlet, but it was true, my clothing did look nice in comparison to my sister's worn coat and scuffed boots.

"You can care a little bit about appearances," I told her. "It won't kill you."

"Is that right, Larissa? Our grandmother cared about appearances, didn't she? And look where it got her."

Her point was valid, but why did she have to bring it up now? Our grandmother, who threw herself under a train just like the one that had stopped before us over a dumb necklace. My sister peered at it like she could see through it, like she was the newly hardened girl standing at the edge of the tracks looking down on our mangled grandmother. And if she were still with us, then who knew, perhaps Polina would have remained frivolous and avoided getting caught up with Bogdan's antics. Her eyes bore into me and I took a step back, not wanting to end our last meeting for a long time on this sour note. I looked back at the parents, who thankfully didn't seem to hear us over the bustle. Bogdan and Misha, who did hear, did nothing.

"You're breaking Mama's heart," I said.

"Soon enough she'll have the baby to play with. She'll be fine," she said.

I moved toward her, feeling choked up, all because of the baby, no doubt. "You know it won't be the same," I said, and I felt her softening momentarily too.

"Look," she said, "I need to go. Ever since the war—well, I just need to get out of this city. I'm not the same person I was when we left here. Everywhere I go, I see Papa and Baba Tonya. I need a fresh start. You can understand that, can't you?"

I looked back at the parents. Of course I understood. I couldn't blame her for wanting to get out—leaving the shadow of Papa and Baba's deaths and our tumultuous country. I wondered what Papa would have made of my sister, who strangely had come to hate frills just as much as he had; the difference was that he believed that the state had done its best to serve him, while Polina saw the state as hypocritical, noting that not all people were surviving on the bare minimum. But Polya didn't want to think of him anymore.

I would be the one to stay in Kiev, haunted by Papa and Baba's ghosts. I wasn't allowed to leave, and never would be. It had been our duty to leave for the mountains to help our country, even if it almost killed us. And now we needed to stay put for our country's sake.

"It's our duty to stay," I said solemnly, and she sighed, thinking

I was just another mindless organ of the state, no doubt, but I had run out of ideas.

She cupped my face in turn. "You are more beautiful than ever," she said, but this did not sound like a compliment. "Look out for my letters," she added.

She leaned in to give me a stiff hug, taking a far wider berth than necessary, as if the thought of brushing against my enormous belly disgusted her. Well, that was that. I knew she judged me for the life I led now, but it was not something I had strived for, the nice coat and bureaucrat husband: it was just what happened to me. But there was no point in trying to tell her this. She had already made up her mind about me. Bogdan, meanwhile, treated me with his usual smugness, never failing to make me feel thoroughly uncomfortable.

He finished saying goodbye to his brother and patted me on the back. "Take care of yourself," he said. It was hard to believe there was a time when he and I spoke nearly every day. I hardly knew him. And I tried to hardly think about him.

They got on the train and did not look back, and I turned toward the parents and my wet-eyed husband; he and his brother were like ice and fire, but he would miss the rascal. I was in a fog for the rest of the day. I tried not to think of the last time I was on a train, during our return to Kiev, when Bogdan kissed me. What if I had truly returned the kiss? Was he just trying to torture me after he heard about my nuptials, or was he giving me one last chance to be his? If I had acted differently, would I be the one running off to Rome, starting anew? These pointless thoughts vibrated through me for the rest of the day and into the night, when I felt my first contractions.

I gave birth to my son almost a month early, likely as a result of the stress of my sister and Bogdan's exit. After my Tolik was born, a tiny, fragile creature who never grew full size, to my mind, I was utterly consumed by caring for him and had no time to care about things like my husband giving up literature or my sister leaving the country or even Bogdan's self-satisfied smile when he announced their departure.

I read to the helpless being in my arms, my boy who happily suckled my breasts; I was delighted to find that, unlike many women of my generation who had suffered during the war, I had no shortage of milk and didn't have to send my husband to the milkman twice a day. Misha would stand over me during this sacred process, as awed as if he were standing before the dawn breaking over a dark sky. So what if we had stopped our nightly reading sessions, or if I was utterly exhausted with my boy, but too stubborn to follow my husband's suggestion of taking on a nanny? We had a good life, overall. Not the most exciting life, but we had decent clothes for ourselves and the child, a dacha outside the city and seaside vacations to boot, access to foreign goods.

Did I think of Bogdan from time to time? When I drank tea, I thought of him pressing those cups to his eyes under the train to make little Yaroslava laugh. When I saw boys shuffling in the streets, I thought of the rascal I knew before the war. And when I saw that my husband was a tool of the state while I had my doubts about the way the country was run, I remembered Bogdan and his critiques of Stalin, and thought he was safer abroad. But did I think of him—that way? I can't say. Sometimes. I'm not certain.

Polya and Bogdan were never married, and all I learned of them came from Bogdan's occasional letters addressed to Misha and me—so much for looking out for Polya's letters! He claimed the happy couple had found more opportunities in Rome than Kiev could provide, that they were thriving in a romantic land filled with pasta and olives and sunlight, but Misha read between the lines. It seemed Bogdan worked for the black market, likely peddling goods, while my sister involved herself in another stinky animal shelter. There was no mention of children, which I thought a bit strange, but then again, my sister and Bogdan fancied themselves iconoclastic bohemians, and perhaps they would hold off on that venture. As the years went on, though, I wondered if my sister had been so ravaged by the war that she was unable to bear children, though I chastised myself when I spent too much time fretting about my careless sister, who only sent me "health and kisses" at the end of Bogdan's letters.

Mama acted as if she were fine without Polya, but I knew she missed her inconsequential banter about her dogs, as if they were the boys who used to walk her to school. My Tolik seemed to help a little bit. The first time she held him, she mentioned my father, for once. "Other fathers were so scared, thinking they would drop their new babies," she had said. "But not yours. He was never afraid of holding you." She still lived in the big room all by herself. The only person she socialized with was Aunt Mila for the occasional tea. She was the one who told me Mama had passed away just after my son's third birthday. "The apartment has been vacated," she told me, and then she asked after several pieces of furniture, and I said she could have all of them, even the divan. I sent news of her death to Polina, but Bogdan wrote back with his condolences, saying they were too tied up to return for the funeral. Only then did I understand that they were gone for good. If Mama's death would not bring Polina back, then nothing would.

Though I should not have taken their stubbornness too personally: when Bogdan's parents passed away when my son was seven—Uncle Konstantin, who I was amazed lasted as long as he did after the war, of a heart attack, his wife of grief a few months later—Bogdan and Polina did not return to Kiev for that either. But my hands were too full to brood over them: the Orlovs had passed on their lavish six-bedroom apartment to us, and Misha and

I set about moving into the cavernous, porcelain-filled place that made me feel ill at ease. It reminded me of my grandmother's luxurious apartment outside Postal Square, which was only a five-minute jaunt from our new home, a place I went out of my way to avoid when I walked home from work. Recalling my grandmother's apartment and its pointless excess, my first act as woman of the house was to fire the maids and the cooks, conceding that my husband could keep his driver. Did he like the life of luxury, my husband? I believe he could have done without it, but he needed to keep up appearances as the new head of the Institute.

When my boy was in his eighth year, a letter from Bogdan arrived. It was addressed to me instead of his brother, and only for a moment did my heart flutter before I understood bad news was coming. *Polina has passed away after a battle with cancer. She was in agony and is better off now. I plan to return to the Motherland—to nurse my broken heart in Kiev. If possible, I would love to stay with my favorite brother and sister.* I took the letter to the gilded balcony outside our dining room, which offered a stunning view of the Dnieper in the distance, and turned it over in my hands. I told myself that my sister had been effectively dead since she chose to leave the country the month before my son was born, so this should not have changed anything for me. And yet—

Tolik played with his train set at my feet, taking in the fresh air. I recalled the day when Polina and I ran down the halls of what was then the vast Orlov apartment, wondering what could possibly be done in so many rooms. After my sister rolled around on the Orlov bed, she and I ran to the balcony I stood on now, and my sister did a dance, the ruffles on her dress bouncing up and down as she cried, "I am queen! I am queen of the city!" I got caught up in her hysteria, though I was at least ten, too old for such antics, and we danced until we got winded, and then my sister sat down. "Look at this

thing," she had said, spreading her arms wide to indicate the balcony. "It's the size of a small country."

I was on edge when Misha left to pick up his brother at the station two weeks later. Nearly a decade had passed since I saw Bogdan, when my heart churned with terrible confusion and longing.
Now I would know whether my feelings had been genuine. I grew
more anxious, not just about what I would think of Bogdan but
over what he would think of me playing house in the cavernous
government bastion I called home. I was still growing accustomed
to it, yet there we lived, with high ceilings, arched windows, and a
fireplace in the parlor with a piano in it, one Misha refused to get
rid of though neither of us could play. What would Bogdan, with
his proletarian beliefs and hatred for all things fancy, have to say
about my new lifestyle?

When he arrived, I felt ridiculous for considering that Bogdan
would care that we had replaced his parents as heads of his former
household. "Larissa," he whispered, and I gave him a quick hug. I
could hardly look into his weary eyes, which hid under his disheveled sandy hair. The broken man who walked through our door
did not seem like someone who could care that he was returning to
his gilded childhood home. He was utterly defeated, nothing like
the mischievous boy I remembered. He was in mourning, of
course, and in a way, so was I, but still, I was relieved to feel no
attraction to him, only pity. He spent his first week in our cabinet,
studying an old atlas from before the Great War, tracing the out-
lines of countries where he had never been, as if to form an escape
route from his hopeless existence. Though he did seem to turn the
corner after a while, and I believe my son was responsible. Bogdan
would take my serious child to the park behind our apartment, and
it cheered him greatly.

My husband was a man of action. He had a barber trim Bogdan's hair and face, and he did shed about ten years, touching his face periodically as if he, too, could not believe it was really his. Though he still moped, he gained weight and looked presentable enough that Misha made him a courier for the Institute's laboratory. His task was to carry boxes of chemicals from various laboratories all over the city to the Institute. He took to the job, though he still believed everyone at the Institute was a Fascist, his brother included. He must have put his rebellious thoughts aside because he realized that getting out of the house was more important than sticking to his principles at that juncture.

He enjoyed the fresh air, the walks punctuated by bus rides, the interactions with the scientists, as if he, too, were a learned man. After several months of stability, he moved into a small apartment of his own, four floors above ours. His final goodbye was sitting down at our untouched piano and playing a perfectly competent rendition of "Für Elise"—this was just one of the many things he must have learned to do while he was gone. Misha was relieved, not only because his brother was thriving but also because we would get some relief from his dark, manic energy. How quiet the house was in the evenings, without Bogdan and his brooding and tales from Rome, his smirking criticism of our acidic red wine!

I still felt it, after all—the improbable pull toward this broken man. I loved my husband, but he worked such long hours and, well, most of our conversations were centered on our boy. I loved my boy, too, but he was such a serious, solemn creature, preferring his toys to people, not as interested in reading with his mama as I had hoped, though he did have a soft spot for his playful uncle Bogdan, who was still more comfortable with children than his fellow man, ever since he joked around with young Yaroslava. Again, I could not help but wonder why he and my sister had not reproduced.

I was bold enough to ask one afternoon, when Bogdan and I

took Tolik to the park. He ran ahead of us to the swings and we watched him from a bench.

"I'm sorry you—could not have children," I said. Bogdan narrowed his eyes and I bumbled on. "That, you two weren't able . . ."

I didn't think anything had the power to truly stun him until I saw the look on his face. He had made it through the war without being shocked. And even though my sister's death had devastated him, he still bore it like a fact of life, something to be expected. But now he jumped from the bench like it was smoldering. I had hardly mentioned my sister to him, and he had likely imagined I would say something tender about her, if I said anything at all.

"Is that what you think?" he said, laughing rather cruelly. "All this time, you thought—well," he said, brushing imaginary dirt off his trousers. "You think you're so special because you walk around quoting old dead bores, but you're not. Anyone can get a diploma, but it takes more to learn how to live. And you, Larissa, should not discuss matters you know nothing about."

He began pushing my son on his swing before I had a chance to apologize.

"You're flying high in the sky, little man!" Bogdan said.

"I'm a rocket!" my son cried.

"You'll blast right to the stars if we keep going like this," said Bogdan, pushing harder, perhaps with a bit too much zeal, but I did not stop him. "You'll go straight into space." He did not look at me again, but I could feel him, daring me to tell him to slow down.

I thought the incident would break us, but it never came up again. We remained allies and continued to spend the late afternoons with my son together when I wasn't working. This continued for the next few years, in fact—Bogdan regaling me with tales of Rome while managing to avoid the topic of my sister, criticizing the Soviet government while I gave my assent by not rebuking him and tried to change the subject by offering amusing tales of my wayward students. How I treasured our conversations! Right up until the day he died.

He was poisoned by accident. I was not there, yet I have pictured the scene again and again over the years. He was carrying a box of chemicals to the Institute and tripped in the snow. Of all the things he had ever carried, he happened to drop several vials of mercury. If he had left the box on the ground, then I might be telling a different story. But he was finally back in the swing of things, eager to please, relishing his status as chief courier. He rummaged in the snow for what he could salvage, placing the few unbroken vials back in the box and carrying it all the way to the Institute. He probably hummed all the way there to keep calm, silver leaking down his hands, staining the white ground. As he approached the majestic building that his father had built from scratch, he might have been filled with a sense of fate, of his small place in the universe.

He began to feel dizzy, but he still made it to the lab, walking up four marble stories. By the time he set the box down on the laboratory table and explained what had happened, his world was a blur. When the concerned scientists sat him down, he began to vomit blood. Misha was summoned to accompany his brother to the hospital, where the verdict was clear: mercury poisoning.

My husband was devastated, of course. "My brother," he kept mumbling as we got into bed. How did this happen? Why was one brother a strong father and capable scientist, while the other festered in his bed? I should not have been shocked by this cruel twist of fate, when my own father was cold in the ground while his brother was alive and well. I held my husband and tucked him in, and then I sat at the kitchen window smoking all night long. I picked up *Karamazov*, but it wore me out. Bogdan had been right all those years ago. Fyodor Mikhailovich did take too long to get to the point.

It took Bogdan almost two weeks to die. At first, he was still himself, and though I knew it was selfish, I finally found the nerve to ask about my sister again. Was she happy, all those years away from home? I didn't dare ask what she thought about me.

"She was perfectly happy," he said. "More with her dogs than me," he added with a smile. "How she loved those foul creatures. But yes, Larissa, she was pleased with her life."

"Good," I said. Was I relieved? Had I wanted her to be miserable—or at least to feel a dull thud of unhappiness, like I did?

"We were perfectly capable of having children," he continued. "It was your sister, Larissa. She didn't want them."

"Why ever not?"

Once I got married and came to my senses, I did not seriously consider childlessness. At the time, this was unthinkable—like deciding to cut off your own breast. I tried to recall my youthful feelings about my uncle never procreating; he saw what having children could do, especially if troubles arose, Revolutions or typhus or the need to send said children to an orphanage. Polya saw what family did to our father. His family failed to care for him; he failed to care for us. I could understand her desire to forgo children after that, to never worry about not giving adequate care. Still, it was terrible that she was gone for good, and soon Bogdan would be, too, that there would be no trace of them.

"She said she already had everything she needed," Bogdan said. "What was I supposed to do, Larissa? I loved her."

"She didn't seem to care about my child, certainly," I said, suddenly angry with my sister for leaving this man to die alone, without a child by his side for comfort. I could have brought my son, a serious teenager, but it was hardly safe. "She loved her rabid animals, but she didn't even bother waiting for my son to be born before taking off. Even that last day at the station—"

"Oh, Larissa," he said, closing his eyes. "Why don't you let it go?"

"Of course I have," I said, hugging myself. "I was just . . ." Only then did I see how selfish I was acting, grumbling about my sister when this poor man was at death's door. This man who found it in him to give me advice during his last days on Earth. Sound advice, at that. Then again, he was the one who declared his love to me in the mountains, when my father was missing, when I was fairly certain he was dead already. He didn't have the most considerate timing either.

"We all would have starved to death in the mountains if it wasn't for you," I said.

He offered me one weak nod that was almost a bow. And then I returned his long-ago kiss from the train—right on his mercury-stained lips. I didn't care if it killed me. I was already dead. He looked a bit stunned but not displeased, and when he closed his eyes shortly after, it took me a moment to realize it was not due to pleasure but because he needed to rest, to prepare his body for destruction. I stood over him for as long as the nurses would allow.

After that, he turned sallow and then gray and then lost consciousness altogether. I still returned every day to see him, recalling what he once said about how it was obvious Father Zosima's corpse would stink to the heavens, no matter how pure he claimed to be. He smelled like nothing, and I sensed that he would continue to be innocent, even when he passed on.

Two weeks later, the Institute gave him a big, hearty funeral. Why wouldn't they? He was the son of Konstantin Orlov and the brother of Mikhail Orlov, its director, never mind the fact that it was exactly the kind of thing he would have hated, all that pomp

and circumstance from the hypocritical bureaucrats he loathed and
yet worked for, the very people who killed him. Misha gave an
impassioned speech on behalf of his brother, about how he was an
original thinker who never followed trends, an inspiration to us all,
a speech that flirted with blasphemy but never crossed the line.
There was a banquet afterward for the hundred or so guests, and as
I studied the caviar and gleaming grapes and deviled eggs and endless bottles of wine, I couldn't help but see it through Bogdan's or
my sister's eyes—thousands of rubles wasted on people who didn't
care for Bogdan, which would have been better spent on the poor,
or the roads, or even homeless dogs.

Uncle Pasha, still a bachelor who would live for another few
years, made it to the funeral from Kharkov, and was a bright spot
on this occasion. "A spirited boy," he had said, putting a hand on
my shoulder. "My princess," he whispered, "has become a queen."
Though he was approaching old age, he still carried that lightness
about him, and did not seem lonely, making me wonder if I knew
anything at all about whether or not everyone needed a family,
though he was happy to watch over Tolik as my husband and I
made the rounds. But you wouldn't believe who else I saw, a far
more unwelcome visitor from the past than my dear uncle.

Yulia Garanina in the flesh—Aunt Yulia, as I called her when I
was a child. She had not aged a day, and in fact looked quite radiant
and plump compared to the woman I had remembered from the
war, though she had never quite looked hungry even then, not like
the rest of us. She was still working in the metallurgy division, and
there she was, with a new husband and a small boy about Tolik's
age who had dark hair and a serious expression, none of the blond
lightheartedness of poor Yaroslava, the older sister he would never
meet. Luckily I had my Misha, because if I had been alone, I might
not have restrained myself. Seeing that bejeweled, heartless woman

who had once called me and my sister thieves for taking two measly pieces of chocolate from her treasure trove made my blood boil.

"Larissachka," she said, holding my hands in hers as if we were dear old friends. "How nice to see you. You're looking well. I'm so sorry about Bogdan, he was such a big, warmhearted boy. We had some good times together, really. Can you believe how long ago it was that we were all in the mountains?"

I released my hands from her icy grip. I could not believe the way she was talking—as if she were reminiscing about a summer vacation! I backed away from her, but she kept going.

"When I think of those years, do you know what I remember most? The sunsets. I have been all over the world since then, all over, but I can tell you that no city holds a candle to Lower Turinsk's sunsets. They took my breath away every time. I have never seen a sky so pink and purple in all my life before the sun went down below the scraggly trees—they were simply stunning, darling, don't you remember?"

"What I remember," I said, raising my voice at this ghastly woman, and then faltering. I remembered the stink of flesh and death and urine and the sensation that we were already walking corpses, that we were living in the land of the dead. In the nearly three miserable years we had spent there, the only sunset I could recall was on the evening after my sister got lost by fainting in a snowbank, clutching her white dog. When I dragged her in, our parents collapsed over her, crying madly. The sun was going down right then. It was something unbelievable—the sky painted orange, so luminous and benevolent. Me and my sister and Mama and Papa and our grandmother and the Orlovs—we stood by the balcony and watched the sun fall below the pines until the darkness filled the room. But I would not share this memory with this self-serving woman, who spoke of sunsets like her time in the deadly mountains was a wild romp.

"What I remember," I said again, catching the alarm creeping into her face. "Is something else entirely."

Misha stepped in front of me. "Thank you for honoring my brother's life," he said. He bowed and pulled me away before I could do any damage. He was grinding his jaw. It was rare that he allowed someone to get under his skin—it was a relief to see it, actually, and it made him seem more human. I saw him as a young man on the evening when Aunt Yulia chastised my sister after we had tried to steal her chocolate, when he had stood by without defending me, and now he was refusing to contradict her again. She walked away with her skirts bouncing behind her. I was tempted to yank her back by her hair, to give her a swift kick in the stomach. That ridiculous woman and her sunsets! It was a blessing I never saw her again.

The next morning, I decided to stop avoiding my grandmother's old apartment on the way to work; the mountain world was dead to me, belonging to ancient times. I walked through Postal Square and was surprised that no fireworks or lightning bolts greeted me when I found the building, which was smaller than I remembered. The two columns still stood at the entrance and the windows were high and majestic, but it was no larger than my home. Through its arched front window, I could almost see my sister and grandmother and Aunt Shura, laughing recklessly as they did the can-can, tangled up in that blasted boa like they were never going to die. After a few minutes, the front door opened and a man emerged holding the hand of a little girl. I watched them cross the street, and then I went on my way. That was the only time I ever stood there.

I do not realize I am crying until the drops hit my keyboard. Natasha has tears in her eyes. Though I must say that in spite of her current pouting, she has appeared to be in better spirits lately, looking less done in. Perhaps my story has rejuvenated the girl after all. But what, I wonder, will bring me back to life?

"That's it," I say as I wipe my face.

"I'm sorry, Baba," Natasha says. "I can't imagine."

"Do not be sorry, my darling. You had nothing to do with it."

I take a long sip of my tea but it has gotten cold, so I put the kettle on once more. It's nearly midnight. A light in the building across the street flickers off, followed by another, the world winding down. Again she tells me she is sorry, and I do not even know which part she is sorry about. The destruction of my city? My estrangement from my sister—or her eventual death? Bogdan's sad demise?

"In fact," I tell Natasha, "it was after Bogdan died that your grandfather bought the cottage on the sea. We always vacationed on the sea, but he thought it would be nice for us to have our own place. Or rather, a place for me and your father to go in the summers while he was at work, a place to call our own."

"I didn't know that," Natasha says. Then she clears her throat and adds, "I guess there's a lot I don't know."

"That's right, my child."

She runs a hand through her hair, looking uneasy, and then adds: "Did you always have affairs, or was it after . . ."

I sigh before I decide to go on. Of course she was aware of my dalliances, though they dwindled by her teenage years. "Until your uncle Bogdan died, I didn't entertain the notion of being disloyal to your grandfather—the biggest betrayal at that point in our marriage was his refusal to read with me. But after I saw Bogdan again—well—I felt that old passion again and needed to do something with it. The seaside cottage appeared like a safe harbor in a storm. I know you can't possibly understand it, but that's the way it was."

"I'm not judging you, Baba. I never have."

"That is kind of you, darling. When I first made eyes at a bachelor by the sea, I thought this was it, that I was living the life my coquettish sister would have lived if the war hadn't ravaged her, making her shift her priorities from flirting to hating the government and caring for dirty dogs. During my first rendezvous, I pretended I was Polina—not shorn-haired, wan Polina who left Kiev for a second time, but the bright-bodied girl with the long red hair who still turned heads when our family arrived at the station to leave for the mountains. I felt alive again, the world heavy with possibility, the future no longer a guillotine slowly bearing down over my head. That's just how it happened. I didn't stop and think about it, really."

"And Grandpa Misha? Did he know?"

"Who could say, dear child? He was brilliant—how could he have missed it? He never said a word about it, all those long years. He only hinted at it at the end of his days, when he became sweeter, more forthcoming. 'I hope you have found the excitement you were after,' he said to me just a few months before he passed. 'Of course I did, my darling,' I told him, because what was I supposed to do, ask for clarification?"

I picture my husband at the very end. His heart was weak, we were in the hospital, we both knew this was it. And as I watched him resting there, I thought that he had not only grown to resemble his serious father but that he had outgrown him. He had outlived him by several decades, and it was as if he had become an even more extreme version of the state-fearing bureaucrat in the process, one who would have raged over seeing his porcelain vases and lacquered dining table carted off forever. One who would have been livid that I was leaving our immaculate home to live out my remaining days by the sea.

I put my head in my hands. "You must excuse me. Preparing for the move has exhausted me."

"Thank you for telling me all that, Baba. You didn't have to."

I laugh weakly. "I bet you got more than you bargained for when you asked, didn't you, darling? I'm sure you have a hard time understanding. You are so devoted to Yuri. It's a beautiful thing to see."

She gives me a wan smile and blinks a few times, a strange reaction. "I understand everything. I had my wild days. Don't you remember?"

"Who could forget?" I say, recalling the endless stream of deadbeats she had dated, some of whom I had the misfortune of meeting. One of them even had a piece of metal going through his nostril like some kind of a bull in search of a matador. I believe he called himself "Rainfeather." It was ridiculous. But now my tea boils and I excuse myself. I have said too much.

Tomorrow I leave for good—Misha's men came this morning to haul everything away. I watched them carry off the drab old landscapes, the uncomfortable velvet dining chairs, the ivory coatrack, things that meant nothing to me while they were a part of my daily existence, and yet I felt heavy as I watched them being wrested from our home, like a part of my soul was being dragged out along with them.

After I began my story, I decided the natural place to donate all the money from the sales. I will be giving the money to the Kharkov orphanage where my father and Uncle Pasha spent their adolescence, if you can believe it. I made a call to confirm that it was still standing, and it was. I considered visiting, but I thought the trip wouldn't do me any good, only adding weight to my old body. "Come on by," the woman in charge kept telling me. "See what kind of a place it is." I told her I was old, too old, but thanked her for the invitation anyway.

I hear Stas entering the apartment before I can mention the orphanage to Natasha. He apologizes for missing the last part of my story; he got a call offering him a new position as a waiter and had a few details to work out. I congratulate him and prepare to tell him that I didn't miss him one bit, though perhaps I did a little, perhaps I am growing a bit fond of the derelict boy. But he looks too solemn for kidding around, and also a bit different. Something is off about him.

"Nice haircut," I tell him. "With it, you almost do not look like a homosexual."

Natasha gives a nervous, gentle laugh. "He's not gay, Baba."

"Whatever you say. This kind of thing does not ruffle my feathers," I tell her, though I am a bit surprised. "In any event, boy, the hair does not look bad," I say.

"Thanks," he says, running a hand through his hair.

I am depleted. I try to focus on the prospect of sinking into my warm bed—a moment of reflection with the dregs of my tea and a few pages of Tsvetaeva's *Moscow Diaries* should do the trick. I long for Misha to rest beside me, to feel his bulk weighing down his half of the mattress, to have his arm draped around me in the night. To hear his heavy snore, which annoyed me every night until I no longer heard it, until I finally learned how loud the night was, how it could keep me up for hours—the planes soaring overhead, the cars roaring by, the cool air hitting the windowpanes— sounds my husband had kept at bay.

"Listen, Baba," Natasha says, inching closer to the screen. "I meant what I said earlier. I'd love it if you came to visit this summer. It would be so good to see you, to have you meet Tally . . . and, well, I'm putting on a play and I'd love for you to see it."

"A play?" I say, intrigued in spite of myself. "About what, darling?"

"A one-woman show," she tells me. "It'll be a surprise. But I think you'd love it."

"I haven't seen you onstage in a while."

"Exactly."

I light a cigarette, picturing the long days ahead. The morning's journey to the sea. The days when I try to relive my long-ago summers, with young Natasha and my lovers at my side, the only place where I felt happy. But the joy I felt beside those crashing waves—it wasn't because of those lovers. It was because I was with my darling granddaughter, a girl whose life I was shaping, who felt at ease with me in a way she never did in her own home. I was saving her, in my own way.

Though I failed my sister, there was Natasha, my second chance. I did nothing for my sister when our father or our grandmother died besides disdain her for not toughening up. I did not carry out my promise to my father to take care of her. I let Bogdan step in and do the caretaking, and where did that lead her? Then I barely tried to keep her in Kiev, where I could have brought her back to life, and instead just watched her walk off to her new life while I only cared about the child in my belly—a child who, it was true, would one day bring me my greatest joy through Natasha, but I could have spent more time caring about my damn sister.

As I stare at Natasha's gorgeous, weary face, it feels ridiculous to live out my end on the sea without the person who made me happy there. I do the calculations. I will still have nearly two months on the water on my own before I take off. And then—another chance to see Natasha onstage. How could I deny her?

"Oh, darling," I say. "I wouldn't miss it for the world."

Natasha

Stas helps me lug a bunch of last-minute crap to the stage two weeks before opening night. As I turn on the lights over the set, I have to say I feel pretty fucking proud. The rusty old train car is on-point. The craggy mountains in the background look almost real from a distance, with the dark, wispy clouds hovering above them. The apartment to the left of the train is just how I pictured it, with its wooden beds and fiery stove and even a broom in the corner. The ground is covered in little pieces of gravel that it will be tough to walk over. The market hides behind the train car, old wooden carts filled with fake rotting onions and potatoes. And I made it all happen, by begging old Babies founder Vadim to use his stage, asking Slavik, another Babies defector who made killer sets and also owed me one, to help put this thing together, but mostly by working my ass off to write the damn play. The last six weeks have been crazy, but in the best possible way. It's amazing, how much I got done while Talia was napping. If only Mama could have seen me, poring over my notebooks, replaying my recorded calls with Baba over and over, crossing shit out, saying words aloud to see if they sounded right, crumpling paper up like a mad scientist, focused as hell on my pages in a way I had never felt about a single assignment in high school, like a good little student-actress.

The last time I was onstage, not long after I got together with Yuri, it was for a stupid *Anna Karenina* spinoff, a story told from the point of view of Dolly, a much more woman-friendly version where Anna gets to run away with her lover and nobody dies, and even old Karenin finds happiness again. It was called *Happy Wife* and it was a bit one-noted. But I missed it, standing under the bright lights as an empowered Dolly, feeling free after kicking my loser husband aside. My grandpa watched a video of that one from Kiev and wrote, *You were too deferential to Anna onstage. You needed to showcase your talents a bit more.* That one cracked me up; as if I hadn't tried! And now I take a photo of the stage and post it: *#curtainsuptomorrow #Iseeyoupostpartum #Sovietstoriestolife*, and wait for the flood of love to pour in; at this point I've stopped posting anything about my family so people know what to focus on. I've got two weeks to go and I want every last thing to sparkle, the show, the stage, the lighting, my costumes, I want the theater to be packed. Since Baba really is going to see it after all, and I want it to be perfect, especially since she doesn't even know what it's about.

Stas stomps around with his hands on his hips, like he has something to say. He was supposed to read over the final version of my play last night but hasn't said anything yet. Maybe he didn't get to it. He's been busy as hell, ever since he moved out of our place last month to crash at the studio of a friend in Harlem who is going to be gone the rest of the summer, close to the restaurant where he's working. I was glad Yuri and I were left alone, finally, but I missed him more than a little, though I tried to tell myself it was mostly because of the help he gave me with Tally. Still, when I asked him to come with me, I thought he was coming partly out of guilt, since I had been with Tally around the clock pretty much since he left, though Yuri's been helping more since his summer classes ended. Anyway, it was a good thing Stas and I hadn't been alone together much because it seemed like some of that heat, or the heat I had imagined earlier, had cooled along with the hint of fall in the late-summer air.

But now, standing on the stage, just the two of us, I feel shaky. I'm still getting used to his short haircut, though he's had it for a while. It makes him look, I don't know, more respectable, less like a fuckboy, which only makes me more nervous.

"Well?" I say.

"Looks good," he says, kicking the boxcar. "It really does."

"That's not what I mean."

"Ah," he says, understanding. "The play wasn't bad, Sterling. Not bad at all."

I feel a flood of relief. He actually fucking read it. And didn't hate it, in spite of his high standards. But he just keeps walking around the stage without looking me in the eye.

"But?" I say.

He smiles. "But nothing. I just thought it was kind of funny that you left out the Orlov family. I mean, weren't the brothers kind of the point?"

I shrug. "It would have been too hard to pull off by myself. I started writing it with them in it and just saw how much easier it would be without them, so I went with that."

"Fair enough," he says. "You think your grandmother will care that you changed the story?"

"She'll just want to see the best I can do," I say.

He makes like he's going to take a step closer to me but he doesn't. "All right then."

He's giving me this intense look that makes me scared as hell. I know I'm being a complete idiot. I must be the only person dumb enough to be capable of flirting this much with an almost-six-month-old at home. Most moms at this stage are probably still tending to their wounded vaginas and desperately enjoying their sad date nights, yet here I am, in need of something more. I know this can't end anywhere good, and that once the play is over, I won't have an excuse for hanging out with Stas solo, that we'll only hang if Yuri is around. Unless—

We climb into the boxcar, sitting down on the one bed with a little window behind it meant to be the place where my grandmother and her sister slept. It's dark in here, and musty. Though I cut my grandmother's return to Kiev, I picture her in this boxcar, accepting Grandpa Misha's proposal in an utterly perfunctory way. With Uncle Bogdan looking over her shoulder, hearing the whole thing. Then he comes toward her, speaking to her for the last time before her wedding, really, and she doesn't know what to do, or how to tell him how she feels.

"Do you think my grandmother should have been with Bogdan instead?" I say.

Stas sighs and looks at the car's ceiling. "Who is to say? What if they got together but got sick of each other after a while?"

"You really think that would have happened?"

"How am I supposed to know?" he says, and he sounds tired, defensive. It has been a long day. Schlepping the last of the props across the city. Sweating like crazy. Wondering what the hell is going on between us.

"I'm not asking you to *know*. I'm asking for your best guess."

"What does it matter? What's done is done," he says. "For her anyway. As for us, I don't know," he adds.

"Us," I say, swallowing hard.

I scoot away from him and then a slow smile rises on his face. He gets up, takes me by the hand, and leads me backstage and I don't even question it. We're standing near a cardboard mountain Slavik painted and then told me to scrap because it looked too cartoonish. But right now, I feel like I could take another step and start climbing it, like I can almost see my grandmother's factory town in the distance. Stas pushes me against it and kisses me, hard. I feel like my legs are going to melt, that I'm just going to turn into a puddle right now and no one will ever hear from me again. I pull away and feel embarrassed and excited and confused, all at fucking once. The smoky taste of his tongue lingers in my mouth.

"Why did you do that?" I say.

"Why did I kiss you?"

"No. Why did you pull me out of the boxcar?"

He laughs. "Because I do have some limits, Sterling."

This makes me laugh, a little. What, he didn't want to corrupt my grandmother's train? There's a sick kind of logic to it. I'm scared of the silence so I feel compelled to talk again, walking back onstage. "When I was a teenager, I'd visit my grandmother in Sevastopol during the summers, and she was always having these 'friends' show up—she'd leave me on the beach and go have her flings."

"Huh," he says. "What about your grandfather?"

"I'm not sure if he knew. There was only one time when I thought he might have," I say, but it doesn't feel like the right time to go on about my sweet grandfather, a kind, thoughtful man who seemed to genuinely care about my acting, through his silly notes. "Baba's not sure if he knew either. Honestly, I have no idea," I say.

"It's better off that way, isn't it?"

I get ready for a whole big conversation about what this meant, what will happen from now on, what is the meaning of a good life, how can it all mean anything, how can we even dare to suffer when we know what our grandparents and parents went through to get us to this fucking country. I'm relieved when he doesn't say anything else, when he takes my hand and leads me back inside the boxcar, where I sigh and rest my head on his shoulder. I have questions for him—how does he really feel about me? What happened with that girl in Boston?—but they'll just have to wait.

What was my grandmother's story supposed to tell me if not

this? A tiny part of me wishes I could ask her what to do, but I'm not nuts, I don't want to let her down. Besides, she's so busy setting up her sea home that she hardly has time for me these days, not that I would trouble her with my romantic problems anyway, since I want her to think I have my shit together. Anyway, could she really tell me what to do—if this was beyond a stupid, meaningless crush? I scan the boxcar for an answer, but I just grab a thin gray blanket and cover myself with it and close my eyes, knowing that nobody, nobody in the world, can tell me what to do.

I'm going out of my mind so I finally take Stephanie up on her offer to get shithoused at the Lair after our babies have gone to bed. She had definitely been my favorite coworker there, probably because she was also an actress, and I was devastated when she quit two years before I did because she got married to a customer who happened to work at JPMorgan and immediately had a baby with him and did the whole thing, a brownstone in Park Slope and all. Though we don't see each other that often, she's still the best friend I've got, and it feels nice, being back at the scene of the crime with her, even if it is where Yuri and I had that terrible fight. Mel's out this time, and there are two hot twentysomethings working the bar who don't know us, and aside from Scotty the regular, who waves at us, we are pretty anonymous and that's how I want it to be. Yuri had to finish planning his fall classes, and I spent fourteen hours straight with Tally, and I'm just pumped to talk to someone who can actually talk back to me.

Steph has had the same spiky black hair since we met, is almost six feet tall, and perfectly angular. Men stare at her everywhere we go, and even now, as we drink gin and tonics, the three men at the bar keep sneaking a look at her. As she takes a big sip of her drink, she nods at the two women working the bar and says, "We were hotter."

"Are hotter," I tell her. "Especially you. You, like, reverse-aged since you left this place."

"I don't want to be that hot anymore," she says. Then she gives me a wicked smile. "And your little houseguest? Is he that age?"

"He's twenty-eight," I say, feeling defensive for some reason. "And he moved out a while ago."

"So that makes it okay to be lusting after him."

"Shut up," I say, smacking her. Those were not the words I used. I told her *I might have a crush.*

"This is so sick," she says, slamming her glass against the bar for emphasis. "I love it."

"What am I supposed to do?"

"Nothing," she says. Then she narrows her eyes and moves her head closer to mine. "That *is* what you're doing, right?"

"Of course. I'm not completely nuts," I say, though I am completely nuts, though I stayed up all night, thinking about that kiss. But I'm not going to tell her that. A full day has gone by and I haven't heard a peep from him either.

"Stay away from him."

"It's a bit hard when he's like a kid brother to my husband."

"Do your best. Just keep it in your pants, Natty."

"I *am*. I told you, I am."

"When I got pregnant, I didn't feel any of the bloating or fatigue or nausea or whatever. I was just so fucking horny all the time, I was like a teenager. I wanted to fuck everything—any man who spoke to me, any woman, anything that moved," she says, tucking a tiny strand of hair behind her ear.

"And it went away?"

"Basically."

I take another sip of my drink and ask for another round. "You miss working here?"

"Not one bit. I know you think I'm boring as fuck but I can tell you, I'm much happier now. You know what I liked? I liked being the star of my high school plays. I liked being the star of the plays at Mason Gross, that was a real ego boost too. But then I moved out here and saw that I was up against a city of sluts who were the stars of their high school plays, and while most of them weren't as talented as me, a number of them were, and so many of them were hotter. And I just didn't want to prove myself against the hotter ones, or hustle to keep up with the talented ones. I hated it. I hated bartending. I hated taking a cab home at four in the morning be-cause I got mugged twice taking the subway back to Bushwick, just me and a bunch of homeless people and a few businessmen who thought I was a prostitute—I got solicited once. I hated all of it. I just wanted to have a nice warm bed and a reasonable sched-ule and reasonable goals, and now I do, I've got my kid, I've got my night classes, and yes, having a rich-as-fuck husband does not hurt, but it's a good life. I fucking love it. There's nothing I want, you see? I just want to keep my universe from exploding. And as long as I do that, I'm good."

"Really and truly?"

"Ninety-eight percent of the time, and I'm okay with that."

"And the other two percent?"

"The other two percent, I'll see a few people from college here and there on TV or on Broadway and I'm like, I'm better than them. Why didn't I do that? Why am I spending all this time hav-ing playdates? But I'm actually not better than them, I remind my-self, because I didn't stick it out and they did—like you're doing," she says, squeezing my hand. "Do you *really* miss this place?"

"I do, actually."

"So tell Yuri you want to work again."

I say, "Ha! He wants me to go back to school."

"And what do you want?"

"To book shit again? And to work at the Lair, at least a few nights a month. Tally's sleeping through the night now. Why the fuck not?"

"You'll be completely exhausted."

"I already am," I say. I finish my drink and signal for another. My fucking milk finally dried up, which I must admit was a relief, not just because I don't have to be paranoid about having more than one drink but because I feel less chained to Tally. "I mean," I go on, "I definitely feel better than I did at the beginning, but how long did it take you to feel like yourself again?"

She smiles. "You won't ever feel like yourself again. At least, I didn't. But how long did it take me to feel okay as this new person I became after having a kid? I don't know, about a year? A little while after I got the job at the theater. That helped a lot."

"You always seemed like yourself."

"I'm an actress, remember? I just knew how to fake it," she says, raising a glass. "You will figure it out, because you are a goddess. Really, you will."

I suck my drink down. "I fucking *hated* those long commutes home after a night at the bar. But the Lair is just down the street. . . . I don't know, I both hated it more than anything and miss it more than anything. I just really hope I'm not done."

"You're not done. You just keep auditioning. There's always a lull, you know that. Plus, you've got your show coming up. Are you all set?"

"Pretty much."

"Great. You focus on that, and then you make your next move."

"I'm trying."

"And in the meantime, Natty, just try to keep your universe from exploding, all right?"

"I'm doing my best."

"You always are, baby girl," she says.

As we get the check, one of the guys at the bar finally approaches us, and I'm flattered but too tired to discourage him without being a bitch. "It's as easy as being a woman?" he says with a sly smile. "That's you, right?"

"Damn right it is," I say, cheersing him when he raises his glass, relieved that this was all he wanted.

Stephanie cracks up as he walks away. "What happened to that company anyway?"

"Lady Planet?" I say. "They went under. It turned out eco-friendly tampons were too expensive."

"Of course they were," she says.

Then old Scotty comes by with tequila shots, and neither of us can turn them down. I let the booze slide down my throat and it feels warm and welcoming, though I know I shouldn't get too trashed. But I need the break, need some time away from Tally and the men in my life. And when the liquor settles in me and I stare straight ahead, it's Stas's fucking face I see, Stas in the boxcar, his arm around me, quiet.

I'm more than tipsy by the time I get home. Yuri's on the couch watching the Red Sox and when he sees me struggling to get my heel off, he smiles like he knows I overdid it and is okay with it, good man that he is. And maybe it's because of that goodness, because he comes up to me and strokes my hair and genuinely seems pleased that I got to have a wild night out with my friend, that I feel like I just can't hold anything in anymore.

"We kissed," I tell him as I finally manage to get my heels off.

"You and Stephanie? Aren't you a little old to get into all that again?" he says, but his smile falls halfway through and he understands me perfectly. He puts a hand to his neck, like he's adjusting a phantom tie.

"It was just once," I tell him. "Yesterday. I—I don't know what it means."

"*What it means?*" he says, backing away from me, toward the couch. He sighs. "Look, I thought you and Stas were flirting a bit, but you flirt with everybody so I didn't really care. I didn't realize—if you don't know *what it means,* then why did you bother telling me?" He stands up.

"I don't flirt with everybody."

"Come on. You do too, but I don't care that much."

"I just wanted to be honest."

"No, you wanted to be selfish. You wanted to burden me with your mistake."

"Couldn't it be a bit of both?" I say. "Anyway, I just—you fell in love with a hard-drinking foulmouthed actress, didn't you? And now you just want me to change diapers all day and become a professional dog walker or whatever."

"That was not exactly how I put it," he says. "And are you telling me that this is why you—"

"I'm not blaming you. I just—he kind of, reminded me of who I was before I got knocked up."

He puts his head in his hands. "I still love that hard-drinking foulmouthed actress. But I also love you as a mother, all right? And I'm not trying to change you, I'm just trying to find a way to make this—new version of you happy."

"Keep looking, then," I say. I sink down into the couch. "You do understand that I've been having a hard time, don't you?"

"I'm not fucking blind, Natasha. Of course I understand. I do what I can when I'm not working. But lots of people have a hard time without—fucking around."

"Lots of people are better at this than I am."

"Stop it. You can't make me feel guilty right now, all right?"

He shakes his head and moves even farther away from me, his back against the balcony door, which I covered in Christmas lights even though he thought it was tacky, while I insisted it was festive, and dressed up our dreary fucking place. His eyes are glazed over, like he can't even look at me. He slides the glass door open and steps outside, and I just watch him standing there with his hands on the railing, his strong back rising and falling as he tries to get ahold of himself.

I hear the jingle of Sharik's bell, and the boy jumps on the couch and then starts the predictable *suck, suck, suck* that means he's going to town on himself. I had three perfectly good cats, some who died even before he did—of all of them, why did the dick-sucking one have to survive? Or was there something about the dick sucking that helped him survive? These questions are beyond me right now.

"Foo, foo, disgusting!" I say, kicking him off the couch, which still smells a bit like Stas's cigarettes. When he sneaks off to his litter box in the bathroom, I regret it, getting rid of my only friend in the world, but he has to learn his lesson. I don't know what else to do so I scroll through my phone. Babies Vera is posting about booking one line on *Victims Incorporated*, as if anyone gives a shit. I like it and even congratulate her.

Yuri returns from the balcony looking even madder than before. In fact, he's not walking, he's more like marching toward me, his fists balled at his sides, looking like a little boy determined to deliver his big line in the school play. The last time he looked like that, his brow furrowed with such intense determination, was when he asked me to marry him, just after we visited my father's grave on his birthday, in the parking lot outside the cemetery on a cold gray winter day. I couldn't help it then, I burst out laughing as I watched him go down on one knee because it was such a funny time to ask someone to marry you and he laughed too and said, "I know, I know, I was going to ask you this weekend, but I couldn't wait another second," and I said, "I know that, and neither can I."

But obviously no proposal is currently forthcoming, though I am genuinely curious about what he will say to me with such determination, given our circumstances. He takes one, two steps closer to me and his lips part. You can imagine my surprise when the words, or rather, the word that comes out of his mouth is a woman's name, and not mine either.

"Evgenia," he says, fists still clenched. I move closer to him, tilting my head, hoping this encourages him to elaborate. But he only says it again: "Evgenia," he says, moving closer to me. "Evgenia," one more time, his hands unfisted by then. I try to rack my brains—do we know any Evgenias? Maybe a second cousin on his mother's side? A long-forgotten friend of my mother's? My father's former teacher?

"Normally," I say, "I go by Natasha." This fails to make him smile.

"Evgenia Kupershteyn," he says, sternly. "Do you know who that is?"

"I would guess she's no American."

"After your father's funeral, when you asked if I was seeing anyone, I said no. But this wasn't true. I was seeing Evgenia Mikhailovna Kupershteyn, a nice girl I met at a faculty mixer, a biologist from Moscow. We had been seeing each other for six months at that point. Though it wasn't the most passionate relationship, we had a good time together and she was a smart and serious woman. But one kiss from you—and I broke it off with her the next day."

"You'd have to be smart, with a name like that," I say. "And?"

"And, I could have been with Evgenia, but I chose you. I have made my bed and now I must lie in it. I knew what you were, I knew you would break my heart, but I just had to have you. Being with you was the only exciting thing I had ever done."

He even raises his voice at the end of this little speech. I don't think I've ever heard him raise his voice before, especially not when Tally is sleeping. It's enough to make poor Sharik slink into the other room, tail raised in objection.

"So that's all I am to you, some exciting thing?"

"You know that's not what I mean."

"And now you regret it. Now you wish you had formed an alliance with Evgenia what's-her-nuts—Mikhailovna Kupersburt."

"Kupershteyn," he says, looking utterly defeated. "And that's not exactly what I'm saying. I just want to tell you that I'm not mad at you. I'm surprised it took this long for you to get sick of me. At least, as far as I know—"

"Yuri, please—"

"I was standing at a crossroad and I took a step toward you. Nobody forced me to do it. Even if you are utterly magnetic, I could have turned you down. I didn't have to see this through. And now—"

"I made one mistake, all right? That doesn't mean I'm going to run away."

Yuri sighs and puts his head in his hands. Though I feel terrible, I'm also annoyed by his little martyr act, like I'm some wild, hopeless creature who couldn't hold herself back. Even if that is how I feel, I wanted him to expect more from me.

"You could blame me at least a little bit," I say. "I deserve it."

"Or I could blame him," he says, his lips set in a firm line. "He's always fucking around like this. He fucked around with every girl in the neighborhood, just so you know. A real heartbreaker—of course, I was off at college, but I heard all about it. I love the guy, but he's kind of a joke."

"Maybe it's because nobody ever gave him a fair chance."

"I see that you think you have a lot in common, but you don't, Natasha, not anymore."

"Maybe not," I say as his eyes flash with anger.

"So what are you going to do?" he says, and only then do I realize I have no idea.

We hear Talia stirring, a welcome distraction. Though she should be able to get back to sleep on her own, I walk into the bedroom to look at her and Yuri follows me. She looks up at us and her lips form an enormous smile, and her fat cheeks rise up to her big ears and her fists come up to her face. As both of us smile and I stroke her now-fluffy little head, I consider that hey, if I was a baby, I, too, would be as happy as a pig in shit because why not be happy when you haven't yet chosen your family, you haven't learned to walk or seen any places outside the city or tasted solid food, you don't know who the president is, and you have no idea that one day, hopefully long after all of your bad decisions have been made, you will be swiftly erased from the planet.

I stand outside Stas's Harlem apartment for centuries sweating like a beast, that garbage-pizza scent rising through the air as the subway rumbles below me, waiting for him to let me up. The perfectly made-up, ponytailed, Uppababy-stroller gentrifying moms pass me with their coffees, laughing to each other like they are gliding on ice, like they never had to wipe shit off their feet or blood off their nipples. Mom friends, mom friends, Yuri and Steph have hinted that I should make mom friends, but what the fuck for? I already spend my time thinking about changing diapers and nap schedules, and why exactly would I want to spend time with a bunch of women talking *more* about the things that are driving me crazy? To each his own, though, I guess, but now I have to focus on talking to Stas and then checking out the stage again, while Yuri's running errands with Tally, which is maybe a nice distraction from hating me.

When Stas finally opens the door, I feel like I'm his mom, showing up at his dorm unannounced, as if he had actively tried to cover up the smell of cigarettes I just walked into. He reaches out, as if he's going to run a hand through my hair, but then he just strokes my shoulder and I reconsider, no, no, I am definitely not his mother.

"Hey," he says, rubbing his eyes. "I didn't expect to see you here."

"Sorry if it's too early."

He laughs. "You've probably been up half the day already."

I follow him up four flights of stairs and walk into a dumpy studio with pizza boxes stacked in the kitchen, towers of thin little books of poetry, and a few plants wilting by the door. The bed is unmade, and there's a pile of clothes by it, and I try to remind myself what the shithole studios I lived in ten years ago looked like and that it was much worse than this, and yet, I can't believe I'm lusting after a man-boy who lives in this place. But by the bedside, I see it, a framed photo of a girl who could only be his sister, standing with him by a lake, looking deliriously happy, a girl with big cheeks and goofy hair. She reminds me how happy I am not to be a preteen anymore.

"Your sister," I say, holding it up and putting it back down.

"Is that what you came here to talk to me about?" he says. He has his hands in the pockets of his sweatshirt, and he looks kind of guilty and ill at ease.

"I told Yuri about our kiss," I say.

He takes a step back, and looks terrified and then a bit excited. "Why the fuck did you do that?"

I shrug. "I didn't plan on it. I just kind of—felt like he should know."

"It couldn't have waited until after the play?"

"Like I said, I didn't mean to. It just came out."

He sighs. "I guess we'd have to deal with it eventually." This is the first time he says *we* and it makes me dizzy. Not to mention the fact that he said *eventually*—that he didn't think this would blow over.

"We?"

He sighs and sits down on his rumpled bed and puts his head in his hands. "You. And me. I don't fucking know, Natasha," he says.

"I don't know either."

"Look, if you want me to fight for you, it's not gonna happen. If you want this, you can decide. But I can't convince you I'm the right person for you or that you should ruin your life for me. I can tell you my feelings for you scare the shit out of me, but what difference should that make to you? I can't predict the future."

"All right then," I say.

"All right," he says. "I wish I could say more. But I have no fucking clue what will happen a month from now, let alone a year or a lifetime. I can say I think I'll feel this way, but I can't ask you to blow up your life on a feeling."

"I never said I wanted you to," I say.

What did he expect me to do, tell him to run away with me and Tally? Where would we go, exactly? How could we make it work? How could we even afford a place in New York? Anyway, I have no plans to leave Yuri because I'm not a delusional psychopath, and it's nice to hear he doesn't exactly think we've got long-term potential either. And yet, I move toward him, remembering the smoky taste of his tongue. It would have been nice if he had tried to make a plan, even if I had to shut him down, I guess.

"I think I'm losing my mind," I tell him.

He nods slowly. "I lost mine a long time ago."

He takes two steps toward me, and I take a few away, until I'm near the tiny balcony, and I open the screen door to get some air. I stand out, looking at the Columbia campus in the distance, a few hopeful students passing through the side gates. I turn from the balcony and see a photo he taped to the wall, of himself standing on some kind of hiking trail. It seems likely that his ex took the picture in question.

"What happened with the girl in Boston?"

"What girl?"

"What do you mean, 'what girl?' Yuri said you left because of a girl."

"That's what I told him. I left because of my sister."

"You what?"

He sighed and sat down. "Our mom—she just can't really take care of her, like I said. She had a bad few weeks where she was in bed almost the whole time and my sister and I had to do everything for her. Well, she climbed out of it and went back to work, but my sister, she—she asked if she could move in with me. For high school. And I know I should have said yes, I know that was the right thing to do, but I just started to panic. Like, who am I to take care of somebody? And how do I live my life with her always around? Our mom isn't a danger to her—she's just kind of out of it. I chickened out and made up some lie about my lease running out, and then really did break my lease and said I was leaving town for a while, but that I would figure out a plan for us soon. And we still talk every day like she never asked, like it never happened, but I know she's waiting for me to come back. I'm a coward, right?"

"I don't think so," I say. I take a minute to process this, to understand there was no mystery ex, that he escaped from something bigger than that. "I think it's okay to want space for yourself. It's a lot to take on. But I know you don't want to leave her alone out there either."

"I miss her like hell."

"I bet you do," I say. "It's okay to take time to figure this out. You're not an asshole."

"I called myself a coward, not an asshole," he says, but he's laughing a little.

"Same difference," I say. I try to think of something brilliant to say about his shitty situation, but he seems to have cheered up a little.

"I'm glad I told you that," he says.

"Me too."

Then he runs a hand through his uncombed hair, trying to look presentable for whatever it is he has to say, and I feel nervous. "I wrote you something," he tells me. He opens a drawer in his night-stand and pulls out a piece of paper.

"You did what?"

My heart is so full, I might die from it. Had Yuri ever made me feel this idiotically giddy? It's hard to remember. Of course, that wasn't the feeling I was chasing when we got together, but here I am, hungry for it again.

"A poem," he says. "I was going to give it to you after the show. But, well, fuck it, why wait?"

"I don't believe it," I say. I didn't think I would ever see a poem of his. When he was passed out in our apartment, I might have searched once or twice but came up empty.

He cringes a bit. "I didn't say it was a good poem. I just—well, here," he says, and then I snatch the poem out of his hands and he starts frantically cleaning up his filthy kitchen, plunking dirty dishes in the sink. He looks so sweet, doing it, so sweet and vul-nerable and a little bit filthy, and I feel pretty vulnerable and filthy, too, and wonder if this is it, exactly what I need, right in fucking front of me. But then I scan the opening line and a sickness washes over me.

> My heart bleeds and bleeds for you, darling
> Rivers of the blackest darkest blood
> My heart bleeds so sweetly, my darling
> That the world is a wild, mad flood
>
> The flood is endless, like my love
> It makes the seas rise and the streets fill
> It reaches the treetops and the skies above
> But for you, my heart is bleeding still
>
> It will bleed forever just for you
> Until it bleeds up to the stars
> It will bleed forever just for you
>
> And in the end, I'll be left with scars
> But that's okay, that's all right
> I will bleed for you all night
>
> I will bleed for you all night until I erase your misery
> I will kiss your eyes until you sleep like a baby, baby
>
> I will kiss your lips until you're never thirsty again.
> I will kiss your forehead until you forget
> Anything that caused you pain

The first thing that sucks the air out of me is how shitty the poem is. I'm no literary expert, but I've read some Yesenin and Tsvetaeva and even remember old Bobby Frost, with his stupid two paths, from high school. I've read my share of plays and well, I know good writing when I see it, and this reminds me of something a high school boyfriend would pass to me in the halls. Actually it reminds me of a drummer named Jake, who was already a college dropout by the time I met him outside my high school, who would leave little notes in my backpack, these humorous little sexual ditties that actually cracked me up, with choice lines like *I would be a rube/to not touch/your boob* and *I would never punt/your cunt,* but actually those were better than this garbage. But the garbage writing is almost beside the point, because he has not only sinned by writing crap but by stealing the song my mother sang, by daring to reference the private moment I told him about, right there with his dumb words. Though then again—I told him about it ages ago, at the beginning of this endless summer. The fact that he remembered who sang the damn song—it's not nothing. But then he had to top it off by butchering the Tsvetaeva poem my grandfather gave my grandmother when he proposed to her—what was the point of that? Why was he trying to combine the messes that all the women in my family had made?

As I meet his gaze, his poor, anxious waiting-for-a-reaction face, I can hear my mother laughing at me, laughing the nasty laugh I remember when I wore an extra-slutty dress to prom, a tight red Forever 21 number I put on just to piss her off. I was only a freshman and going with a senior who called himself Axel but was really named Alex, wearing a dress that was all ass, which happened to rip down the middle as I stepped out the door. My date and I stared at each other, bewildered, as a terrible shriek erupted from Mama's mouth. It was one of the most awful sounds I had ever heard, a delighted shriek no daughter's mother should ever make at her expense, but I deserved it completely, because she had been right about the dress. It was too cheap and too tight and it would not last the evening, let alone the night. And now I hear her laughing again because I've gotten in over my head with this twenty-nothing idiot.

I don't want Stas to mistake the tears in my eyes for love or fucking sentiment.

"What the fuck is this?" I say, tossing him back the poem like it's on fire.

His face shifts. He reaches out to tuck a strand of hair behind his ear and realizes it isn't there. But I say it again, I don't care how it makes him feel.

"What the fuck is this?"

"I'm sorry," he says. "I thought—"

"I tell you something about my mom, something really private, and you put it in a poem?" I say. I don't even bother with Tsvetaeva.

"I didn't post it on Facebook. I just thought it would be nice to, I don't know, pay some kind of tribute to your mom—"

"You didn't know her," I say, taking a few steps away from him. "You aren't family."

He follows me and then stops in his tracks. I see how much I've hurt him, but I don't care. "I wasn't trying to be your family. I was trying to be nice. To share my work—"

"It isn't your work."

"It's a compilation," he says, reaching out for that phantom strand again. He swallows hard and his face gets all pale, as he really gets how much he fucked up. "I don't understand why you're acting like this. I was trying to do something nice for you." I look at him, into his eyes, and wonder if he's really the man I kissed. If he knows anything about me. If he did, then he never would have done anything so stupid.

He comes toward me, brushes hair out of my face, but I don't feel like kissing him anymore. I feel sick, actually. Like I have eaten all the old pizza in the kitchen and need to puke it up.

"Please," he says. "I'm sorry about the poem."

"Let's clean up this mess," I say, nodding at his kitchen. I don't have the energy to discuss it further. Then, when he looks genuinely hurt, I add, "Thank you."

"Thank you?"

"For trying," I say.

"Yeah," he says. "I did *try*."

I wash the disgusting dishes and he dries them, and then he sweeps his tiny kitchen, I feel tense when he's right behind me, brushing up against my back. As I'm finishing up with the dishes and asking myself why the fuck I'm still here, his phone rings, and at first I wonder if it's Yuri, but when I see him smile at his screen, I know it's his sister.

"Answer it," I say.

"Why?"

"Because I want to meet her."

"Fine," he says, and a cute chunky little preteen appears on the screen. She has his pretty eyes. "Sonya, this is Natasha. Natasha, Sonya."

"Hi," she says. "She's pretty," she tells him.

"I know it," he says.

"You should have seen me before I had a kid."

She laughs and says, "Are you ready for your big show?"

"Sure," I say, but I'm lost, I'm not thinking of the show exactly, I'm thinking of my grandmother, of her own sister, Polina. It's so obvious my grandmother misses her every day, that she would give anything to be with her again, but she doesn't see it. So I look at Stas's sister. "Are *you* ready?" I ask her.

"For what?" she asks, and her brother gives me a big nervous look.

"For your brother to visit you when it's over," I say.

I can feel his spirit falling, but he gives her a big smile, and directs that smile at me with hatred in his eyes. "That's right," he tells her. "I can't wait."

The girl is so excited, the joy on her face is so real, that I don't regret what I've done. She shrieks and squeals and says oh my God she can't believe it, she's missed him so much, and then he tells her he's gotta go.

"I love you," he tells her, and she says, "You have no idea." He hangs up and I refuse to meet his gaze.

I just shrug and say, "Only trying to help." I imagine this was what he was thinking when he told Yuri about the play idea before I had decided to go all in on it. But he doesn't seem mad.

"It's fine, Sterling," he says.

Then he puts his arm around me and I let him keep it there. I know it's not going to go any further than that, this time. I thought he'd be livid after what I had just done, but he just seems tired. "Are you really ready for the show?" he asks.

And I just stand there, I can't even think of an answer.

"Sure," I tell him. "Sure I am."

Then I see he's still clutching that stupid poem, and I'm mad at him for writing it but also sorry for being so mad, so I snatch it out of his hands and walk away without even looking at him. He doesn't say anything as I stumble out. All I hear is Mama laughing at me all the way out the door.

I was livid the summer Mama decided to invade me and my grandmother's trip to Sevastopol, or rather, when she finally accepted my grandmother's standing invitation to join us, because why the fuck not, she was starting chemo in a month, and it was her last summer on Earth, just a few months before I would catch her singing and bury her not long after that—though we didn't know any of that at the time, of course. Not only was Mama encroaching on my very sacred grandmother time, but I was also particularly mad at her then because she basically ended my latest relationship. My college dropout drummer-slash-poet boyfriend Jake, the non-cunt-punter, and I were making out in his car outside our house when Mama yanked open the door in her stupid bathrobe, looking beautiful and furious, and declared, "It's past your curfew." The comment scared him off for good, reminding him that I was still in high school, after all, adding poor Jake to the list of men Mama had gotten rid of as swiftly as she killed those poor sick animals of my childhood, clobbering them with a frying pan in the yard during the night while I watched from my bedroom window, too scared to say something because, what—I was afraid I was next?

Cut to two weeks later, when Mama and I got to my grand-mother's seaside cottage after the boy stopped returning my calls. There I was, alone and drummerless on the Black Sea, gritting my teeth around my mother, trying to enjoy myself around my grand-mother, but mostly ignoring her too as a result, finding refuge with Ivan the bartender on the beach, a hairy bear of a man who barely spoke a lick of English, which was just fine for my purposes. I hated Mama for ruining Jake for me but was also freaking out about her impending procedure, wondering if that was what she thought about anytime she looked out at the ocean, but I was too afraid, or maybe just too self-absorbed, to ask her.

Most of the time that trip, she was laughing away at one thing or another with my grandmother, but one morning, my grandmother said she was taking a few hours to "meet a friend," and went off on her own. Though I hated her for being disloyal to my grandfather, I knew there was nothing I could do about it; if hosting a dying woman didn't stop her from running off to one of her men, then nothing would. Mama and I exchanged glances but did not say anything about it, and until then I didn't realize that this wasn't just a secret I had kept. My parents had long known about it too. And I was sad for my grandfather of course but happy that Baba was still able to chase after a bit of joy. Except this meant I was alone on the sea with Mama for basically a lifetime, hours and hours of just getting baked by the sun and saying almost nothing, until Mama stood up, as if summoned, to stare out at the water.

I watched her at the edges of the waves, just staring out with her long soon-to-be-gone wavy black hair falling on her pale back, like she was the last person on Earth. I followed her to the water, though I didn't have anything to say. And she turned to me with a big smile, like she had been waiting for me to come to her, even if she had spent all morning beside me on a towel saying nothing.

"When you were a little girl, I was out of my mind with sadness," she said. "It took me years to find work in America because I had such a hard time learning English. It was just full-blown depression, I see that now, but at the time, I just felt like my thoughts were the truth, that I needed to take myself out of the equation and that you and your father would be better off. Thank God we didn't have guns lying around! That would have been the end of me. . . ." she said, laughing a bit.

I could see how the general coldness I remembered from her when I was a kid was more like sadness, but the whole suicide angle was too much and I was both horrified and annoyed. Who wants to talk about almost-attempted suicide on vacation, let alone her own mother's? I was still feeling pretty sorry for myself, after Jake dumped me, and having a mother with cancer and all, so this was just too much to take. I was glad, after a moment, when I saw that she was not waiting for me to say anything, that she was just thinking.

"Your grandmother saw how upset I was, more than your father, I think. Remember that first dump where we lived in America, that awful-smelling apartment next to the big dirty swimming pool? She would see how sad I was and would say, 'Oh darling Valentina, why don't you just go for a swim in the pool?' Like that would solve anything! I never set foot in that dirty pool, it was beyond me, but your grandmother swam in it every day when she visited. . . ."

I laughed a little bit. "I do remember that," I said. "She had a big smile on her face the whole time, keeping her head above water."

"Exactly," Mama said. "And then, one summer, we took her to Wildwood, but I didn't think she'd actually go in the dirty water, though she did. And you followed her! I trailed along and I watched you going into the water. You were maybe nine and a good swimmer, but I was still nervous as you walked farther and farther into the choppy waves. The sun was beating down on me, everyone was in a good mood. But there I was, thinking, no, I can't kill myself, Natasha still needs me, I still have to look out for her, I can't let her drown. But then you swam on just fine, right toward your grandmother, and I thought again, no, Natasha's a big girl now, she can take care of herself, she doesn't need her mother anymore after all . . . and, well, that fall, your grandmother knew someone who knew someone who got me my first part-time accountant job, and she basically saved my life. No, no, she did save my life, I see that now."

I was standing there, tears streaming down my face, while the sun was shining down on us just like in the story, mad that I was feeling so much, that I never knew the depth of the pain I had caused her until that moment, wishing I could help. What was I supposed to say—what difference does it make that she saved your life if you're just going to go and die anyway?

"The water's pretty warm today," I said pointlessly, but Mama looked at me directly now, the spell was broken. She was no longer reminiscing, and she was maybe even mad that she had let herself reveal so much, let her guard down instead of being tough, tough, tough.

"What happened to your drummer?" she said, a bit meanly even.

"You scared him away," I said, swallowing down everything she had told me.

A thin smile crept along her face. "Good."

"Why do you like seeing me get my heart broken?"

"He's not good enough for you," she said. "None of these men are. What do you want from them?"

Her question struck me as ridiculous. I looked up at the birds high in the sky, the crags sticking out of the water in the distance, and three blond siblings fighting over a sand castle. Men—they gave it all meaning. Without them, the world was fluff.

"Everything," I said.

"But why, kitten? Your father loves you. Your mother loves you. Why do you insist on chasing after these deadbeats—what are you trying to prove?"

"You can't love me like they can," I said. "It's different."

"No," she said, shifting her gaze away from me. "I guess I can't."

And then she looked at the water again, but it was clear she had nothing more to say, that she was embarrassed about having said anything at all, and even resented me a little bit for hearing it, as if it was my fault she had decided to talk about being suicidal or whatever. And then she put her hands on her hips and stared at me, like she was waiting for me to reveal something in turn, and for a second I even racked my brains for something embarrassing I could tell her to make up for her revelations.

But I wasn't as dumb as she thought I was. I knew what she was doing, distracting me with her stories of sadness when we both knew what the problem was. She was the gatekeeper between me and my men, and she was determined that if she had to suffer, then I had to suffer too, that there would be no love in my life as long as she was clinging on to hers. We both turned to see my grandmother strutting toward us with her swim cap on, looking refreshed after her day of romance.

"What's the matter—why are you two just standing there?" she said, shaking her head. "Isn't it time for a swim?"

I don't feel ready at all to see my grandmother by the time Yuri tells me to get up. I stayed up for most of the night, sweating and tossing and turning and feeding Tally once and thinking of Mama, of how cruel I had been to her that summer, caring only about what she said about my stupid boyfriends instead of hearing how hard it was for her, the whole fucking motherhood business in a new country. But how could she have expected me to understand then? There's nothing to be done about it now, obviously.

I manage a shower-and-coffee resuscitation before we haul ass to JFK to pick up Baba in our rental car on a thankfully not-too-hot morning, to snatch her up before she does something stupid like take the train like she did the last time she visited, saying it was because she didn't want to trouble us. But really she had done it out of her fake proletarianism, her need to be a woman of the people though she's basically Kiev royalty. I'm hoping she doesn't even think about it this time, that she knows she was way too old to pull that stunt before and is definitely too old now. I'm so nervous and strung out after the sleepless night and my talk with Yuri and then Stas and not knowing what the fuck I'm doing that I realize I'm actually saying some of this stuff out loud.

Yuri says, "I don't think she'll take the train at this point."

"I hope not," I say. I'm in the back with Tally, watching her gnaw on her plastic keys, relieved to be sitting away from my own husband.

"You haven't told her about us, have you?" he says, and this nearly makes me choke.

"Of course not," I say. "Plus, I'm not sure what I would say."

"Me neither," he says.

He turns onto the highway and as we crawl forward, I wonder if he's going to tell me what I should have said, if he knows our status better than I do and has already made all the decisions. Since I told him about Stas, he hasn't exactly stopped talking to me, but he won't look me in the eye and only talks about Tally-related matters, like I'm one of his problem students that he's just being cordial to because he's stuck with her for the rest of the semester, except he knows he can't get rid of me quite as easily. And it's not like I've tried to have long soul-searching conversations either; I've just been working on getting the play right, hoping we'll figure it out once it's over.

"Listen," he says. "Next week—"

"Can we not have some big serious conversation right now? Can we give it a few days?"

"Next week, after your grandmother leaves, I'm going to Lake George for the weekend."

This cracks me up. "You've got your poles ready?"

"I'll figure something out."

"I guess it'll just be me and Tally," I say, brushing some hair out of my girl's eyes.

"If you say so."

"Stas is visiting his family after the play anyway."

"You don't need to tell me that. You're the one who said we should give it a few days."

"Fine."

I have an image of my father coming back with his fishing poles to his tiny Jersey City apartment, looking lovesick after hanging out with Yuri. I would ask him what they did there, what they talked about, but he would never tell me much, reminding me of the way I would act when I came home from a date and Mama gave me the third degree, though much less kindly of course. "We talked about life," he would say. "What about it? Did you figure it all out then?" He would smile big. "For that, we'd need to fish at least a few more times, darling."

As we cross into Queens, I stare at my daughter and the Hudson and wonder how I got to this fucked-up place, how I could have treated Yuri like such shit without even thinking twice about it. No, I can't blame my hormones or weakened mom state, because there are millions of moms out there who don't kiss and develop crushes, or worse, on their husband's best friend. A guy who I'm more confused about than ever since he messed things up by giving me that stupid poem, making me wonder if I ever knew him at all.

I need to get back to where I was, to the person I used to be before I had this fucking baby, the baby who is sweetly sleeping in the backseat, just minutes away from meeting her great-grandmother. And actually, I do think she looks like her a bit—when she's fussing over something, I can see it, that look on her face that so reminds me of my baba. The girl has become a wonder this summer, rolling over, babbling a bit, shaking rattles and chewing on everything in sight, even eating bananas. She's come such a long way from the human puddle I gave birth to, though she's got a long, long way to go. And yet, there are so many things my daughter can do that I wish I could—sleeping through the wild street sounds, facing the brutal, cold world with absolute wonder, smiling for no reason at all—but I have unlearned all of her survival skills, and one day, she will unlearn them, too, and there's nothing I can do about it.

She opens her eyes but doesn't cry out, she just stares at the cars flying by the window. Such a patient little thing, a girl I'm starting to feel somewhat connected to, a girl whose hair is getting a gorgeous fiery tint to it, beginning to cover up her enormous ears. I don't know if it's the fact that I've been busy working on my play and have actually had a chance to miss her, or if it's my hormones returning to normal or what. At least there's somebody around me who I feel somewhat certain about.

As I stroke Tally's hair, Yuri puts his face in his hands at a red light. "Fuck," he says.

"What?"

"I forgot to get flowers," he says. "How could I have forgotten the flowers?"

"That's all right," I say, and for some reason his genuinely distressed face over this non-issue when I am contemplating how cosmically I have failed makes me laugh. "She won't care."

Standing at arrivals with Tally strapped to me, I'm anxious as hell about seeing my grandmother, because she'll be able to tell that something is off. During our Sevastopol summers, she could always tell if I had snuck off in the middle of the night for a liaison, though she didn't make a big deal about it. One time, when I returned to the cottage after spending all night hooking up on a sandy blanket with a lifeguard, I thought my grandmother was asleep. But as I crept toward my room, her sharp voice pierced the darkness. "You might want to shower first, darling," she had said.

We watch the rumpled travelers descend with their small bags, rushing into the arms of the people who love them. There's a man in uniform, a tiny pink-haired woman hugging a surprisingly large dude with all her might, and a mother and her two children reuniting with a husband in a sweater that looks out of place in late August. And there she is, my dear grandmother, looking much frailer than she does over Skype, descending from the escalator like a spirit from the heavens, her silver braid still silky and falling past her shoulders, her pearls on, a grim little frown on her face, looking like she means business. My only blood besides my daughter, who is curled up against my chest in her carrier, a little dazed as she blinks up at the bright lights. The tears well up in my eyes, not just because it's been two years since I've seen her, before I was pregnant and when she and my grandfather were both healthy and happily eating at the little kitchen table I miss with all my heart, before I had fucked everything up. She really is the one soul on Earth who knows me, who knew Mama and of course Papa, who was proud to see me come out of my dark, dark twenties, though I'm doing no better now than the younger, flightier girl I was back then.

And in her face, I see Papa's, and just a touch of my own, and yes, even my daughter's, confirming that all of our genetic soup is as intermingled as I imagined. I rush toward her, forgetting, for a moment, that my daughter's strapped to my body, not understanding that the joy and wonder on my grandmother's face is reserved for her, this new miracle, not old-news me. She hunches slightly to get a good look at her.

"She looks better in person, actually," she says, stroking the top of her head, turning to the left and the right to inspect the girl. "One ear is a bit smashed in, have you noticed that? She was probably all jammed up, down there," she adds, gesturing at my lady parts, and for the first time in a while, Yuri and I both laugh. Tally, meanwhile, is staring at Baba with an open mouth, a black *O* of incomprehension. She looks up at the bright lights of the airport, the people rushing about, hugging loved ones and dragging suitcases and whipping out tickets, all of them with someplace to go, reminding me that I haven't left town since I played a runaway who was found belly-up in a lake in Chicago before I got knocked up.

"You made it," I say, giving my grandmother a big hug, smelling her thick perfume, and my eyes sting as the tears fall down my face.

"You haven't aged a day," Yuri says as he embraces her, and when he emerges from her grasp, she takes a step back and inspects us with the same suspicion she gave poor Tally. I know my hair's a mess, my last night's makeup is smudged, there's spit-up on my too-tight T-shirt, and my sandals are caked in playground muck. Baba is soaking all of this in, rearing her head back like I've stepped in dog shit.

"The child looks good," she says. "But what happened to her parents? Look at you—an old lady comes halfway across the world, and you don't even bring her flowers?"

PART IV

SUNSET

Larissa

My arm is linked with Yuri's as we stroll to the theater. The poor boy parked two blocks away and repeatedly asked if I was comfortable walking, as if I were some kind of invalid. And while it has been more and more difficult for me to walk lately, I am determined to make the most of my final trip to America, to welcome the challenge. I have spent so many days sitting by the sea, lapping at the waves, reading under the sun, waiting for my soul to regenerate. Of course, I loved being on the shore with a good book, but I had delved back into *Onegin* and it all just seemed mannered and silly to me, Onegin was just an old dunce for trying to get Tatyana back after all that time; he would have been better off staying home. I had already begun to feel—to say the least—a bit restless.

But my week in America isn't quite lifting my spirits either; it has been a strange one. I knew Natasha would be busy with her rehearsals, but she was not only busy but utterly distracted, barely even looking me in the eye, giving me far less attention than she offered during our Skype sessions, which did make me wonder once or twice why I even bothered going across the ocean for a face-to-face encounter. Though baby Talia! I must admit I've had a few fair moments with her, which is partly because I had been asked to watch her more often than I expected. In fact, the six-month-old child has been smiling and even laughing at my antics and generally giving me more attention than her distracted mother. Though her father, darling Yuri, had been as affectionate as always, just as he is at this moment.

"A gorgeous day, isn't it, Larissa Fyodorovna?" he says, gesturing at the ocean with the flowers in his other hand.

"Indeed," I say. "I will not have many more of them. When the play is over, you can bury me right on the beach."

He laughs and says, "But what about the after-party?"

"I suppose we can scope it out first, see how good the drinks are. . . ."

Natasha and her vagabond Stas have been preparing at the theater since morning. Talia is at home with the manager of Natasha's former bar for this special occasion. I am finding it hard to catch my breath, but I am happy to be out and about with a handsome man by my side.

Brighton Beach hasn't changed much since my husband and I visited my son in America just before his untimely death. The storefronts still boast their names in Russian. Occasional food wrappers and plastic bags float through the streets. The sand on the beach is dark and filled with branches and women who are too old to be showing so much of their sun-bronzed bodies. Women not much younger than me sit on their stoops, gossiping loudly. "I told my Marina one million times, Boris is no good for her, no good at all, but does she listen?" one of them says, and we pass them before we can hear a response, though I can well imagine it.

The last time I was here, my son had taken me and Misha to sit by the water at a restaurant with a slatternly name like Tatyana or Ruslana, and we were served warm beers in tall glasses and a perfectly decent meal. Though I had to do most of the talking, as usual, I remember enjoying myself, feeling as if there was nothing else in the world I wanted, even if the sanguine middle-aged man I had birthed across from me seemed to lack for everything as he picked at his meal, mayonnaise from Salat Olivier stuck to the corners of his mouth, without a woman to reach over and wipe his face for him. He did not soar like a rocket, my Tolik—he did not even come close. A man whose sadness predated his birth, whose movements even in my womb were so infrequent that I was surprised and delighted every time I felt another flutter in my abdomen after a long respite, relieved he was still alive.

My husband looked a bit melancholy as he gazed at the water, and I wondered if it was because he found the beach to be an inferior specimen, because he, too, pitied our poor boy and wondered how we could have raised such a lackluster being, or if he was just afraid of dying. I asked him about it later that night, as we settled into our son's puny guest room. "Oh, Larissa," he said. "You read too much into everything. I don't even know what you're talking about. I was perfectly happy to be there. It must have been a bit of indigestion." I did not believe him for a second, but I did not press on. I only went back one more time after that—for Natasha's wedding—and I told my husband to stay home, citing his health, though to be honest it was because I did not want him to bring down my mood. Staying cheerful at my age was a hard enough business as it was.

"Does it feel anything at all like home?" Yuri says as we pass a stand with an old man selling dried fish and sunflower seeds. Here, beer cannot be sold in the streets, a true travesty.

I laugh. "Who knows what home feels like anymore?"

"I suppose you're right," he says. This time, he is not playing along and looks a bit lost himself. I can't blame him, with his wife either tied up with the baby or at the theater, while he blunders on at the university. It has not been the easiest summer for him. Perhaps it is a blessing for him, for Natasha, for me, for all of us, that the summer is coming to a close, that the days have been getting shorter.

"I bet you're ready for the show," I say, and he smiles.

"Definitely," he says. "I'm ready for Natasha to relax a bit. She's been working so hard."

"So have you."

His eyes twinkle at my bit of mischief. He knows I love Natasha but that I am also aware of how hard he is working, that she is not the only one with responsibilities.

"I'm so happy you were able to come. I know it means the world to Natasha," he says.

"It was nothing," I tell him. "What else do I have to do? Rework my will?"

"That is only necessary if you plan on leaving more for us," he says.

"I will leave you everything, little fools."

"Stop the nonsense," he says, patting me on the back. "You will outlive us all."

What a kind, well-mannered boy—one with a sense of humor, at that. A loving husband and father. And yes, one whose sense of duty and politeness is not unlike my Misha's, but yet, who appeals to me utterly. A man who does not seem prone to bouts of abyss-gazing, though that may very well come later.

We are fast approaching the theater, which is spray-painted a tacky gold-and-red color meant to look regal. The marquee boasts the title SUNSET, which it takes me a moment to realize is the name of dear Natasha's play, unknown to me until now. When we enter the auditorium, I begin to feel nervous, though I have utter faith in my granddaughter. I must say the place is much larger than I expected, based on the previous hellholes I had crawled into to watch my sweet girl perform, places with beer-stained seats, cracked toilets, and moldy ceilings. There are velvet curtains and dim lights on either side, and the place is quite cozy, the seats warm and inviting.

There must be at least three hundred seats in the place, but only two dozen of them are filled, at most. I check my watch and see that we are quite early, that the crowd still has fifteen minutes before the curtain opens, but when I look behind me, I don't see anyone coming. Yuri is concerned about the lack of crowd too—for weeks Natasha has been promoting the show on the Internet—but it feels taboo to mention it.

"It's not an utter hellhole, after all," I tell Yuri, and he gives me a small laugh.

"Definitely not," he says. "A nice place," he adds pointlessly, also looking over his shoulder for imagined guests.

There are only a few minutes left and only a handful of people have trickled in since we arrived, a few of them waving at Yuri, which means they are simply friends who have taken pity on my poor granddaughter, not discerning theatergoers. What is poor Natasha thinking backstage? Is she also feeling a pit in her stomach as the emptiness of the room dawns on her? I hope she is too focused on getting into character, getting her show on the road at last, to notice. Or perhaps when she comes onstage, the lights will be too bright for her to even see the lackluster crowd.

At last, the lights dim slightly, signaling that there are only minutes before the show begins. Then I hear a clanging of high heels and Yuri and I both turn around to see three extremely dolled-up young women in high black boots and black dresses, and enough makeup that they themselves should be onstage. Behind them, I see at least a half dozen other young women and men who are dressed in a similarly garish manner, and I understand that these are Natasha's former theater colleagues. Well, I think her Baby Borsches are better than empty chairs, and I hope she thinks the same.

Yuri gives them a faint wave. "The whole gang is here," he mutters, but he does not look entirely displeased. And then he squeezes my hand. Before I have time to say anything else, the curtain falls and I realize the show is going to start on time. Natasha has refused to tell me much more about the play than she did when she first invited me to see it; all I know is that it's personal to her, and that she hopes I like it.

When the curtain opens, I don't believe what I'm seeing. Natasha stands onstage with a long braid in her hair and books under her arms. She looks right at the audience, and in the faintest Russian accent, she begins to speak.

"Leave Kiev?" she says, to no one in particular. "Tell me, how can I leave Kiev? Kiev is the only city I have ever known. The Nazis, at least they are a known evil, but who knows what will happen in the mountains. . . ."

I gasp and put a hand to my mouth. Can it be true? Natasha appears to be playing a young version of me. Yuri squeezes my hand and says, "I hope you like it," confirming my suspicions. But I'm not so certain I do like it. My granddaughter looks comical up there, like a child playing with her mother's makeup, and I can't help feeling like I'm being mocked.

Then the lights flicker and she runs in circles to strange music and when they return, she is transformed into my grandmother. She wears the white boa and the frilly hat and coat and though she did not have time to put on more makeup, she looks all dolled up now, indeed different from the girl she had played moments ago. It is something unbelievable—truly! How could the girl not tell me? How could she hide it from me all summer long—how dare she put my story onstage for strangers to scoff at?

"Leave Kiev?" this old-woman Natasha asks again, her voice heavy with disbelief. "I almost left Kiev during the Revolution. This is different, I suppose. . . ."

I am angry, I am ecstatic, I am captivated. Who could believe it? The family boards the train, where there is hardly any talk at all, just rattling and whooshing and younger Natasha talking to her parents and sister. But only when the train arrives do I realize that the Orlov family has been cut out of the picture, there is no second set of parents and no brothers, which seems to miss completely the point of my story. I know it can be difficult to embody many personages during a one-woman show, but without the Orlovs, my story of the mountains means nothing, or that is what I have believed up to this point. I suppose I should not blame the girl for cutting back on them for the sake of simplicity. It is difficult to make room for all the people in our lives. But most of the stories I have painstakingly told without knowing their purpose have been thrown out the window. Yuri keeps looking at Natasha and then back at me, watching my expression.

"It's fine," I tell him. "I'm fine." He begins to relax slightly, though I am still bewildered.

We have already begun to settle into our mountain apartment, and Grandmother Natasha flails her boa around and complains while scrawny me tells her it will all be fine. The parents leave for work, me and Grandmother Natasha are alone, and we bond over stories about the glory days of Imperial Russia, and she even teaches me a bit of French. My stage self's relationship with her grandmother is far warmer than I could have ever hoped for. And then, in comes Licky—or, rather, a stuffed version of my dear family bobcat, who just sits there, accepting his fate. That is where Polina comes in and has her shining moment. And as Natasha twirls around, impersonating my gorgeous, ailing sister, I am no longer mad at her, and I get caught up in her spell—truly, she looks just like her, and it makes my heart curdle. I feel faint. I want to embrace her. I want her to run off. I want to tell her how sorry I am. I never want to see her again. Natasha lingers on the role of my sister for far too long, in my opinion. Who needs to see Polina's transformation from a beautiful girl to a cynical, stony woman? What a sweet relief when she turns into me again!

Though I was nervous for the girl at first, noting some uncertainty, some chaos in her movements, she begins to hit her stride after the cold winter, when she clutches at her stomach and moans for food, worrying over my sister's condition with more love and understanding than I was ever able to give my own blood. I do not even know how long I have been holding Yuri's hand. Did I reach out to him for comfort, or did he anticipate that I needed some and reach over to me instead, the poor boy?

You know the rest—a touch of starvation, a crescendo of cold nights, long days at the factory for my father, the poor kitty boiled in a stew by my stern mother, another overlong monologue by my gorgeous sister, who seems to never want to get offstage, my father dies, and then Grandmother and I are at the market, where we happen to hear that the war is over, it's time to go home, which is not exactly how it happened, but then, there she is, holding my hand, preparing to fall to her death. "My train," Grandmother Natasha says, looking off into a dim, unknowable future. "My train. That's my train. My train is coming for me at last." And then I close my eyes, because I do not want to relive my own grandmother's death, but after a moment I open them, because I sense that nothing's happening.

My grandmother is staring up at the ceiling, at an imagined sky, where the lights behind her turn pink and purple to imply that the sun is setting. "Will you look at that?" she says, to all of us. Then the stage goes black as we hear the rumbling of a train, followed by a crash and a scream. My grandmother is dead. The curtain falls. The play is over. I can feel my heart beating in my throat.

She gets a standing ovation from the few dozen people who

have turned up, and Yuri and I rise to join them. The business was a bit messier than her other shows, less polished than her long-ago *Karenina* knock-off, but who could blame her, having done this all on her own, as a new mother at that? Her performance was a bit rough around the edges—yes, she stuttered a few times, forgot her lines a time or two—but it had more soul than all of the work I had ever seen her do put together, though I may be biased, of course. I clap as loud as the youth in the audience, and my face flushes with pride. Natasha returns to the stage, glowing as the audience stands. I hope the girl feels the good work she has done, I truly do. I hope she is not discouraged by the half-empty seats.

So far, she is still smiling, glowing from her success. And then Stas emerges from backstage, where he has been helping out, and is clapping for her, wildly. And once more, I am hit with another surprise. When the two of them look at each other, I feel as if I have been slammed over the head with a pot of Stroganoff. How did I not see it all along? Her gleaming eyes and enhanced makeup, his wild, desperately not-homosexual visage—how did I not see that these two were as entangled as me and Ivan Dolgorukov, a bureaucrat who visited me on the sea from time to time, always leaving me with another shiny bauble to remember him by, even if it would be indiscreet to wear it?

First, the fact of her putting on a play based on my story—and now this. Too much for this old woman to bear.

My cheeks burn with shame. Of course I have missed this, along with so many other things that were right in front of my nose. The fact that Licky was being fattened up for the slaughter for all those months. Bogdan's nighttime affairs. And perhaps that I had once been the true object of his affections, though he told me so plainly. And what else? That my sister had needed me, and I had failed her. But what can I do about any of that now?

I glance at Yuri, who continues to clap with an unreadable look. Is he excited for Natasha? Disappointed about the crowd? Or is his soul crushed by a much larger disappointment?

Natasha grabs the microphone and I panic, thinking what, are they going to announce their mad love? But of course not, she thanks the audience and her husband for their support, introduces Stas and so on, though what happens next is almost as awful.

"This may be a surprise," she says. "But we have a special request. I wouldn't have been able to tell this powerful story if it wasn't for my grandmother, who graciously told us everything that happened to her before and during the Great War. Without my grandmother's strength, well, I wouldn't be standing here today. I wouldn't be alive, let alone an actress. I wouldn't be who I am. So please join me in welcoming her to the stage and give her a round of applause."

Utter humiliation! Natasha says my name, and then Yuri helps me trudge up to the too-bright stage. I stand up there squinting at the audience, and everyone cheers and claps so loudly that I think it will knock me over, but I remain where I am until the crowd begins to rustle out of their seats, approaching the stage with flowers. Natasha gives me a hug and then studies my face.

"I hope—" she begins.

"It was fine, darling. I am not angry with you, you naughty girl. It was shocking, but a nice surprise, a nice surprise," I tell her.

"Really? I was worried. I was going to tell you, but then I thought it would be fun to have you see it without knowing what to expect."

"No need to worry about me, dear. I thank you for the tribute— truly. And the show itself—it was quite good. Your best work by far."

"Thank you, Baba, thank you! That means so much." I try to read her face—for what? To see if she is disappointed by the turnout? To see if she is madly in love with Stas? To confirm that I have failed to care for her after all?

"You were dynamite," Yuri tells her as he hands her his flowers and gives her a kiss on the cheek. But I am uneasy now around these three, and I watch Stas watching him and feel even more convinced that there is something going on between him and Natasha. Yuri looks at him warily, or perhaps I am inventing drama where none exists, but I can say that this would also explain why things had been so tense around the household. I had assumed Natasha was just exhausted from mothering and play-mothering, but there seems to be more at stake.

"Thanks, babe," she says to him, but she keeps her eyes locked on me. "You really didn't hate it?"

"Of course not, darling. You did well for yourself. I am proud. And you too, my boy," I tell Stas, though it hurts even more than normal to look at the creature, who has been surprisingly kind to me since my arrival. "I heard you helped out."

"Only a bit," he says with a bow.

"I hope I did your story justice, Baba. I wasn't sure what you'd think," Natasha says.

"As much as you could have," I say. "You cut some of it out, didn't you?"

"I hope you didn't mind," Natasha says, looking at Stas carefully. But he will not look at her: he only looks from me to Yuri.

"Not at all," I say. "I thank you for it."

But the admirers have lined up, ready with flowers and lavish praise for my girl, and I want to give her time to enjoy this moment.

Yuri and I return to the sidelines, sitting down again to watch the fans flattering Natasha, and only when I see her nervously tapping one of her heels do I understand that of course the girl is devastated, that she saw the half-empty seats in the audience, that she is waiting to be alone to give out an inhuman cry, to wonder what exactly she had worked for, and what unintended consequences it might have had. The poor darling! I may still be emotional over her play, and furious about her affair, but my heart still bleeds for her. Her face is glazed over in an expression I remember all too well from the summer after her mother died, when she and her father joined me in Sevastopol—how the girl joked around to lift her father's spirits, though I was not oblivious to the makeup stains on her pillow every morning.

The girls from her former theater troupe pull her aside, and they seem to be begrudgingly paying her compliments, which she even looks slightly pleased to hear, because this is better than nothing, and maybe she has made a small peace with the made-up girls. She is gorgeous under the blinding lights, even if her face is still half-covered in old-lady makeup.

But her play's reception, I remind myself, is not what is at stake here. I watch Yuri watching her and wonder: how much does he know? He puts his arm around me and continues to watch the stage with a bemused expression. Does he know he is in the thick of disaster?

"I know Natasha and I make a strange pair," he says. "I know she has a wild heart and desires I cannot help her attain. I married her knowing that, because she was special, not like the girls my mother set me up with, who were perfectly nice but never made me feel a thing. I loved Natasha right away because she was so different from those girls, and so different from me. But I knew my choice could lead to problems down the line," he said. "I'm not blind."

"I never said she was a perfect girl," I say. "But you have given her everything she has expected from you. And more. Do not be so hard on yourself. There have been many benefits for her, to be with someone like you instead of . . ." I trail off, gesturing at the undereducated aesthetes on the stage, making certain to avoid Stas with my gaze. But then Yuri sinks into his seat and returns to his standard tone. The man who had spoken moments ago has retreated.

"I'm so proud of her," Yuri says. "She was amazing up there. Of course I want this show to open up more possibilities for her. But I wish she could see that she already has so much to be grateful for. She has me, she has our daughter. I wish I could be more than a professor at a community college, that I could give her more. But if only she would see that we already have everything we need, when it comes down to what's important."

"Of course she already sees that," I say carefully. "She treasures her life with you, dear boy. Before you, she was so lost."

"You helped her too," he says. "I hope you know how much she loves you. All those summers she spent with you were not lost on her. She has learned all of her strength from you. And her values. You've taught her how to live."

This makes me lurch back a bit. Is he speaking sincerely, or is there a tinge of accusation in his voice? Those summers indeed! Is it more than a tinge—a complete denouncement?

"Nonsense," I say. "She has done it all on her own. Do not give me so much credit."

I spend the last night of my visit on Natasha's balcony with a glass of cognac and a cigarette long after Yuri has gone to bed. Natasha is still out at the bar, a loud, seizure-inducing faux-Russian place near the theater where I lasted all of twenty minutes, long enough to watch Natasha take three shots of vodka while Yuri and Stas had a somber conversation near the bathroom, and then Yuri drove me home with a tremendous pile of flowers in the backseat, to where Natasha's former manager, Mel, was watching television while the baby slept. The flowers are in a pile by the door now, and I can smell them from where I sit.

Now old Sharik and I regard the street below us, its narrow sidewalks and teeming plastic garbage bins, scraggly trees that fail to disguise the ugliness of the dirty streets, and the lights in the building across from us lit up like buttons on a switchboard, so many strangers out there in the large and confounding world. It is well past midnight, yet a few couples and a gaggle of young women wander down the streets in search of fun, and I can't blame them for chasing after it while they can. The balcony can barely contain the three neglected potted plants and empty bird feeder and me and the cat, and yet it has been my refuge since I arrived. The cat brushes up against me, as if he knows I am leaving.

"You will be lost without me, boy," I tell him, and he brushes more furiously in response. He has been sleeping at my feet every night, and I will miss his warm and smelly presence in my sleeping quarters, even if he has some nasty habits. I put out my cigarette, drain my glass, and leave the balcony. Sharik follows me out and jumps on the couch as if to encourage me to rest along with him on the sad piece of furniture that is nearly as old and saggy as yours truly.

Though Natasha and Yuri had insisted I take their bed, I took the couch so they would have some privacy in their tiny bedroom. Besides, the living room is quite cozy, with its lampshades draped in scarves, holiday lights framing the windows, coffee table adorned by the stubs of purple candles and glass bowls of rocks, with a photograph of my nasty grandmother lording over it all. Natasha has tried to give the little place some character, reminding me how few are the things that truly belong to us, no matter how we try to dress them up. This is the kind of life I had pictured for her all those years when I did not send along vast swathes of money, the same way my father did not spoil me. In some ways, her big, open living room reminds me of my childhood apartment. And yet, the girl has found a way to get in trouble without extravagance. A girl who I hope is on her way home now, to her husband, avoiding an interloper's charms.

The bedroom door is slightly open, practically beckoning me, and I approach, though I know it is a transgression. I rarely enter the room where Natasha, Yuri, and little Talia sleep, and it is neater in there than I expected, relatively spare compared to the cheerful chaos of the rest of their home. Talia's crib is by the door, blocked off by a Japanese curtain as an attempt for some privacy for the happy couple. Yuri snores gently, a tempered man even in repose, one arm splayed out, as if to fill the gap where Natasha's body should be. I lean over my great-granddaughter's crib and stare at her sleeping form. Toward the end of Natasha's pregnancy, she would cry out during our Skype sessions, her eyes large as she placed a hand on her belly, telling me how hard the girl was kicking her, and I was glad the child had some fight in her already. Though it should not seem like such a miracle at this point, the girl traveling from Natasha's womb to this crib, it still fills me with wonder.

The girl has come a long way from the rat-faced thing she was the first time I laid eyes on her over the computer screen. She has hair now, little brown-red ringlets, and her eyes are big like her mother's, dare I say a bit like her great-grandmother's, and she is gaining a semblance of silly personality, a mischief around the eyes, even when they are closed. Perhaps this was why I was so repulsed when I first laid eyes on her. I knew I would never see her grow into a young woman or find her way in the mystifying universe, so I decided not to bother. And then, out of nowhere, her eyes pop open—I am caught! I hold my breath and wait for her to cry and rat me out, but she does no such thing. She simply holds my gaze. We are co-conspirators.

I reach into my pocket, pull out the velvet pouch, and, from that, the ruby necklace. I dangle it in front of the child. Imagine, a necklace belonging to the Empress Maria, passed on to my great-grandmother, in the reach of this American-born child, light-years ahead of the first known necklace owner, a serf-owning woman married to the second-to-last tsar of Russia, the mother of Nicholas, Russia's final monarch. The baby girl I see is a universe away from serfs or tsars, and good riddance, and yet, her eyes light up as she reaches for the necklace. It is a heavy object, one that must have weighed down my grandmother considerably during the war, when her form shrunk from plumpness to skin and bones, and now it is the perfect bauble for a baby. The child's face is flooded with so much delight I worry she might laugh.

I know there will be no more visits, that this is the last time we will see each other. What will the world hold for this tiny creature after I am gone? What ties her to me? What will she take from her mother, and what has her mother taken from me? All of the wrong things, I am afraid, but it is too late to do anything about it. Oh, what difference does it make? Dust is a must. I have reached the edge of my grave and am gazing into the abyss with longing. The infant will have to fend for herself, just as I did. I stroke her delicate hair and take the necklace away, and then I sneak out of the room and prepare to rest.

As I climb under my covers on the couch, next to Sharik, I picture Natasha onstage as my grandmother, feeling the silliness of seeing my life play out before my eyes. It was fine that she had changed the story, mind you, that she had simplified it, which is something I wish someone had done to my actual life. Though the story was even more complicated than I had let on—I had not told Natasha everything. She would not have known what to do with it. I did not want to overwhelm my poor granddaughter, or to make her think less of me.

I see myself onstage again, before the gullible audience, except this time it is truly me, a young Lara, and instead of Babushka Natasha, I see long-dead Babushka Tonya, the genuine article. The audience fades, and so does the auditorium, the stage. We are back in the mountains.

I have been seething ever since my grandmother not only failed to praise my father during his funeral but also had the gall to say that going to the orphanage was the best thing that ever happened to him. My anger reaches a fever pitch when she begins speaking to him during her mad rants, telling him he once had the rosiest cheeks. How could she dare to address my poor dead father as a boy—a boy she had treated so poorly? No, no—she had taken things too far. Once I hear her speak to him, I decide she needs to be punished.

That night, I wait until my sister's restless body settles above me, and I confirm that my grandmother is sound asleep as well. Then I slither out of bed. I hover over my grandmother, take a deep breath, and reach under her filthy boa to unclasp her necklace. Her thick, snakelike skin brushes against mine and nearly makes me leap—I have never truly touched her before. I stuff her necklace into my underwear. And then I sleep the sleep of the dead.

In the morning, I wake up to my grandmother's cries.

"Where is it? Where is it?"

I watch her go on with her wild accusations, watch her mind completely dissolve, watch Polya and Bogdan become as fused as the welded components of a steel bridge, watch Mama become even more immobilized by heartache. I keep the necklace in my underwear during the first day of the search and the next night, once everyone is asleep once again, I go outside to dig up the portrait of Papa and Mama and bury the necklace underneath it.

"I know you never cared for riches, Papachka," I say. "But I hope you can keep this safe."

I did not and do not believe in God or an afterlife, did not think Papa was prancing around with the angels while waving the ruby necklace in the air, or using it to buy himself endless Champagne and caviar, or that it made a lick of a difference, as if dead wasn't dead. As if putting a portrait in the ground meant any speck of my father resided there. No, he was but a corpse in the mountains in a place I would never see, a mean wind whistling above his cold bones. Still, taking the necklace away from my grandmother and giving it to Papa makes me feel better for a while.

I do not feel sorry for my grandmother, not even when she starts wandering outside and babbling to her long-dead relatives, it only fills me with a sharp joy.

But after a few weeks, even this pleasure fades, and I want to dig my claws in even more.

I hear a rustling in the middle of the night and watch my grandmother rise in her nightgown and wander outside to where Papa is buried. I follow her, while Polya sleeps on. For a moment, I worry that she has discovered the location of the necklace, but once I hear her mad babbling addressed at her daughter, I realize the jewels are safe.

"Shura," she mutters under her breath when she reaches the grave, calling to her long-dead daughter. "Dear Shura. Why aren't you here to save me?"

This old, tired woman in a boa, babbling in her nightgown—I almost pity her, but I do not lose my resolve.

"Maybe Papa could have saved you," I say.

"How's that, my dear?" she says. She wipes her forehead with her coal-black boa. It takes a moment for her eyes to settle on me, for me to be certain she knows I am not Shura.

"Papa could have saved you, maybe," I say. "But you killed him."

"How's that?" she says again, genuine confusion furrowing her ancient face.

"You killed him slowly when you trucked him off to that orphanage, when you made him a caretaker of Uncle Pasha and all those lost, lonely boys. Then you killed him again, last month, when he saw another crowd of helpless boys and could not help but save them over himself. You exiled him from his own family and made him think his life was worth nothing—even at his funeral, you couldn't be bothered to say a single kind word about him! You're the most selfish woman I've ever met, but Papa was utterly selfless because of you, don't you see? Just like Polya is utterly spoiled because of you! You are hideous and vile and have never done anybody a lick of good!" I say.

She tilts her head back and lets out a long, maniacal laugh. I can see a sliver of her white throat, bare without its necklace.

"Selfish?" she says. "You think I am selfish?"

And then she gives me a hard, cold slap. She had not hit me since she mocked me for wanting to touch her necklace when I was a child. I enjoyed the familiar bitterness of the sting.

"Who are you?" she says then. "Who are you to understand the decisions I have made? To know what I have suffered? You don't know anything about the world. I am not selfish in the least—if I were selfish, I would have fled to Odessa with my children and set foot in the free world, but I did not know what life would be like there. So what did I do for them, instead? I married a monster!"

"A monster?"

"A man whose monstrosity I did not understand until my boys had been living under the same roof with him for a few months. It was too late to take my choice back, but not too late to send them away! What else could I do—leave him and my daughter and go back out on the streets? I couldn't do that on my own."

"So you're the one. You're the one who sent them away."

"It was best for everybody."

"You're crazy," I say, stepping back. "You're a crazy old lady. You're the monster!"

I could not believe what she was telling me. I searched her face for hints that she was crazy, that she was the same person who was babbling to her dead sister just moments ago. No, her story was reasonable. It made sense of her comment that entering the orphanage was the best thing that ever happened to my father. I recalled how Papa always stood an arm's length away from Dimitrev senior any time we visited his lavish apartment, his body stiff like he was bracing against an icy wind, his knuckles white against his sides. How could I have misread his hatred of him—I assumed it was because the man had him sent away, not because he had degraded him. My poor Papa! All those evenings spent enduring this bawdy man with his vodka as he flirted recklessly with Polina and Baba Tonya. Twisting his silver mustache around his dirty finger. The more he twisted it, the longer—

Could it be true? Of course, it was beyond me to show my grandmother that I believed one shred of her story. It was too late. I had already made up my mind about her.

"Go back to bed, Baba," I say. "Come on, let's go back to sleep."

She looks up at me like she has an endless river of things to tell me, her eyes wet but lucid, and I do not want to hear it. Instead, in a small voice, she says, "I am exhausted." And then she follows me back to the apartment.

Which is where I lie, wide awake, waiting for signs that my grandmother is asleep—but she continues to toss and turn until I hear Uncle Ivan and Snowball stepping out for a walk, and then I hear Mama and Aunt Tamara stirring, so I lose my chance to creep back under the linden tree to dig up the necklace, which is very unfortunate, because when everyone gets up, Mama insists that Baba accompany me and my sister and the brothers to the market, where she dies before I have a chance to return her finery.

I leave it resting under the linden tree until we prepare to leave the mountains. Then, while my sister and Bogdan sleep above me, I sneak out to dig it up, pausing to run my hand over the Papa and Mama portrait packed in the dirt. Though the town is silent as I claw through the earth, when I look up at the apartment, I think I see it: a tiny rustling of the curtain on the balcony. Did Polina hear me leaving the room and go out there to see what I was doing, suspecting that the only thing worth digging up in the middle of the night was the damn necklace? Or was I just seeing things? The next day, she treats me with her usual indifference and does not seem particularly suspicious, though she is so weak that it's hard to see how she feels about anything.

I keep the necklace hidden in Kiev for the next decade, until Bogdan dies and we buy the cottage by the sea, and then I hide it under the floorboards there, not knowing what to do with it for all these long years until I began telling Natasha my story and understand where it must go. I resurrect it during my return to my seaside home, finding it waiting for me there, as shiny and formidable as it had been in my youth. At first, I am almost afraid to touch it, as if it is haunted. As if my grandmother will materialize out of the ether to slap me for taking it away, and tell me, one more time, "Why Larissa. I did not think you cared for nice things."

My edges fade by morning. All night long, it is not the conversation with my grandmother that flits before my eyes, but my last conversation with my sister. I see Polina, shorn-haired, standing beside me at the Kiev station as she prepares to board the train that will take her away from her Motherland for good. After I told her to keep up her looks a little more and she scoffed at me and said, "Is that right, Larissa? Our grandmother cared about appearances, didn't she? And look where it got her." I wondered—had she seen me digging up that necklace, just before we left the mountains, understanding what I had done? Or was she just commenting on our grandmother's frivolous nature—one she had decided to forgo, and one which she believed, with good evidence, that I carried on?

I have tried to return to that night again and again over the years, to stare up at Building 32 after I unburied the necklace to see if someone was watching me from the balcony. Sometimes I saw my sister in her nightgown, but more often I saw nobody. Once the ghost of Papa appeared, staring out into the dark woods, eyes tinged with disappointment at me for not taking care of my sister. Yet another time, a ray of light shined on the balcony and revealed Licky merrily rolling around on his back, his belly basking in the glow. My grandmother and horse-faced Aunt Shura made an appearance once, doing the can-can with their arms around each other, their skirts flying up.

And truly, what did it matter? It is as pointless as trying to recall whether I ate fish or beef on my wedding night. There is no getting Polina back. Though I have my doubts, if there is something on the other side of this life, then perhaps I will find her again. Perhaps I will walk toward her, and tug on her arm as she had once done to me as we were leaving the city. "I'm scared," I would tell her, while she would give me a triumphant smile and say, "Well, don't be!" It would serve me right.

Though there is one thing I can do when I return to my country, I decide. I can make a trip to that orphanage in Kharkov, after all. Why not poke around there? It could not hurt to see the place where my father and uncle spent their formative years. I have seen a photograph of the endless gray building and have pictured all the little bunk beds inside, though I hope they have been updated since my father told us about them in the mountains. There is nothing to fear. I picture myself opening the door and stepping into the warm, welcoming light.

Just after I hear Natasha stumbling in, I manage to drift off at last, floating on a stormy river on a tiny boat with my sweet father, who is troubled by the roiling waters. We're wearing heavy winter coats and wool scarves. Papa kisses my forehead and tightens my scarf and says, "You need to bundle up, Larissa, the winter is going to be colder than ever this year." Then he closes his eyes and begins to cry, which I slowly understand is not my father crying, no, it is the baby stirring, followed by the even-sweeter sounds of her mother waking up to care for her and that, I think, is not the worst sound that could interrupt your slumber.

Natasha

"And then Babies Vera was like, 'Wow, with all that makeup, you actually managed to look like you were on the brink of starvation—very impressive!' Can you believe her? She called me fat the last time I saw her too. It's like, I get it, I get it—why don't you try having a kid and see how you come out? And it's not like those girls are hot shit themselves—with all that makeup, they all look about forty-five, but do you see me insulting them?" I say, trying to keep things light, like I don't care that nobody came to the play, as Yuri and my grandmother and I dig in to our last breakfast together, one I prepared with some difficulty, due to my brutal hangover and lack of sleep.

The sky was already turning pink when I got home from the after-party and I just curled up in bed scrolling through my phone, counting the likes on my *#curtainsup #Mamasback #grandmotherland #brightlightsBrightonbeach* posts, trying to feel happy that anyone at all cared at least a little bit, even though a picture of Tally sucking on her foot would have gotten more traction. Though I knew I killed it, I wished the people who liked my damn post had just come to see the play instead. My one comfort was that I think my grandfather wouldn't have found a thing to criticize. I could almost picture his letter to me: *You were perfect. Just the right amount of emotion. And you did it all yourself!*

Yuri shakes his head as I continue to make fun of the Borsch Bitches. "You should be happy the Borschies came at all. That was nice of them."

"Stop being so reasonable," I say.

"What is wrong with looking like you're forty-five, dear girl? I would amputate my left foot to be forty-five again," says my grandmother.

"You look much better than those girls, Larissa Fyodorovna," Yuri says with a wink.

"And who cares how much you weigh?" Baba says, ignoring the flattery. "You were phenomenal. Truly. And I have seen quite a range of your previous work, so I can say this with confidence."

"Thanks *a lot*."

"What? It is a compliment, darling. You are evolving, and I am so proud."

"It was your best work by far, Natashka," says Yuri. "You should have seen yourself—it was like you were possessed. The part where you ate the cat? You were amazing."

His eyes are somber but sincere. Though he said the same thing last night, I didn't really hear him. "Thank you."

The rest of breakfast is quite pleasant. Tally's sitting in her new high chair, picking at a bowl of berries, smacking away happily, while Baba fusses with her. I stick my tongue out at her and she gives me a little monkey laugh.

Yuri and I chuckle back at her, but we can't think of anything to say next. We have decimated everything on the table so there's no food to distract us, so we just watch our daughter finishing up her food. Last night at the bar, he and Stas had words near the bathroom, and after that, Stas said he was leaving to see his family in the morning, that he wasn't sure when he would be back. But I was okay with that. I told him to take his time, and I would take mine. But the rest of the night, after Yuri and my grandmother left, he was by my side, though Stephanie kept coming between us, raving about how I killed it onstage, but she eventually told me to take care of myself, took a shot of tequila, and went home. Stas and I closed down the place, and though we split an Uber, he didn't ask me to come up when it stopped in Harlem. He just took my hand and lifted it to his mouth and gave it one long kiss. "Until next time," he said.

My grandmother gets up and opens the fridge to unearth the chocolate cake we brought to the after-party last night, all covered in pink-and-white icing and far too sweet for more than one bite, though almost two-thirds of it was devoured. She carefully cuts herself a slice, plops it on a plate, and eats it standing up.

"What?" she says as Yuri and I watch her, mesmerized. I know what she's going to say before she says it: "It's never too early for dessert."

Yuri laughs and says, "No, I suppose it isn't." He forks a piece of the cake in solidarity. The two of them are just standing in the kitchen chewing together, looking kind of forlorn, because it's time for them to say goodbye. We had already planned this—he'll head out and Tally and I will walk Baba to the train to say goodbye.

Yuri gives my grandmother a big hug. "Remember," he tells her, wagging a finger, "you promised to update your will for me."

"Of course, dear child. I will leave you all of my horses and carriages, and a room of Roman statues."

"Anything else?"

"Chests full of gold. You'll never have to work again."

"Wonderful."

I hate when they talk like this, but I don't stop them for once, I let them do their weird morbid thing, though it hits too close to home. Who knows when—or if—we'll see Baba again? I stand by the mirror and fuss around with my hair, with old Great-Great-Grandmother Tonya looking down at all of us, her gaze striking me as more bewildered than cold, right then, wondering what the fuck any of us are doing. Then I get Tally out of her chair and hold her chunky little body in my arms, feeling the weight of her head on my shoulder, which makes me feel less hungover and nauseous for one sweet second, like all is right in the universe.

Yuri lifts a finger and runs into the hallway and brings back a huge bouquet of flowers I advised him against buying, which are more majestic than the ones he gave me after my performance, though I can't blame him.

"Some flowers to see you off," Yuri says with a shy smile as he hands them to my grandmother. "Since we failed to greet you with them."

"Foolish boy, you expect me to drag these all the way home?" Baba says, though she is pleased.

"It's the thought that counts," I say.

"These are quite nice," she says, and she gives them a big long sniff. "And they will look great next to Natasha's flowers," she says, and she takes the bouquet and drops it on top of the flower pile by the door.

"Can't blame me for trying," says Yuri.

He gives my grandmother one more hug before stepping out the door, to begin a slew of errands to keep the house in order before he leaves for his fishing trip. Sharik skulks in from the bedroom, gives the new flowers one big sniff, and turns away, unimpressed. He plops down next to them, sitting right up, and begins going to town on himself. My grandmother and I laugh at the loud, sucking sound. I feel sorry for the old motherless cat, right then—nursing on his dead mom as a kitten, how could it not fuck him up? Still, I reach over to discourage him, but my grand-mother lifts a hand and stops me.

"Let him be," she says. "Why rob him of his pleasure? Here's a creature who actually knows how to make himself happy. If only we all could be so lucky."

I get Tally in her stroller and we walk Baba to the train. I tried one last time to convince her to get a cab, but she insisted on "riding with the people," and there was nothing I could do to change her mind. Though there's another week until Labor Day, it's starting to feel like fall already. A crisp breeze fills the air as we pass old men playing chess in the park, women not much younger than my grandmother peddling apples and berries on the sidewalks, a coffee shop filled with people my age furiously typing into their laptops. We get to the platform well ahead of time. Three trains could go by before Baba is late, even on a Saturday morning. We sit on a bench and stare at the buildings in front of us, with only two teen-age girls and a bunch of pigeons for company. Baba leans over and tickles Tally under the chin, and she gives her a little laugh.

"I have grown quite fond of this child," she says. "Now that her rat face is gone, she is quite handsome, like her parents, I can see it as clearly as the sun in the sky."

"I have too," I tell her. I'm trying to hold back a flood of tears. I don't want to spend our last moments together blubbering like an idiot. I want her to feel like I am in control, like I will figure every-thing out.

"It seems you have grown fond of someone else too," she says without looking at me.

I feel my face shifting into an attempt to deny what she has said, but I decide there's no point. "You don't miss a thing, do you?"

"There are plenty of things I have missed, my darling."

I wipe Tally's face just to stall. "You must think I'm ridiculous," I say finally. "*I* think I'm ridiculous. But it's like—this tide just washed over me and all I could do was drown." I don't add, *Until recently. Until I read his dumb poem and saw how clueless I was.* Then again, there was the feeling I had when he stood by my side the whole night at the bar, the hairs on my arms feeling electric from him, and I was back where I started.

"Who am I to judge? I know the feeling," she says. I feel the tears stinging my eyes and only then does my grandmother look at me. "What are your plans, dear girl?"

I take a deep breath and say, "As if I know." Then I add, "Can I ask you something?" I continue before she can say yes or deny me. "You had a nice long life with Grandpa Misha, even if it wasn't perfect. But do you think—I mean, if you could go back and do it all over again, would you have chosen Bogdan?"

My grandmother sighs and shakes her head. "My darling, don't be ridiculous," she says. "If I had not married your grandfather, I would not have had your father, and he would not have had you."

"Is that an answer?"

"My life would have been completely different."

"But you might have had other children, other grandchildren."

"I might have given birth to a one-eyed donkey, but I didn't, so what is the point of mulling it over?" she says, and I feel her temperature rising.

"I'm sorry. I just . . ." I say. "So does that mean—do you mean to say you're glad your life turned out the way it did?"

I imagine my great-great-grandmother standing on a platform over a century ago, with nothing to guide her but her intuition. What would she think of what became of my grandmother? What would she think of me? Baba and I both know that there's a good chance this is it. She could certainly go on and live a few more years, maybe even to be a hundred, but she could also leave the world any day now, and who knows when we'll have another visit. I want to tell her that she was everything to me, that those trips to Sevastopol were everything, that I didn't judge her for having affairs, not really, that I never expected her to be perfect.

My grandmother sighs again. "Who is to say? I have lived my life the best I could live it, but not without my share of mistakes. You have made them, too, and will continue to make them. Most of them won't kill you," she says. She smiles and adds, "If what happened between me and the brothers is so important to you, then why did you cut them out of your story?"

I laugh. "The story wasn't really about them."

"I suppose not."

She reaches into her pocket. She pulls out a pouch, and from that, a string of red jewels that it takes me a minute to understand is the ruby necklace she had been talking about all along. The one that had been stolen from her grandmother. The one that led the woman to go completely mad and end her life.

"But how did you . . ." I say, staring at her hand, the bright jewels in it that look cartoonishly lavish, sparkling like crazy. Before I finish asking the question, I realize I don't want to know the answer. Or, rather, that I can figure out what happened without my grandmother telling me, without her confirming she had stolen the rubies from her grandmother out of spite. How can I blame her for hating the woman, after all she had done to her father? And as she herself had just said, who am I to judge?

At last I hear it, the train chugging toward the platform, and see it snaking around the bend in the distance.

"I have made my share of mistakes," she says again. "At least this one was valuable. Please, take it. It can give you the freedom you seek."

I slowly take the necklace out of her hand just as the train comes to a halt and opens its doors. It's even heavier than it looks and it makes my hand tremble, either from the weight or the thought of touching something that my great-great-grandmother had worn for years like a second skin, something that the woman in the photograph on my wall had loved best of all.

"What should I do with it?" I say.

"Be careful with it," my grandmother says, closing my hand around it and kissing my fist. "It is a very precious thing."

And with that, she gives me a big hug, strokes my daughter's cheeks, and disappears through the jaws of the train.

I give Tally a bottle after the train pulls away, and then we keep walking, walking, walking. The girl is smiling, cooing, staring at everything with her mouth open in unabashed wonder, like it seems impossible that all of these things can exist: the two red-haired children trailing their mother, the woman in the pink dress smoking a cigarette on the street corner, the leaves on the trees fluttering in the wind, the two tired men entering an Irish pub, the light hitting the store windows, the big garbage trucks and their loud, loud roar as they pummel down the street. As we wait to cross it, my girl looks so perfect sitting there in her little green jumper, the light in her reddish curls, that I bend down and take a picture of her, and capture her smile perfectly.

I open my Instagram but decide against posting it, and send the picture to Yuri instead. I wait a few seconds to see if he answers, but he does not; he's probably too busy packing for his trip any-way. I scroll and see that I got more likes on my play post—I'm up to four hundred—and try to remind myself that I'm not going to get any validation or love from the Internet, that those likes didn't translate into asses in seats. Fucking social media is like a bad boyfriend who won't change his ways, no matter how much I beg him to, and the only real love I can try to get right now is from the sweet little lump in the stroller.

My phone dings with a text from my agent, not Yuri. He's telling me I have been cast as the orphaned sister killer in L.A.—filming starts next week. I assumed I didn't book it because I sent in the tape weeks ago and forgot all about it. I can't help but laugh and laugh, which makes my girl smile hard. After being my grandmother and great-great-grandmother, do I really want to stoop to being a murderer, as Stas would put it? I straighten Talia's little barrette and stroke her face. I do, I do, I do, I know that I do. Somehow, I—we—will do it. I can't turn it down. And it may just be the break we need. And after that—what do I do? Return to life with Yuri? Ask Mel if I can pick up a few shifts at the Lair? See if I can enroll at the community college? Take Stas by the hand and ride off into the sunset? Pawn the necklace and leave them both for good?

When we stop at a streetlight, two women look down at Tally and coo, because having a baby is apparently an invitation for everyone to talk to you.

But then, from the confused smile on one of the women's faces, I think she might recognize me.

"Tampon commercial?" I say to her. "You know, it's as easy as—"

"That's not it," she says, cocking her head at me. "Russian prostitute?"

"Is there any other kind?"

"Good work. I loved *Seeing Things*."

"Thank you so much," I say. "Really."

The other woman seems to have no idea who I am, but she's interested in Tally.

"How old is this darling?"

"Almost six months."

"They're already a lot of fun at six months, aren't they? Watch out, the next thing you know, she'll be going off to college," she says.

"You spend the early years being like, when will she walk, when will she talk? And then the next ten you just want them to sit down and shut up," the other one says.

"I'll try to slow down," I tell them, and as I push Talia ahead of them, not even that annoyed by the assumption that everyone will go to college, I hear her say one more thing.

"Congratulations!"

I thank her and push on, past a father and his two sons. It's been a while since I was congratulated for having a daughter. I thought she was too old for that, and it feels nice. Tally paid the woman no attention, or me, really, and continues to stare out with her mouth half-open. Over the last few months, my daughter has gotten more entranced by the outside world than by me, not as desperate for me to hold her anymore.

She's becoming less like the baby I was, if Mama described me correctly. "Always wanting to be held," Mama had said, shaking her head. "If I left the room for a moment, you would scream bloody murder! I don't think I emptied my bladder until you were two. It was awful." But I see now that she didn't think it was awful at all, that maybe she even longed for a time when I needed her like that, or at all.

Talia does give me a smile, though, when we pass the dog park, probably more at the big shaggy gray dog than me, but it does melt me like they said it would, her smiles always melt me now even though there was a time when I didn't think this would ever be possible, when I was convinced I must have been immune to her.

How did it happen? As Baba would say, it's something unbelievable. This sweet little girl, who just months ago felt like a gooey
alien in my arms, became my favorite little person, the only one I
can really talk to besides said grandmother, the only one whose
eyes hide nothing and who understands me. I pull her little blanket
up to her chest, mostly so she can suck on it more easily. Baba is
probably boarding her plane by now. The sun is rising but it's still
pretty crisp, too crisp for early September, but I'm ready for the
change, the summer has been endless.

"Endless summer, am I right, Tally?" I say. "Though I guess
you've never known another season, have you? You have nothing
to compare it to. Well, I promise you'll have some good summers
ahead, but this one has just been weird."

My daughter is staring out at the sunlight, the people passing by,
the boats chugging down the river, the taxis honking, the surly girl
at the overpriced vintage boutique on the corner arranging the
mannequins in the windows to lure customers in. I never woke up
before ten in the morning until my daughter was born, and never
went to bed before two, but now, I have to say I like this schedule.
There's a hopefulness to the mornings, the day spread out before
you like a cozy blanket, the sense that there's plenty of time to do
it all, to make some decisions. Time to start over, to unfuck everything you had fucked.

I don't realize how far we've gone until I see the water, the
Hudson gleaming in front of us. We're miles from the apartment
now, but it doesn't matter, I could use a long walk home. I push her
up to the rocks that overlook the dark-blue water, a few sailboats
drifting along as the sun rises higher in the sky. It's not swimming
water, no, but a teenage couple kicks at it, their shoes piled up behind them. A big cargo ship passes by, covering one of the sailboats
for a moment. Usually, when I take her this far out, my daughter
gets tired and starts to fuss. But this time, she's not complaining.

This morning, as I push her toward the water, she likes it. She looks from my face to the sun and back at the water again.

"What do you think, darling?" I ask. And then I stop to watch her taking it all in.

After Mama's first and only trip to the sea with me and my grandmother, we returned to Kiev to see my grandfather, but we got off to a rough start. When he picked us up at the station, he gave my grandmother a once-over and said, "That's a lovely bracelet," and she clamped a hand to her wrist like she had been burned, because she had forgotten to take off what was no doubt a gift from her latest suitor. "Just a silly thing I got from a stand by the water, it's nothing," she had said, charging ahead with her suitcase.

But that evening, after a stilted dinner in the formal dining room with the too-big chandelier instead of the cozy kitchen just to please my grandfather, he and I were alone on the gold-framed balcony while Mama and Baba cleaned up. I thought he must definitely know about Baba's affairs and worried that he might even ask me about it. He was quiet for an interminable amount of time, watching the apartment buildings across the street and the Dnieper in the distance and the sky turning this beautiful pink and orange as the sun inched toward the horizon like he could do it until I was an old woman myself, while we heard the clanking of my grandmother and Mama clearing the plates on the other side of the glass door.

"Your mother loves you, Natasha. You must take care of her," he said.

"How?" I said. "How exactly do I do that?"

"You do what anyone can in this situation," he said with a shrug. "You do your best."

A moment earlier I had felt sorry for my grandfather, but now

I was angry. I thought of all of his thoughtful critiques of my acting, and expected him to tell me what to do in the same way. "More feeling at the end," he could have said. "Give those tears everything you've got. But also, honor the complexity of your role." But he came up empty this time.

"That's it? That's all the advice you have for me after, what, seventy years of living? Mama's going to die, and all I can do is—my best?"

He winked at me and laughed. "If I live any longer, I'll have even less advice to give."

Now I laughed, too, forgiving him, feeling choked up all of a sudden. We looked over our shoulders to where my mom was throwing back her head and cracking up at something my grandmother said. Mama stopped in her tracks and looked right at me, her smile disappearing like she was caught doing something. Then she stuck her tongue out at me and laughed again. She was stunning with the dusky light falling on her wavy hair, her face suntanned and fresh from the sea, and I knew I would never be half as beautiful as she was, even if I spent my whole life trying. I turned back to my grandfather.

"One more thing," he said, and I thought he'd come up with some profound advice at last, something meaningful about the eternal bond between children and their parents, but he didn't say another word, he just pointed at the sky, where the sun was finally setting below the buildings, casting the river in its early summer evening glow. He opened the door and Mama and Baba stopped what they were doing to join us, and we all watched the sun dip down until we could only see a hint of its bright, burning light.

Acknowledgments

This novel wouldn't have been written if my grandmother, Lana, hadn't stoked my imagination with stories of her Soviet upbringing. After she passed away five years ago, her sister, Tanya, and niece, Natasha, continued to tell me stories that kept me going. My parents, Olga and Alex, read through several drafts of this book and gave thoughtful feedback about historical inaccuracies, and I am very grateful to them for this, and for raising me to be fascinated by the place we came from, and so much more. My brother, Andrew, supported me in countless ways as well.

I'd also like to thank everyone at the Iowa Writers' Workshop, which made it possible for me to share a short version of this project in Ethan Canin's Long Story Workshop. Ethan and my sharp classmates helped shape the project and made me see that it had potential to be a novel. My agent, Henry Dunow, read many drafts of this novel and put it in good hands, keeping me sane along the way, and Andrea Walker and Emma Caruso, my tireless editors, helped it find its final form. Emma was a superhero, particularly in the home stretch of this project. Jess Bonet and Carrie Neill were always there to answer my endless questions and helped in endless ways. Cindy Berman helped this book fall into place.

My husband, Danny, offered tremendous support to me as I plugged on with this project in ways that leave me speechless. And my daughter, Dasha, kept my spirits high as I wrote, both in utero and in this unbelievable world.

ABOUT THE AUTHOR

MARIA KUZNETSOVA was born in Kiev, Ukraine, and moved to the United States as a child. Her first novel, *Oksana, Behave!*, was published in 2019. She lives in Auburn, Alabama, with her husband and daughter, where she is an assistant professor of creative writing at Auburn University. She is also a fiction editor at *The Bare Life Review*, a journal of immigrant and refugee literature.

ABOUT THE TYPE

This book was set in Fournier, a typeface named for Pierre-Simon Fournier (1712–68), the youngest son of a French printing family. He started out engraving woodblocks and large capitals, then moved on to fonts of type. In 1736 he began his own foundry and made several important contributions in the field of type design; he is said to have cut 147 alphabets of his own creation. Fournier is probably best remembered as the designer of St. Augustine Ordinaire, a face that served as the model for the Monotype Corporation's Fournier, which was released in 1925.